Pocketful of Sand

A Novel

By

M. LEIGHTON

To my amazing husband, *Kevin*, who asked me to write this book. I never expected it to creep into my soul the way it has.

This one is for you, babe. I'd build sandcastles from here to eternity to spend one more day with you.

ONE

Eden

October

EMMY'S FACE LIGHTS up when she runs full speed toward the water's edge, chasing the tide out. My heart warms with her squeal of delight as it chases her right back in. Back and forth they go, engaging in the never-ending dance of ebb and flow.

Few times in her six years of life have I ever seen her so happy, so carefree and animated. That alone makes this move worth it. Maybe we won't have to leave this place. At least not for a while.

Tirelessly, her little legs carry her as she flees the frothy waves, sandy water splashing up from her feet as she runs. I watch her play, more satisfied than

I've been in a long time. Maybe this will be good for her.

Finally, winded, she doesn't turn to run the tide, but keeps coming toward me until she can launch her small body at mine like a tiny bullet. I catch her, hugging her close so that I can bury my nose in her neck and inhale the smell of baby powder, fresh air and little girl.

When she pulls away, she's smiling. "That was fun, Momma. Did you see me run fast? Even the waves couldn't catch me."

Her lime green eyes are twinkling and her cheeks are rosy from the fall nip in the air. Her hot breath mixes with the ocean's breeze to sooth my insides, like maybe happiness, wholeness is finally blowing in.

"I did! You ran *so fast* I could hardly keep up."

She claps excitedly. "Can we walk before we go?"

I glance at my watch. We are supposed to meet the landlord at his office at three, but we should be in good shape as long as we head back to the car within the hour. "Sure, but we can't stay too much longer."

I've barely finished my sentence before she's out of my arms, on her feet and blazing off down the beach, her long hair flowing out behind her like midnight flames.

This straight stretch of beach is practically deserted, so I let her run as fast as she wants to. There's a great likelihood that I'll have to carry her back, but I don't mind. I treasure any chance I get to hold her close and pretend that nothing in the world could ever take her away from me. Plus, all this exercise means she'll probably fall asleep in my arms tonight. She'll be exhausted. I smile at the thought. The perfect end to what's looking like a nearly perfect day.

Up ahead, Emmy stops several feet from what I now recognize as someone building an elaborate sandcastle. I see her pop her thumb in her mouth, so I speed up. That's a sure sign of distress for her. That and the way she goes still as a statue, not moving a single muscle. Those are the only outward signs of her condition.

Without looking back, as though she can sense my presence when I stop at her side, she reaches for my fingers with her free hand, squeezing them as tightly as she can.

I squat down, something I've learned is soothing to her. When she's anxious, she likes to be able to hide. While she'll tuck herself behind my legs if I'm standing, she relaxes more quickly if I'm down on her level where I can hold her.

She surprises me when she doesn't turn into my chest and bury her face like she usually does in these situations. Instead, she stands perfectly still, watching the man who's on his hands and knees constructing the castle. His back is to us and I doubt he knows we're here, he's so intent on what he's doing. Obviously he takes his castling seriously, which gives me ample time to study the scene.

The castle is taller than Emmy and has at least a dozen spires and turrets of various sizes. It's probably taken him all day to construct it. There are even trees in the "castle grounds" that lead down to the edge of the mote he's currently digging. The whole thing is pretty impressive. But not nearly as impressive as the guy who's building it, I learn once I turn my attention to him.

His hands are broad and long-fingered, tanned and capable-looking, as though they're used often and probably calloused. I follow them up muscular forearms roped with thick veins and bands of sinew, to biceps that bulge against the dark blue cotton of his T-shirt. The material is stretched tight across his wide shoulders, too, which only further accentuates his narrow waist.

I evaluate the man in the same clinical way that I do the castle–with an appreciation for form and structure. Nothing more.

That is, until he turns his shaggy blond head to look at me.

I can tell by the frown that creases his forehead and shades his bright blue eyes that we took him by surprise. Normally I would do the polite thing and apologize, but at the moment my thoughts are as scattered and hard to catch as my breath.

He's handsome, yes. He's built well, yes. I'm sure in another life or if I were someone else, I'd be very attracted to him. Only I'm not attracted to men. Or women. Not anymore. I'm not attracted to *anyone* anymore.

So then why can't I breathe? Why do I feel like I just fell into a black hole that sucked all the air from the world and dropped hot boulders into my stomach?

He rocks back on his haunches, brushing off his hands almost angrily. My insides do a funny little quiver as he watches me. It's not really fear or embarrassment; it's more like...*awareness*. *Extreme* awareness.

Emmy stirs where she had gone around behind me to peek over my shoulder, and her movement draws his piercing eyes. After that, I think *I* cease to exist.

As he stares at her, the color leaves his handsome, golden face, taking with it the frown that he was wearing. His mouth drops open a little and I hear the huff of a breath as he releases it. If I didn't know any better, I'd say he looks shocked. I just don't know why he would be.

He gapes at Emmy for a few long seconds before, wordlessly, he turns away. At first, he does nothing. Doesn't move, doesn't speak. Doesn't even appear to breathe. Just continues to kneel, facing away from us, staring at the sandcastle. But then, after a bit, he returns to his mote. He digs into the sand fiercely, almost angrily, and I wonder that his fingers don't bleed.

I don't really know whether I should say something or not, so I opt with not. Already he doesn't seem too thrilled with our presence.

Another interruption might be even more poorly received.

Just as I'm rising to sweep Emmy into my arms and carry her back, the man pauses, his head turning as he catches a glimpse of the clump of daisies buried stem-deep in the sand in front of the castle. His shoulders slump visibly. I see his hand start to jut out and then stop, and then start again. He reaches for one flower, plucking it from the bunch and twirling it in his fingers. I know I should leave, leave him to whatever he was doing and thinking before we arrived, but I can't. Not yet. I can't, but I just don't know why.

Finally, he glances back at us, at Emmy. His gaze isn't too direct, almost as though he knows that too much attention is hard for my daughter. I watch as he extends the flower, his hand shaking the tiniest bit as he holds it out to her. I start to reach for it, but Emmy surprises me by grabbing it herself, her slim little hand easing out to carefully take the daisy from his grasp.

The stranger gives her a small smile and turns away again. He doesn't get to see the way Emmy's lips curve around the thumb still stuck in her mouth. He doesn't get to see the way she watches him afterward.

"Thank you," I tell him quietly.

He pauses, turning only enough that I can see his strong profile–straight nose, carved mouth, square chin. He nods once and then returns to his excavating, as intent as he was before we interrupted.

Puzzled and flustered, I turn and carry my daughter back the way we came, the scent of fresh-cut daisies teasing my nose and the quiet hum of my child tickling my ear.

TWO

Cole

*W*HO THE HELL was that? I think, wondering why I feel like I just got sucker punched in the gut. I resist the urge to turn and watch her walk away. Or go after her.

Who the hell was that and what the hell did she just do to me?

THREE

Eden

A CLUSTER OF bells jingles overhead when I push through the door of Bailey's Quick Stop, which is the address that the landlord gave me when he told me where to pick up the keys to our cottage. A quick glance around shows me the place is empty. I take a tentative step forward, practically dragging Emmy along. She's hugging my left leg so tightly I can hardly walk.

"Hello?" I call quietly.

"Hiya!"

I jump when a woman with wildly teased brown hair pops up from behind the counter where the cash register sits. She's smiling broadly and holding a frosted glass in one hand. I'd estimate her to be in her early thirties, maybe ten years older than my twenty-three. With her button nose and big brown eyes, she's pretty despite the trouble she seems to be having remaining upright.

"Hi, I'm looking for Jason Bailey. Am I at the wrong place? This is the address–"

"No, sweetie, you're at the right place. Come ooon in," she says, laughing as she throws up an arm and enthusiastically urges me forward. I hobble toward her, Emmy clinging to my leg as I do. The woman notices her, brown eyes lighting up when she sees my daughter. "And who is this?" she asks in a gentle voice.

I reach down to smooth Emmy's hair, not at all surprised when I see her sucking her thumb. She's just staring at the woman like she's a frightening alien.

"This is Emmy. She's very shy," I explain. That's what I tell everyone. It's much simpler than the truth.

"All the princesses are," the woman says, unfazed. "I'm Jordan. What can I help you two lovely ladies with today? We've got everything from paint to wine and bait to bread. We've got a grill if you're hungry and a bar if you're thirsty."

"Just Jason Bailey please," I repeat, watching as she tries to collect herself, tugging at her disheveled shirt and smoothing her disheveled hair.

"Oh, right right." She turns her face partly to the side and yells, "Jasonnn! Get out here," the smile never leaving her face.

As is the case with most small towns, new people stick out like sore thumbs, and Miller's Pond, Maine is no exception. It had a population explosion in 2001, bringing the town tally up to a whopping three thousand four hundred people. And, now, three thousand four hundred and two. I guess that's why this store has a little bit of everything. No big chain supermarkets or stores have found their way here yet. From what I could see on the map, the closest super center is at least thirty miles away.

"So, what brings you to Miller's Pond?" she asks.

I smile and clear my throat, uncomfortable with her questioning. But I have a carefully composed history rehearsed for just such an occasion. "Uh, I was born up in Bangor. Just getting back closer to home."

"Close, but not too close, eh? Smart girl."

I smile at her observation and add, "Plus we love lighthouses and Miller's Pond has one of the oldest ones in the country, or so I hear." It's a pat enough answer, hopefully pat enough to stop her or anyone else from asking more questions. It's all fiction, of course. 100% untrue, but that's the way it has to be.

"That's right, sweetie. You've come to the right place. Annnd, you've just made friends with the one person who can tell you anything you need to know about this town and the people in it. Besides that, I make a kickass rum and Coke," she says with a wink, her voice dropping down to a loud whisper. I assume that was in deference to Emmy.

"The village idiot can make a rum and Coke, Jordan," a man says as he appears in the doorway behind the counter. He looks to be about the same age as Jordan and, based on his light brown hair and same color eyes, I'd say they're related. "Or, in this case, the town lush."

Although his words are biting, he smiles at Jordan and she laughs, playfully punching his arm. Her fist slips off and she nearly falls, but the guy grabs her by the shoulders and more or less props her back up. He's shaking his head when he finally looks up to me.

"Jason Bailey, Jordan's brother. You must be Eden."

"I am. It's nice to meet you."

"Is that a bit of the south I'm hearing?"

My lips curve nervously. I've tried very hard to drop any hint of accent from my voice, so his observation flusters me. I don't have a lie ready for that. "It is. I wasn't there long, but it must've rubbed off."

He nods, seemingly satisfied with that.

"And this is her daughter, Emmy. She's a shy princess," Jordan provides.

I can't help noticing the appreciative way Jason's eyes sweep from my chest to my feet and back again on his way to see Emmy. He simply smiles at her, doesn't try to engage, which is best. When his warm eyes lock onto mine again, I think to myself that he's handsome and pretty obviously interested. At least superficially. Only I'm not. A normal woman probably would be. But I'm not normal. I'd like to be, but I'm not sure I ever will be.

"Well, it's a pleasure to meet you both. I look forward to getting to know you."

While his smile is as polite as his words, something tells me his insinuation is anything but innocent.

I just nod, thinking to myself that he won't ever get to know me *that* well. "It's been a long day for us. If I could just get the keys..."

I figure offering up an excuse for my lack of interest is the best way to avoid bruising his ego, and I'm okay with that. Anything to keep out of trouble.

"Of course. Come on back to my office," he says, walking to the end of the counter and indicating yet another door. Once inside, I dig in my purse for the form I filled out. It's a single page, nothing too invasive or complicated. In fact, the...loose requirements for the rental of this cottage were big factors in choosing Miller's Pond. Jason let me secure the lease via a faxed agreement that didn't ask for my social security number and he allowed me to pay six months in advance via a cashier's check that I mailed in. Now I just have to pick up the keys.

Jason grabs an envelope from his top desk drawer. It has Eden Taylor and the cottage's address scribbled across the front. He opens it and dumps keys out into his hand, makes a few notes on a paper or two and then hands them over.

"You know the address?"

"Yes, we drove by on the way in."

"Then welcome to Miller's Pond."

And just like that, I exhale. Maybe this will finally be a place we can call home. Home *safe* home.

FOUR

Eden

Thirteen days later

OUR LITTLE COTTAGE is quiet when I get up. I pull Emmy's door shut on my way to the bathroom. She sleeps like a rock unless she has a nightmare, but I like to keep her cocoon as peaceful as I can until she wakes.

The hardwood floors are chilly under my feet as I pad silently to the stove and grab the hot water kettle. I love our place. For whatever reason, be it the charming wraparound porch or the big oak in the front yard, or the soothing beige walls and cozy old fireplace, this feels like home. Already. And we haven't even been here two full weeks yet.

I glance up as I pour water into the kettle. My stomach flutters when I see him. He's there. I hoped he would be.

Every morning since we moved in thirteen days ago, the man we saw building the sandcastle has been working across the street at the cottage diagonal from mine. Rain or shine, he's there. I don't know who he is or why he draws me to my window each day, but he does.

I find myself peeking out at him often. More often than I should, probably. But as hokey as it sounds, something about him speaks to me. Calls to me almost. And I can't shake it.

I mean, he's a pleasure to watch, of course. And that's saying a lot coming from someone like me. Physically, he's all that a woman could ask for–tall, fit, ripped in all the right places. Most days he wears nothing but faded jeans, work boots and a tool belt. Sometimes a baseball hat. Rarely a shirt. And if ever there was a body made to go around shirtless, it's his. But that's not what pulls me to the window time after time, day after day. It's not even the tattoos scrawled up his ribs–the one on the left reading "always", the one on the right reading "never". No, there's something else that brings me here to watch him. Something…more.

I've noticed that whether he's hammering or scraping or carrying something through the door, he has this intense solitude about him. It's as though the world has abandoned him. Or maybe that he's abandoned the world. I can't put my finger on it. I only know that it's decidedly incongruous with a man who looks like he does.

I think about him being on the beach that day. Building a sandcastle like it was the most important thing in the world. It was strangely haunting for a man who looks like he does to be so…alone.

Maybe that's what draws me–his isolation. I can't be sure of course, but something tells me that he doesn't have much of a life outside his job. He arrives sometime before I get up, which is early, and stays to work late, long after I give Emmy her bath. He eats lunch on the lawn by himself and I've never seen him talking on a cell phone or engaging the few people who pass by. He just appears to be alone. All alone.

We've fallen into a strange rhythm of sorts. It's just one small thing, but it seems significant somehow. Every day, at some point, he will catch me watching him. Every day, he has. And every day he holds my gaze, even from so far away. It gives me chills, the way he stares back at me. But then he frowns, just like he did at the beach that day, before he turns away. It's like I make him think of something he doesn't want to think about. And my need to know what that is increases with every day that passes. *Need*, not want.

I'm not sure if brokenness is discernible with nothing more than our casual contact (if you can even call what we have "contact") or if this is all in my head, but for some reason that's the word that comes to mind when I see him–brokenness. Someone who's broken.

From the outside, he's practically perfect. Well not even *practically* perfect. He *is* perfect. Flawless.

Breathtaking. But he's too quiet, too withdrawn, too...solitary for someone as handsome as he is. Maybe that's why I think he's broken. Surely in a town this size, every single woman within ten miles would be banging on his front door, offering to help with whatever he might need. Or want.

And yet, he doesn't seem to have anyone. I've noticed that his ring finger is empty, too. As empty as his life appears to be.

Maybe he's got dark secrets that keep the town at bay. A scary skeleton in his closet, a maniacal monster under his bed. That's probably reason number one, the only one I should need, to stay far, far away from him. And that's exactly what I'm doing. Mostly because he stays away from me, never offering to come over or speak when we go outside. He just keeps to himself and I do the same.

But still, he pulls me.

So here I am. Watching. Waiting, it seems. On what, I don't know. But I often get the feeling that something is about to happen. Only it never does.

A loud banging at my front door startles me and I spill coffee down the front of my shirt. I grab a napkin and wipe at it as I run, rushing to the door before whoever it is can wake up Emmy. She's a late sleeper. Sometimes I think God made her that way to protect her.

I peek through the square of glass at the top of the plain wood door and find Jordan smiling up at me. She looks surprisingly bright-eyed and bushy-tailed this morning, considering how she most likely spent her night.

I snap open the dead bolt and unlock the knob. "Hi, Jordan."

"Hiya, sweetie," she says, pushing past me and carrying a brown cardboard box into the living room. From that first morning when I met her, she's taken to me like her long lost best friend.

She's never come to my house before, but evidently she's been inside it at some point prior to my arrival. She plops the box down on the coffee table and then perches on the end of the sofa like we do this every day.

"I always loved this material," she says, rubbing her hand over the velvety cinnamon-colored upholstery.

"You've been here before?"

"A time or two. I dated the guy who lived here before you."

"Dated?" Jason says from behind me as he walks in carrying another box. "You don't date."

"Why the hell don't I date?"

"You're like the town bicycle. You give rides. You don't date."

"Uh!" Jordan squeaks, insulted. "Are you hearing this?" She seems incensed, but then, just as quickly as she got riled, she waves him off and her smile returns, feathers no longer ruffled. I can't decide if their mean banter is all teasing or if they have a love/hate relationship. "So, your landlord had some things ordered. Wanted us to bring them over when they arrived."

"Landlord?" I ask in confusion. "I thought Jason was the landlord."

"Nah, he's just a lackey."

"I'm a property manager, not a lackey," Jason replies sharply. Then he turns to me. "The *owner* was going to replace a few things before you moved in, but there was no time. Better late than never, though, right?"

I nod, a little uncomfortable with my space being so abruptly and unexpectedly invaded. "What kinds of things are we talking about?"

"New microwave," he says, indicating the heavier box he was carrying, "new blinds for the kitchen and a new coffee maker."

I perk up at the mention of the coffee maker. "That's nice. I've been boiling water every morning."

"Well, not anymore," Jason says with a smile.

Jordan gets up and wanders to the kitchen, stopping to stare out the window as I so often do. I wonder if she sees the sandcastle guy. Then I wonder if she knows him.

"Damn," she says on a sigh. "It's a shame to cover that view with new blinds," she says. That's how I know she sees him. There's nothing spectacular about the view except him. She turns her big smile back toward me. "Unless that's why he sent the new blinds."

"Why who sent the new blinds?"

"The *owner*," she answers emphatically. "Cole Danzer. He must've noticed they were missing."

I join her in the kitchen, glancing out to where the gorgeous handyman is measuring a piece of wood.

"How would he know?"

"Well, I guess Cole's not blind and can see from a hundred feet away," she declares with a laugh, tipping her head toward the window.

"Wait, so *he* is the owner?" I ask, admiring the way the muscles in his shoulders shift as he works.

"Yep. Cole Danzer." There's a dreamy sigh in her voice that matches her expression.

"Crazy Cole is what we call him," Jason says as he reaches between us to lay the blinds across the sink.

Jordan gasps. "We?"

"Yes *we*," Jason confirms with a frown. "You're the one who started it."

"No, *I* call him Crazy *Hot* Cole. But you've never called him crazy *at all*."

"That's because I work for him."

"So what, you don't work for him today?" To this, Jason says nothing, but I can see his nostrils flare. "Ohhh, or is it because you like our lovely little miss Eden? And you don't want her getting any ideas about the beautiful hunk o' man across the street?"

"Jordan, just shut up. You don't even make any sense," her brother replies petulantly.

When Jason bends slightly to apply himself to removing the blinds from their box, Jordan points down at him and mouths behind his back "He likes you!"

"Jordan, go open the store. Come back for me in an hour," Jason snaps.

"Fine," she huffs. "Walk me out, Edie."

Edie? That's a new one, I think.

Jordan reaches for my arm and loops hers through it, practically dragging me to the front door. She pulls me out onto the small wraparound porch, but doesn't stop there. When she keeps walking, I start to resist.

"This is far enough, Jordan. I'm a mess!"

I think about my straight black hair in a ponytail, my oval face and hazel-gray eyes devoid of makeup, my coffee-stained T-shirt and pink shorts that say "Juicy" on the butt. I feel my face heat with embarrassment.

She stops and stares at me. "You're gorgeous. Now come with me."

Before I can argue, she tugs me into the yard. Automatically, my eyes find their way to Cole the instant he comes into view. He's still in the yard, but now he's moving his ladder.

"Hi, Cole," Jordan bellows, causing my stomach to drop to my bare toes. The grass is covered in a chilly, early fall dew that coats my feet. I catch my breath when Cole glances up at us, his brow drawing immediately into a frown. He doesn't respond. He just holds perfectly still, his long fingers curled around the ladder, forearms straining and biceps bulging. "Have you met Eden yet?"

As Jordan drags me across the pseudo-cul-de-sac, I can feel his eyes on me, the startling blue penetrating all the way through my clothes to my skin underneath. Goosebumps break out on my legs and arms and, to my utter humiliation, my nipples pucker. The heat of his gaze and the cool of the morning is too stark a contrast for my body not to notice.

When we stop within a foot of him, I see his hooded eyes rake me from head to toe. My nipples strain against my T-shirt, catching his attention on the way back up. I cross my arms over my chest, praying for this moment to just be over.

He's silent for a long time. Long enough to be rude, but I don't get the impression that he is. I get the impression that he's just thinking. His frown deepens and for a second it appears he's going to just turn away, but he doesn't. Instead, he props the ladder against one shoulder and sticks out his hand.

"Cole Danzer."

His voice. God! It makes me want to groan. It's like a silk sheet draped over jagged gravel. It belongs in a bedroom. A dark, warm bedroom. Where pleasure and pain peacefully coexist, heightening the senses and curling the toes. It would be sexy in any circumstance, even if he were reading the encyclopedia aloud or explaining an insurance plan.

Reluctantly, I straighten my right arm and slip my hand into his. His palm is calloused, his fingers rough, just like I knew they would be. From the moment I saw them expertly crafting a sandcastle almost two weeks ago, I suspected they'd feel this way. They rasp against my sensitive skin, setting the walls of my stomach into a flurry of rippling activity.

"Eden Taylor," I reply.

Despite his cool exterior and his less-than-friendly expression, his touch is warm and somehow reassuring, like he could fix or heal or bring back to life whatever he set these hands to.

Which is ridiculous and the first indication that I'm probably losing my mind.

I'm not this girl. I'm not the kind of woman who melts over a man. Any man. But this one does something to me. I get the feeling that, if the circumstances were right, I'd melt for him. Or *with* him.

He nods once and quickly releases me. I wonder if he felt something, too.

"Jordan," he says abruptly, nodding once before adjusting his grip on the ladder and resuming his work as if we weren't standing in the yard.

Jordan, still smiling, takes my arm again and leads me back the way we came, as if that was a perfectly normal greeting from this mysterious man. When we pass ear-shot distance, Jordan saves me the trouble of having to bring up Cole.

"Why do all the hot ones have to be so damn crazy?" she asks, sounding exasperated.

"Why do you say that? I mean that he's crazy?"

Without looking at me, she answers. "Because he *definitely* is. He's, like, talks-to-dead-people crazy. One-flew-over-the-cuckoo's-nest crazy. Twelve-monkeys crazy." She stops in the middle of the road and looks me in the eye. "Not that it makes him any less attractive. I mean, God, what I wouldn't give to get that man naked. I'd do him six ways from Sunday."

She smiles wistfully and continues walking, half-dragging me along behind her. My mind is spinning with a million questions.

"Does he really talk to dead people?"

"Yep," she replies. "Well, supposedly. *I've* never heard him, but it's pretty common knowledge."

Holy shit! That's pretty crazy!

"Who does he talk to?"

She doesn't answer me until we are back in my yard, and even then she lowers her voice. "His daughter. At least that's the only one I know of."

His daughter is dead?

I close my eyes, resisting the urge to bend over and put my head between my knees. *Oh sweet God!* I feel like someone punched me in the chest, all the air whizzing out of my lungs in a harsh hiss.

"Hi-his daughter?"

Jordan nods. "Yep. I think she might've died in a car accident. Nobody seems to know much about it, though. That or they just don't talk about it. You know, out of respect."

I want to ask more questions, but I can't. The words won't come past my lips. All I can think about is my Emmy and what I would do...how I would feel if she...

No. I can't think that way. I couldn't live without her. I just couldn't.

"I guess in a lot of ways, his life ended that day. Had the world in the palm of his hand. Rich, hot, successful football player, beautiful wife, adorable daughter and then bam! Gone. Everything."

"How did it—"

My question is interrupted by Jason. "Jordan, I told you to go open the store. Strom Tuggle just called. He's been waiting in the parking lot for fifteen minutes."

"Oh screw Strom! He's just there for his daily glance at my ass. He can wait." Jordan gives me an apologetic look and twirls her keys on her finger. "Stop by the grill sometime. I'll buy you a drink and a chicken sandwich."

"I can't really...not with Emmy..." I hike my thumb back toward the cottage, my heart aching as I think of my little girl, my whole world, sleeping peacefully inside. Alive and well.

"Oh, right right. Well, I'll come to you then. I need a new girlfriend. This town's in dire need of some *not* bitches," she declares with a grin.

"Jordaaan," Jason prompts warningly.

"I'm going, I'm going."

As Jordan saunters to the truck, I stand staring after her, wishing she'd come back and answer my million questions.

FIVE

Eden

THE OLD OVEN is preheating and I'm stirring muffin mix when Emmy comes racing out of her room.

"Good morning, sleeping beauty," I call over my shoulder when I hear the patter of her feet. "What's got you–"

"Momma, look what I drew!" she says excitedly, stopping at my side and stretching up on her toes to shove a piece of paper in my face.

I set the bowl down and take the crayon picture from her fingers. Although it's rough, as the drawings of most six year olds are, it's easy to make out the sandcastle and the oversized daisy poking out of the top of one turret.

"It's beautiful, pumpkin!" I exclaim, my heart hurting all over again when I think about the man across the street. "Maybe we can try to build one the next time we go to the beach."

"Can we go today?"

"No, you've got schoolwork today, young lady. But maybe tomorrow. If it's not too cold."

With a squeal, Emmy snatches the picture from my fingers and runs to the refrigerator, where she yanks a drawing from two days ago out from under a magnet and replaces it with this one. When she starts to walk off, I stop her.

"Emmaline Sage, pick that up and put it in the drawer, please." I'm already stirring again, so I tip my head toward the picture, which now rests on the floor. It's the crayon rendering of a dog we saw trot by the other day.

Emmy doesn't complain; she simply scoops up the paper and deposits it in the kitchen drawer where all her other artwork goes when she's tired of seeing it on the fridge.

She skips off and, seconds later, I hear the television click on followed by the musical sounds of her favorite cartoon. I pour the blue-tinted batter into a muffin tin, scraping out the last blueberries from the bowl. I lick a bit of the mixture from my finger as I set the bowl in the sink and run water in it.

When I open the oven door to slide the muffins in, a cloud of smoke wafts out to choke me. Coughing and sputtering, eyes watering, I set down the pan and wave my hands in the air so that I can at least see my way to the window to open it.

Of course, it's stuck, a thick layer of fresh paint sealing it shut. I run to the front door and yank it open, pushing back the screen door in hopes that the smoke will make its way outside. I grab a straight-backed rocker from the porch and wedge it in the opening so the smoke can drift out while I go back inside to shut off the oven.

I've got a magazine I'm using as a fan when stomping draws my attention back toward the door. I stop everything–moving, thinking, breathing–when I see him. It's Cole Danzer, bigger than life and twice as beautiful, walking into my kitchen. He looks around for a second and then reaches over the sink to wrench up the sticky window. He does it with remarkable ease and, for a few seconds, I'm focused only on the sleek muscles of his biceps.

In addition to being lustily mesmerized, I'm stunned. Of course. He just appeared out of nowhere. And now he's here. In my house. In my personal space.

And I realize how very much I want him here. In my house. In my space.

I guess that's why I just stand statue-still in my stained T-shirt, holding a magazine, mouth hanging open, staring at him. I'm not as surprised by his surly demeanor when he turns his nearly-furious gaze on me, though. I'm beginning to think he's always this way.

"I thought your house was on fire," he growls in his bedroom voice. "What happened?"

He's like a thundercloud, popping and crackling with irritable electricity. He even makes the hair on my arms stand up, like he's reversing the polarity around me. I think it's his proximity. His face is within a few inches of mine where I'm still tucked into the corner of the cabinets. I *was* fanning smoke toward the door. Now I'm just standing here, oddly mystified.

He seems to be even taller, even broader standing in front of me here in my tiny kitchen. And despite the gagging smoke, I can smell the clean scent of his soap–fresh and piney. I make the mistake of inhaling deeply, which only makes me cough.

His ever-present frown deepens initially as I sputter, but when I catch my breath, it softens as he raises his brow. Without uttering a word, it says, *Well?*

I can't even remember the question when he looks at me this way.

"P-pardon?" I stammer, continuing to stare despite how rude I must seem.

Good Lord, he's gorgeous! I mean, I thought he was incredibly handsome the first time I saw him. And he still is, whether he's angry or frowning or pretending to ignore me. But like this…when he's *not* scowling at me… he's the most magnificent thing I've ever seen. His blue eyes are bluer, his lips more chiseled, his jaw even stronger. The pull of my body, of my *soul* toward him is magnetic. Gravitational. Irresistible.

"What happened?" he repeats, helping to shake me from my stupor.

"I-I don't know. I was preheating the oven to make muffins." I glance at the pan where it rests on the counter. "And then..."

Since most of the smoke has cleared out through the now-open window, Cole cracks the oven door. Another, smaller gray cloud belches up out of it. He just waves it away and bends to look inside.

"There's something stuck to the broiler. Didn't you clean it before you turned it on?"

His question makes me feel defensive. It's my turn to frown. "As a matter of fact, I did. I guess I just didn't think to check the heating elements. Why would I? Who gets food on the broiler?"

"Well, it's too hot to clean now. You'll have to wait until it cools off," he announces, closing the door and straightening.

"Thanks for that piece of wisdom," I retort, my voice dripping with sarcasm.

Cole's brow furrows into its frown again. "I just didn't want you to burn yourself." His concern seems genuine.

Oh.

Now I feel like an over-sensitive ass. "I know. I'm sorry. It's just...it's just been a long couple of weeks."

With his mesmerizing blue eyes narrowed on mine, Cole watches me. Without saying a word, he just watches. I can tell he's thinking. His lips move as though he's biting on the inside of his cheek.

"What brings you here? To Miller's Pond?" He finally asks, almost grudgingly, as if he really didn't want to ask but couldn't help himself.

"Fresh start," I respond, forgetting all my carefully rehearsed half-truths and full-lies.

"What was wrong with the old one?"

I think vaguely to myself that I should kindly berate him for his nosiness, so as to dissuade him from asking so many questions in the future. But before I can, I see a curious little face ease slowly into my line of sight behind Cole.

Emmy.

This must have her all out of sorts.

I drop my magazine and squeeze out from between Cole and the counter so that I can make my way to my daughter. Her thumb is already in her mouth.

She turns her head and presses her cheek to mine when I pick her up, both of us facing Cole. Her big green eyes are trained unwaveringly on him. "This is Mr. Danzer," I tell her, not bothering with the normal mommy things like *Can you say hi*. She won't. And the doctors tell me not to try and make her. It only adds a sense of pressure, and she doesn't need more anxiety. "This is my daughter, Emmy."

Cole's color fades a little. He doesn't look quite as...*unhealthy* as he did the day we ran into him on the beach, but he still has a haunted look about him, one that I now understand. I wonder about the child he lost–how old she was, what she looked like, if they were close. My guess is that they were.

"Hi, Emmy," he greets, his voice softly scratchy as he addresses her. It brings chills to my arms and a lump to my throat. I imagine this is his daddy voice, the one that says you are loved and I would never hurt you. I hear it as plain as day and my chest aches for his loss.

Cole doesn't approach us and Emmy, of course, says nothing. After a few seconds of staring him down, though, she lifts her free hand and points toward the refrigerator. Cole's intense blue eyes swing in that direction and settle on the picture hanging there. He approaches it slowly, reaching out to drag a single finger over the Crayola daisy. "Sand and daisies," he says, his voice barely above a whisper.

He stares at the image for several long seconds, during which I'm at a loss as to what to say. I can feel his sadness filling my kitchen with a fog as thick as the smoke.

When he finally recovers, he turns toward us and, God help me, he smiles. And what a smile it is! It changes his face completely. He was gorgeous before. Breathtaking even. But when his lips curve and his teeth gleam and his eyes light up, he's the most potent male force I think I've ever encountered.

I stare helplessly as he speaks to my daughter. "It's beautiful, Emmy. I'm glad you liked the castle."

With her eyes stuck on Cole (and I can't really blame her for that), Emmy wiggles until I set her down. She backs up slowly, never looking away and never taking her thumb out of her mouth. When she reaches the edge of the kitchen, she raises her fingers in a gesture for him to follow her.

Cole looks to me for approval. I nod, having no idea where this is going, but anxious to find out. Emmy doesn't engage anyone. She hasn't since we left home.

For that reason alone, my heart is so full of hope right now that I can practically feel it trembling, like it's teetering on the cusp of something wonderful.

Cole follows Emmy, and *I* follow *Cole* back to Emmy's room. She stops just inside the door and points to the daisy Cole gave her. She wanted to frame it so we could hang it on her wall.

She didn't let go of it until we got home that day. When she finally did, she insisted that we preserve it. I let her help me press the flower between newspapers and cardboard, and then we set a heavy book on it for a week. When it was ready, I used one of my old frames to display it for her. She wanted it hung right across from her bed, where she could see it every day, she said.

Cole squats down in the hall outside Emmy's room, never getting too close to her. "Did you do that yourself?" She shakes her head and points to me. "Your mom helped?" She nods. "Moms are good helpers, aren't they?" She nods again. "Well, you did a good job. Maybe one day you can help me make one like that. For a present."

Emmy says nothing, just stares at our big interloper like a tiny fawn caught in headlights. We all hold perfectly still in this oddly poignant moment. Eventually, Cole slowly stands and says to no one in particular. "Guess I'd better get going."

He turns to squeeze past me in the narrow hallway, his soap teasing my nose and his warmth teasing the rest of me. I flatten my body against the wall, afraid to touch him. Whether for my sake or his, I don't know. I just feel like that would be opening the door to something I can't control.

Emmy comes out into the hallway and we both watch him go. Just before he disappears, I call, "Thank you."

He turns, gives me the same straight-faced nod I've gotten before, and then he's gone.

As my daughter and I stare through the empty door out into the empty yard, I wonder to myself if it was a good idea to let him get close to Emmy, to let him see her room. I mean, if he's crazy, who knows what he's capable of?

Normally I don't scoff at my paranoia, but this time I do. Something tells me that Cole would rather die than see Emmy shed a single tear. Or any little girl for that matter. I'd say if she were ever to be in good hands, crazy hands or not, those hands would belong to Cole Danzer.

I just wonder if the same thing applies to me.

SIX

Cole

I KNOW THE little girl isn't Charity. She looks like her. Almost exactly like her. She even smells like her, that sweet powdery scent that I'll go to my grave remembering. But I know it's not her. It can't be. I *know* that.

I'd give anything if she was, though. To have another chance. To be a better father. To spend more time, pay more attention, do all the things I should've done. Could've done. Didn't do. I missed my chance, though, and I'll never forgive myself for that. Never. I can't.

That's why I can't let her go. Not this time.

Despite what people say about me being crazy, despite what the doctors say about what I see and hear,

I *know* that my daughter is gone. I *know* that I can't hear her or see her or talk to her. Yet I do. I do because I'm afraid if I don't, I'll lose her forever. And I can't risk that. I can't let her go.

I never wanted to feel again. Anything. Anything at all, other than the gut-wrenching sadness that reminds me of what happened. Of who I am and what I did. I never wanted to feel hope or love or desire again. I don't deserve to feel. At least not anything good. I only deserve pain and heartache and sadness. And guilt. Suffocating guilt.

But damn her, she's making it so hard! Watching me like she does, tearing me up with her soulful gray eyes. Laughing with her daughter, with the girl who looks so much like everything I lost.

I knew when I first saw them that day on the beach that they'd be trouble for me. And I was right. Already, I can't stop thinking about them–the little girl who looks like mine and the woman whose face I dream about.

SEVEN

Eden

IT'S SUNDAY AND we've been in Miller's Pond for exactly one month on the nose. Today, Emmy and I are visiting the beach. I figured we had better enjoy it while we can. It seems the weather is getting colder by the day. Plus, I needed to get out of the house. I found myself watching obsessively for Cole to show up for work across the street, but he never did. It's the first morning he's missed since we've been here and for some reason, it has me all out of sorts.

I spent the first two hours continually glancing out the windows for his arrival. Then, when he didn't show, I spent the next two hours wondering why. Is something wrong? Did he finish his work? Where will he go now? Will I get to see him again?

Of course, I got no answers, which only left me more frustrated. So, Emmy and I decided to go for a jaunt outside.

I bundle her up with a hoodie over her sweatshirt before we strike out on the short walk to the beach. I wanted her to wear gloves, but she loves the feel of the sand and since I won't let her go barefoot, we compromised by me carrying her gloves in my pocket. She might need them before the day is out.

"Can we build a sandcastle today?"

"Not today. It's too cold. The water might turn you into an Emmy-sized ice cube and what would I do with that?"

She giggles. "You can't put me in your drink. I'd drown."

I smile. "Yes, you'd drown if I put you in a drink, so let's save the sandcastle until it's warmer, k, doodle bug?"

"Okay." She doesn't seem overly disappointed.

On the beach, Emmy chases the waves in and out, but not as long as usual since she can't get her feet wet. She picks up some wet sand and throws it into the surf a few times, but that doesn't last long either. Within twenty minutes, she's running up to me so we can go for our walk.

"Can we walk now, Momma?"

"Sure," I tell her. "Let me check your hands."

Obediently, she lays her fingers in mine so that I can feel the temperature. They're freezing.

"Time for gloves." I take them from my pocket and hold them out for her to shove her tiny hands into. She flexes her fingers several times until the knit fits just right. I touch her nose and her ears next. "Let's put your hood up, too. Your ears are cold."

"Mooom!" she whines. I know she's not happy when she calls me Mom.

"Don't 'Mom' me. It's hood up or head for home."

With moody eyes locked onto mine, she pulls up her hood and hands me the strings to tie under her chin.

"Thank you."

We start off down the beach, Emmy shooting up ahead into the empty straight stretch. She runs as fast as her little legs will carry her on the hard-packed sand.

I think we both see the castle at about the same time. I'm thankful that Emmy slows so I can catch up to her and stop her before she gets too close.

"He's building another castle, Momma," she says, excitement widening her eyes when Cole's head appears on the other side of the structure. "And there's more flowers!"

She starts to walk on, but I stop her. "Maybe he likes to do this without people watching, Em. Let's let him build this one and we can come back over tomorrow to see it when it's all finished. How about that?"

"But he has flowers," she argues woefully, pointing at the bunch of daisies buried in the sand. "And he gave me one last time."

"I know, baby, but I think he likes to leave them there for someone special."

I wonder if this has something to do with his dead daughter. It's obvious that his castling is more than just a pastime. Even from this distance, I can see how red and angry his strong hands look. I can only imagine how cold they must be working the wet sand on this chilly, windy day. Yet he has been here for who knows how long, building another castle.

It's every bit as elaborate as the first one we saw. Maybe even more so. Why does he do it? Who does he build them for?

Emmy must be wondering the same things because she starts asking questions as I tug her around to start back the way we came.

"Who does he leave the flowers for, Momma?"

"I don't know, sweetie, but I bet they're for someone very special to him."

A thoughtful pause.

"Where's *his* little girl?"

I slant a look her way, to her wise green eyes staring up at me. She's growing up so fast. Tears blur my vision as I catalog every detail of this moment–Emmy's rosy cheeks, strands of her dark hair peeking out around her hood, her gloved little fingers squeezing mine. She's my reason for living. She has been since the day she was born. Everything I've ever done has been for her. I can't imagine my life if she weren't a part of it. I don't even want to.

"What makes you think he has a little girl?"

She shrugs, not answering my question. She's very perceptive, but still, I can't help wondering what brought her to this conclusion. "Does he?"

"Not anymore."

"What happened to her?"

"I don't know."

"Is she in heaven?"

"I think so."

She falls quiet for several minutes as we walk, her fingers firmly clutching mine. When she finally speaks again, her words break my heart.

"Some babies aren't meant to stay down here with their mommas. And their daddies. Some babies are angels. And angels are meant to be in heaven."

She's not asking me. She's telling me, as though she's the mature one trying to so delicately explain it to me. Like she's helping me to understand.

"Maybe they are, sweetie."

"Some of them are only 'posed to be here for a little while and then go away."

"Maybe they are."

I wonder at her train of thought, at how she's justifying the death of a child in her head. I don't know at what age most kids are able to really understand death, but Emmy has enough issues to work out right now. I don't want to add more stressors by over-explaining senseless tragedy.

Another long pause while Emmy examines the toes of her shoes as she walks. "Would you be sad like him if I went to heaven?"

My heart seizes in my chest. The mere thought...it steals my breath in the most painful way.

"I would never be the same again," I tell her, trying to control the tremble of my voice.

"But I don't want you to be sad. I want you to be happy, even if I'm not here to *make you* happy."

"I could never be happy without you, Emmy. You're my whole world. My sunshine."

She digests this in silence and I immediately regret being so honest with her. I don't want her to feel the burden of keeping her mother from falling apart. No child should carry that responsibility.

"Maybe I can stay until you have other happy things, then."

I stop walking, squatting in front of my daughter, taking both her hands in mine. I blink back tears. I don't want to scare her. "Emmy, you aren't going anywhere. His little girl died in an accident. Sometimes that happens, but that doesn't mean it will happen to you."

"But I won't always be around, Momma. And I don't want you to be sad." Her heart is in her eyes. She's truly worried about this. About me. About what would happen to me if she weren't here.

I stroke her smooth, cold cheek. "Don't you worry about me, baby girl. It's *my* job to worry about *you*. Not the other way around."

She stares deep into my eyes, her young mind spinning with thoughts I'll probably never understand. "Momma?"

"What, sweetpea?"

This whole conversation is terrifying me. I'm resisting the urge to drag her into my arms and hold her so tight that she becomes a part of me, the way she was when I carried her for almost nine months.

"Will you promise to try?"

"To try what?"

"To be happy when I'm in heaven."

"Emmy–"

"Mom!" she snaps desperately.

"Emmy, what on earth is this about?"

"Promise!"

I swallow the lump in my throat. I've never outright lied to my daughter. Until today. I make a promise that I have no hope of ever being able to fulfill. "I promise."

She pats the back of my hand with her own, a gesture far too old for someone so young.

"But that's a promise neither of us has to worry about. You're meant to be right here with me, Emmaline Sage. Don't you think any different."

Neither of us speaks on the way back to our cottage, but the air is heavy with enough emotion that we don't have to.

EIGHT

Eden

EVIDENTLY IN MAINE, the weather can change overnight. While it was very chilly yesterday, that wind must've been blowing in winter, because today it's downright cold.

Since I homeschool Emmy (mostly out of necessity because of her anxiety and our frequent moves), it's vital that we find things to do outside of our house, wherever that might be located at the moment. Here in Miller's Pond, I've used walks down the road or to the beach as our escape since the nearest town, Ashbrook, is thirty plus miles away. But now, with the weather turning, the beach is out of the question, so I find myself looking for reasons to venture to Bailey's.

Today, I decide to take Emmy out for lunch. And Bailey's has a grill.

Jordan, the ever-present fixture at the everything-store, greets us from behind the cash register when we walk in.

"Well, hiya, ladies!" she says, her Northern accent shining in the way she says it. It might be even more pronounced if she weren't slurring.

Drunk at noon?

I'm beginning to think Jordan might have a bit of a drinking problem.

"Hi, Jordan!"

Emmy, as always, hugs my legs.

"What brings you two in today? My stunning conversational skills? My incredible sense of humor? My unshakable balance?" She says the last as she pretends to walk a tightrope and nearly loses said "unshakable" balance. She laughs when she does it and I can't help smiling. At least she's a pleasant drunk.

"Her uncanny ability to aggravate the customers?" says Jason as he appears from behind the counter, like he so often does. Jordan gives him the stink eye, but he ignores her, smiling at me. "Hiya, Eden. Good to see you."

"Hi, Jason."

"I stopped by your house last Sunday. Thought I'd take you and Emmy on a picnic."

That takes me by surprise.

He stopped by? For a picnic? Without even asking in advance?

I guessed when I first met him that Jason was a bit on the cocky side, but this is a little too...presumptuous for me. And I'm not particularly fond of it.

"Oh, uh, we weren't there."

"Yeah, I kinda got that."

I laugh, feeling silly. I'm a terrible liar on the fly. I have to have time to think and plan and rehearse. Although that wasn't a lie. But for some reason, he makes me feel like I'm on the spot all the time. Like he wants to know too much about me. It's there in the way he looks at me and the way he follows me with his eyes.

"We went to the beach."

He nods and, as the silence stretches on, I try to think of a good way to dissuade him from just dropping by like that. Before I have to come up with something, he gives me an opening.

"I would've called, but I don't have your number."

"Oh, I don't have a phone."

His brow wrinkles. "Is that wise, with a child in the house?"

I can't explain my reasons, of course, but even if I could, I wouldn't appreciate his comment. Evidently Jordan doesn't either.

"Because *you've* got so many kids to take care of. Idiot! Why don't you shut the hell up and stop antagonizing my customer?"

"Your customer? The only reason you haven't drank us into bankruptcy is because of me. I think you need to check the attitude at the door."

"At least I don't piss off everybody who walks in here, you asshole."

Emmy's hold on my leg gets tighter as their bickering escalates. "I think we're just gonna grab a seat," I say quietly, steering my daughter to a stool at the diner-style bar.

Their voices drop to heated hisses as I take Emmy's jacket off and lay it across my lap. As I'm opening a menu for her to look at, Jason comes to perch on the stool beside mine.

"Did I piss you off? Seriously?" His expression seems contrite, sincere.

"It's fine," I reply noncommittally.

"I didn't mean to. I swear. I was just...I was just showing some concern. That's all. What I was going to say is that I'd be happy to get you a phone put in if you want."

I feel Emmy's head hit my arm, pushing it to the side to lean against my boob. It's like she's trying to shrink into me in order to hide. Raised voices make her anxious. And she doesn't need any help with anxiety. "I appreciate that, but we're in good shape."

"You sure?"

"I'm sure. We just came in for a bite of lunch today. That's all." I add a smile so that my remark doesn't seem rudely pointed.

"Oh right right," he says in another colloquialism that sounds just like his sister. He slaps the bar and stands. "I'll leave you to it then."

He nods and turns to leave just as the door opens with a jingle, drawing every eye. In walks Cole Danzer in all his amazing, masculine, heart-stopping glory. His eyes find me immediately, holding on and refusing to let go. I feel short of breath all of a sudden, like he let all the air out of the room when he opened the door.

Seeing him again hits me like a physical blow. I haven't laid eyes on him in a week. Since the weather has cooled off, he must be doing something else. That or he's working inside and I just never see him come and go. And I've looked. Often. Believe me. But there's never a car or truck outside, so if he *is* there, he must live close enough to walk over.

The thought sends thrilling fingers dancing down my spine. Just the idea that he could be that close to me...all the time...day or night...

"Hoooly shit," Jordan mutters, probably louder than she intended to. Alcohol-induced lack of inhibition, I suppose. "Hiya, Cole."

Cole lets my eyes go long enough to glance at Jordan and nod. Then they're back on mine as he approaches.

I'm so absorbed in his arrival, I forget Jason is still close. "And Eden," Jason says, bending toward me as he speaks. "I'm here if you need any help. The weather can be brutal this time of year."

I clear my throat and drag my eyes to him, leaning away until he straightens. "I think we'll be okay, but I know where to find you if not."

Jason doesn't make a move to leave. He just turns to face Cole and crosses his arms over his chest. I get the sneaking suspicion it's his way of staking a claim or something. "How goes it, Cole?" he asks pleasantly enough. While his question is innocent, his body language says all sorts of other things that concern me. It says *She's mine,* which I'm not. It says *Back off,* which I don't want Cole to do. It also says *I'll fight for her,* which I'd hate. All in all, I don't like what I'm seeing.

Cole stops a few feet away, his blue gaze flickering to Jason. He nods again. "Jason."

The room is filled with tension. Cole's expression is much as it always is–curiously blank. Except for the frowns he gives me sometimes, this is the face he wears most often. But it's not his expression that brings tension to the room. It's the way he stands in front of Jason, like he's waiting for him to move, that gives me the sense that, despite the fact that they work together, there is no love lost between these two.

Emmy, as if she can sense the sliceable strain in the air, crawls into my lap and pops her thumb in her mouth. Cole catches the movement in his periphery and glances over at her. His rigid expression softens and his lips curl up. Just at the corners. It's not a smile, but it must be enough for Emmy, who is peeking up at him from where she's resting her head against my chest. I see her tiny hand rise and her fingers fold one, twice, three times in a wave.

He glances back up at Jason. No words are exchanged, but Jason shifts to the left, moving out of Cole's way. Cole straddles a stool two down from the ones Emmy and I are sitting on. He picks up a menu as if to say that whatever else might be going on, whatever undercurrents are drowning the rest of us, are of no consequence to him.

Jason walks off without a word and Jordan makes her way around to drool over Cole, a bee drawn to his unusual brand of honey. She stares at him unabashedly, leaning one hand and one curvy hip on the bar. All she lacks is a wad of bubblegum to pop. "What can I get for you, handsome?"

Cole doesn't even look up. "I think they were here first. Take their order, but put it on my bill."

"That's not necessary," I say.

Cole shifts his beautiful blue gaze over to me, pinning me with his stare. He doesn't speak right away. Just melts me with those eyes. "I know. But since you didn't get your muffins..."

"But that wasn't *your* fault."

He shrugs, his eyes dropping to Emmy. He winks at her before returning his attention to his menu. I look down to find her grinning behind her thumb. What is it about him that fascinates her? I can see it on her face as plainly as I can *feel* it on mine.

Maybe it's a genetic weakness that I've passed on to her. Like Cole-holism or Cole addiction. He seems to draw her as inevitably as he draws me.

"That's good enough for me, girls," Jordan chimes in. "Never argue with a gorgeous man who wants to buy you things." She beams a bright smile at Cole, who seems not to even notice as he continues studying the menu.

I end up ordering Emmy a grilled cheese and tater tots, not sure that she'll even eat now, and I get myself a chicken sandwich. Jordan assures me that it's to die for and the only thing that could make it better is a bloody mary.

"I'd better not, but thanks," I reply mildly.

"What can I get for *you*, Cole? Anything you see making you hungry?" she asks, unflappable in her pursuit of his attention. I'm a little embarrassed for her. I'm thankful for her sake that she seems too intoxicated to really care if she's making a fool of herself.

"Double cheeseburger combo. To go," he says, putting the menu back in its place and standing. "I'll be right back."

He walks off, heading toward the universal sign for the men's room. Jordan and I watch him go.

"Damn that man! He's so good at resisting my charms. I do everything but throw it up on the table for him, but…nothing. Nada." Her sigh is exaggerated. "I'll wear him down eventually. He's my Mount Everest."

"How's that?"

"He's the one thing I'm determined to climb on top of if it kills me."

She winks at me and then turns to yell at whomever does the cooking, someone named Raul if I understood her correctly. Then she sashays away, whistling and swinging her hips as she picks up her covered drink cup from behind the counter. I know she's drained it dry when I hear the straw start sucking air. I can only imagine what was in it.

She carries away the cup, disappearing into the back, probably to refill it from her own stash. While she's gone, Cole returns from the restroom.

He slides back onto his stool and, when he speaks, it's without even looking at me. "I heard what Jason said."

His voice is a quiet rumble that brings chills to my arms. I don't think it would matter what he said, or where he or when he said it. I think I'd always react to that damn voice of his.

"Oh?"

He nods. "I don't live far. Just up the road from you. The cabin on the beach," he explains. I know exactly the one he's referring to. It's the only one that actually looks like a cabin. Emmy and I have passed it each and every time we've walked that way. "If you need anything when the weather gets bad, come find me."

Somehow knowing where he lives seems...intimate. I'd say many people know where this man can be found, but I'd wager that he only *told* a very few of them. Yet here he is, basically inviting us into his life if we have a need. I feel honored almost, like he's gifted us with something rare and precious.

"Thank you. I appreciate that."

He turns to meet my eyes. And, again, I'm held. Effortlessly yet completely. Mercilessly. I feel like I can't look away. Or maybe that I don't want to. As though in doing so, I'd risk losing something exquisite. I don't know why, but it feels...important, like we are slowly building something priceless.

"I can come by and check on you when the snow comes. If you want."

"I'd hate to put you out."

But I'd secretly love it if you showed up at my door. Every day. Forever.

He watches me intently before he replies. He says so little, chooses every word so carefully it seems, that it makes me wonder even more about him. Makes him even more fascinating.

"It's no trouble. I promise," he says in his rich, gravelly voice. A chill streaks down my arms again and I shudder the tiniest bit. Enough for Emmy to notice, though. She picks up her head and looks at me. I brush several dark strands from her cheek, stuck there where she was pressed against me.

"We certainly appreciate that, don't we, Emmy?"

She turns her big green eyes to Cole and nods, her lips curving behind her thumb again.

He nods to her just as a bell chimes from somewhere behind the window that leads to the kitchen. I still haven't seen anyone back there, although an explosion could've happened a foot away and I might not have noticed. That is how this man affects me. I should probably be afraid. Only I'm not. I'm more intrigued and more…captivated than I can ever remember being. Than I ever thought I *could be.*

Jordan comes rushing out, tucking her presumably full cup back behind the counter. She reaches in through the window and takes a bag from a hand that appears to come from out of nowhere. Maybe Raul is just really short.

She carries it back to Cole, holding it out like it's an invitation to a sex party. "Enjoy," she says in her throatiest voice.

Cole nods, impervious to her efforts, and throws a bill onto the bar. "That ought to cover it. Thanks, Jordan."

"Anytime," she says as he stands and picks up his bag.

Then, without another word or backward glance, Cole walks right out the door. All three of us watch him go.

NINE

Eden

AS MUCH AS I love our little cottage, it must have cracks galore. It seems impossible to heat. No matter how high I turn up the thermostat, it never gets any warmer. It's not freezing, but it's not toasty either. Emmy and I both wear sweaters even when we're inside.

I glance out the window as I pass on my way to the living room. It's habit now, even though I haven't seen Cole working across the street since the weather turned so cold. But still, I look...on the off chance...

And today, I hit pay dirt. Through the front window of the cottage diagonal from mine, I see him. My heart flutters in my chest, making me feel breathless for a second.

The heat must be on over there because he's only wearing a white T-shirt. I can just see him from the waist up, but it's enough. It's enough to give me butterflies and warm my cool skin. Cole is standing in front of the window with a few nails clamped between his lips, hammering something above his head. I let my hungry eyes drift over him, drift over his god-like face, over his peaked biceps, over his narrow waist. The material of his shirt has ridden up as he stretches, revealing the very last row of muscle on his chiseled abdomen. My stomach turns a flip as I imagine what that skin must feel like–smooth and hard. Probably warm. Hot even.

"What is it, Momma?"

I jump guiltily, so enthralled I didn't hear her approach. "You scared me! What are you, a ninja-in-training?" I tease.

Emmy's eyes light up. "Like a *Teenage Mutant Ninja Turtle?*" she asks.

"Even better! You're not green and you don't have to carry that heavy shell on your back all day. But if you want to try, maybe you could start with carrying me." I grab her and pretend to try and climb on her back. She squeals and wiggles, so I end up tickling her instead.

"Your hands are cold," I tell her when she runs her icy little fingers up my neck in an attempt to tickle me back. "How about a hot bath to warm you up?"

"A bath?" she asks in horror. "Ewww!" Like every other child in the world, baths rank among Emmy's least favorite things.

"A clean little girl? Ewww!" I dance my fingers up and down her spine and she twists and turns to avoid them. "Fine. I guess I'll have to settle for a clean *and warm* Momma then."

"That sounds better," she admits with an impish grin.

"And after that...lunch. Then school work," I warn.

I see Emmy's eyes roll before she turns away from me to scamper back into the living room. School work, especially since she's homeschooled and has no playmates to soften the blow, falls right above baths on her "list of things I loathe." Getting her to do either is like pulling teeth.

In the bathroom I turn on the hot water spigot and temper it with just a little bit of cold as I wind up my hair and shed my clothes. I think *my eyes* roll back into my head when I stick my toe in. The moan that rumbles out of my throat when I sink down into the warm liquid is uncontainable. "Holy crap, that feels good!" I say to the empty room. It's fairly quiet in here, only the muted blare of the television interrupting the tranquility.

I let my eyes drift shut, visions of Cole dancing through my thoughts. His beautiful face, his incredible body, his overt strength. His hidden vulnerability. He's like all things delicious—and gorgeous, and capable, and mysterious—wrapped up in a package that has KEEP AWAY scrawled across the front. It makes for one of the most irresistible combinations I've ever encountered. It's so easy to picture him sweeping me off my feet, holding me in his strong arms, crushing my mouth with his perfect lips, warming my skin with his calloused touch. *God!*

I don't know how much time has passed in my fantasy world when I lift my head to look around. Emmy is happily singing along with one of her favorite DVDs and my water has cooled considerably. Not ready to give up Cole just yet, I hook my toe in the drain plug and yank. I let out a couple of inches of tepid water before I re-plug it and twist the hot water knob to add more heat. I hear a dull clink and practically the whole thing comes off in my hand and then, a deluge of water.

The hard spray hits me right in the face. I squeal and press my hand in to cover the pipe hole. Water is in my eyes, shooting up onto the ceiling and spilling from the tub out onto the floor before I get it somewhat under control. And even then, it's still spewing like crazy. And it's getting hotter.

"Mom! What happened?"

Emmy is standing in the doorway, wide-eyed. I flatten my palm over the pipe end to stem the flow as I look around for some kind of shut-off valve. The only one I see is for the toilet right beside the tub.

My mind races. I'm no plumber! I have no idea what to do in a situation like this other than let it flood the house, which would be a nightmare! One thought, one person, pops into my head. Whether advisable or not, I cling to that image.

"Emmy, I need you to run to the cottage across the street. You know the one where Mr. Danzer worked this summer?"

"Yeah, I know which one."

"You go straight over there and knock on the door. Don't stop and don't talk to anyone else, do you hear me?"

"I won't, Momma." Her eyes look frightened, but she's already backing out the door.

"Emmy, get Mr. Danzer and bring him over here, okay?"

She nods and then turns to run.

"Emmy!" I yell. I sigh in relief when she appears in the doorway again, cheeks already flushed. "Hand me two towels," I say. She grabs one from the sink where I left it and another from the cabinet underneath and hands them both to me. Water leaks copiously from around my fingers when I ease back to wind one around my front, half of it dragging in the water, and then stuff the other one on the pipe to staunch the flow of hot water. "Okay, go, go, go!"

She races off and I pray that sending her after him was the right thing to do. This would be a terrible time of year to have to find alternative accommodations. But if anyone can fix this, I bet Cole can.

I snatch the plug out of the drain again and listen to the water in the tub gurgle away, my stomach twitching with anxious anticipation.

TEN

Cole

PART OF ME is glad that Eden isn't at her window anymore. It's hard enough to keep my mind off her as it is, but when I can see her...when she stands so still in her kitchen and watches me...

I close my eyes and grit my teeth against the unwanted sensations that tear through me. I don't want to feel anything for her. I don't want to think about her or imagine what her soft lips would feel like against mine. I don't want to lie awake at night and wonder what she's doing, what she wears to bed, or what she looks like when she sleeps. I don't want any of this.

Not that it matters. I'm getting it anyway. No matter how hard I fight it, she's all I can think about. Accept on beach day.

I almost don't hear the knock at the door. I'm too deep in thought and the sound is too soft. I stop hammering for a second to listen, thinking I might've mistaken some other noise for a knock. But then I hear it again, hesitant but insistent.

I lay down my hammer and walk to the door, cracking it to look outside. Standing on the porch is Eden's daughter, Emmy. Her eyes are as big as saucers, her thumb is stuck snugly in her mouth and she's wiggling one foot where it's being swallowed whole in what looks like her mother's shoe.

A searing streak of panic blazes through me. I fling open the door and drop to one knee in front of her. "Emmy, what is it? Is your mom hurt?"

She shakes her head slowly, eyeing me suspiciously, like I might try to grab her and run away. Relief washes through me and I drop my head for a second. I shouldn't care. I shouldn't care more than in the polite way that people care about what happens to someone they hardly know. But that's not what this is. This relief...the panic that I felt initially...it's much more than just polite. It's a helluva lot more.

And I have no idea why.

I think again, briefly, vaguely, *What the hell is she doing to me?*

Emmy raises her arm and points back to her house. Her message is clear.

I would've responded, but the words get stuck in my throat when she surprises me by reaching out and curling her small fingers around mine. Something in my chest seizes. The world becomes uncomfortably emotional for a few seconds. I have to take my time before speaking.

Anxiously, she tugs.

"You need me to come back with you?" I finally manage.

She nods.

I reach behind me to pull the door shut so that I can follow her. She keeps a hold on my hand, her fingers tightening as she navigates the steps in her too-big shoes. They clomp on the boards and I walk slowly at her side, careful that she doesn't fall. It's a bitterly familiar sensation, one I want to both revel in and turn away from.

Only I can't. This little girl needs me. Her mother needs me.

As we walk across the street, my focus is torn. Part of me is wondering what I might find in the cottage up ahead, but another part of me is remembering why I never wanted to feel again. If I feel *anything*, I have to feel *everything*. The good and the bad. The peaceful and the painful.

At her own porch, Emmy releases my hand, kicks off her shoes and bounds up the steps. She throws open the door and races through the house, sparing a glance back to make sure I'm following her.

I toss her mom's shoes, which I picked up on the bottom step, beside the door and make my way inside.

Emmy runs to the bathroom and stands to one side looking in, still sucking her thumb.

"Hello?" I call to announce my presence.

"In here!" comes the harried response.

I head to the bathroom, not knowing what to expect. What I find nearly buckles my knees. Holy mother of God! It's Eden. In the bathtub. On her knees. Dripping wet. Covered only in a soggy towel that outlines her every curve in the most mouthwatering way.

It takes me a second to speak. I feel like I've been punched in the gut. What is it about this woman that makes me want her so badly? After all this time, after all the women who've tried, why her? Why now?

I don't have the answers to any of those questions. I only know that my whole body is tight as a damn drum just looking at her.

"Can you please shut off the water?" she sputters, drawing me back into thinking mode.

Immediately, I turn and head back outside, around to the side of the house to the water main where it's buried in the yard with the meter. I twist the handle to close the valve and turn to go back inside, leaving the cover off until I'm ready to cut the water back on.

In the bathroom, I find that the flow is already tapering off and Eden is breathing a little more easily. The muscles in her thin arms are straining under her water-slicked skin. Her breasts are heaving behind the knot in her towel. It's hard as all hell to drag my eyes back to her face.

But her face...God, she's beautiful! Her hair is jet black, like her daughter's, and her skin is porcelain cream. Even when it's not wet, it has a satiny sheen that makes my fingers itch to touch. Her nose is small and delicate and her lips are pink and lush. But it's her eyes that get to me. The way she watches me, the look that shines from the hazel depths. It's like she can see right through me.

Even now, when she turns to me after the water has stopped and she has let her tired arms fall to her sides, her eyes draw me in. Hold me right where I'm standing. They won't let me go. And part of me doesn't want them to.

Her lips break into an exhausted smile. "Phew! That was quite a bath." Emmy giggles around her thumb and Eden winks at her. An odd contentment spreads through me, like the steamy warmth of the bathroom is heating my insides. My heart ties itself into a knot of a million emotions. And my stomach clenches around only one.

Betrayal.

Betrayal of my daughter. Her memory. I can't be happy. Not without her. If she can't be here and be happy, then neither can I. I made her a promise. And I intend to keep it.

ELEVEN

Eden

FOR JUST A second, I thought I saw something flash in Cole's eyes. Like ice thawing. Or resolve softening.

But then it was gone. Almost like I'd just imagined it. Now he looks like the same heart-stoppingly gorgeous, aloof man that he always is.

"I'll need to get some things from Bailey's to fix this. You'll be without water for a while. If that will be a problem, you're welcome to go across the street. It's warm and the water's on."

"I think we'll be okay for a while," I tell him, shivering without the hot water to keep me warm.

Cole frowns as his eyes rake me. Despite his expression, my skin tingles hotly everywhere his gaze touches. "You're freezing."

As if on cue, my teeth chatter, the coolness of the ambient air like ice on my wet limbs. "If you'll give me just a minute to dress…"

I don't want him to rush off. I'd rather be freezing and without water for a few minutes than to let him go just yet. But that's not to be.

The crease in his brow deepens. "Oh. Sorry. I, uh, I'll be back." And with that, he's gone, once again leaving Emmy and me watching after him.

⌘⌘⌘⌘

An hour and a half of sitting on pins and needles later, I hear an engine roar up to the house outside and then shut off. Emmy runs to the window, but I *make* myself remain seated. He can knock and *then* I'll go answer the door. I don't want him to think I've been sitting here waiting on him all this time.

Which is exactly what I've been doing. From the moment he tore his hot-and-cold blue eyes off my wet skin, I haven't been able to get him off my mind.

Who the hell am I kidding? I think about him too much all the time!

"It's Jordan, Momma," Emmy informs me.

My mood plummets. I don't know how to take Jordan and I don't really trust her, so any time spent with her isn't exactly pleasurable. That's doubly the case when I was expecting Cole instead. Not a fair trade. Not a fair trade *at all*.

This time, I do get up and go to the door, peeking out before I swing it open. My stomach does a little flip when I see Cole walking along behind Jordan as they approach my door. I can tell by the exaggerated way she's swinging her hips that she's hoping he's looking at her butt.

When I open the door, she gives me a wide grin and a wink, as though she knows that *I* know exactly what she's doing. "Is he looking?" she whispers when she stops in front of me.

I glance past her to Cole. His eyes are focused squarely, disconcertingly on me. His ever-present frown is in place, but his blue gaze is blazing up at me. For a second, I have to work to breathe, to make my lungs expand and contract, expand and contract.

"Is he?" Jordan hisses before Cole climbs onto the porch.

I just smile and nod, trying hard to keep my eyes and my attention on her rather than the man coming up behind her.

"I gave this handsome man and all his plumbing goodies a ride back here since he doesn't drive."

Doesn't drive?

Although I've never seen him in a vehicle, it never occurred to me that Cole might not drive.

"I told you I could walk," he says flatly when he stops behind Jordan.

Over her shoulder, she turns a million-watt smile on him. "And miss an opportunity to flirt with you? Not a chance."

When she faces me, she rolls her eyes and then mouths an excited *Ohmigod!* Based on the flush of her cheeks and her uncharacteristically bright eyes, I'd say she's pretty happy today, with or without alcohol. If she *has* been drinking, as per her usual, it's not obvious.

"Can we come in?" Cole asks, his voice rife with irritation. I get the feeling he's not too pleased about his predicament.

I suppress a grin. "Of course."

I back up and open the door wide. Jordan wiggles in first, followed by a lagging Cole. My lips twitch as I look up into his scowling face.

"Don't you dare laugh!" he leans down and whispers to me as he passes. That only makes my mirth harder to contain.

As I close the door behind him, I'm having trouble not smiling from ear to ear. Not because his reaction to Jordan is funny, which it sort of is, but more because I'm warmed from head to toe, inside to out, with how he shared it with me. Almost like a private joke. It makes me realize that I like sharing things with this man. And that I want to know him better.

A lot better.

I get the feeling that the number of people Cole trusts in his life are about as many as the ones I trust in mine—none. Well except Emmy.

But something tells me that I can trust him. And that I *want* to trust him. I want to be able to trust somebody. It's been so long...

Cole makes his way straight to the bathroom. Surprisingly, my daughter is right on his heels, leaving me alone with Jordan, who doesn't appear in any big hurry to leave. She has already made herself at home on the sofa, so I resign myself to spending time with her until she decides to leave.

I curl up in the big chair facing her, tucking my cold feet up under me. Jordan notices.

"Don't you have heat in here?" she asks bluntly.

"Yes, it's just not a particularly warm house."

She shivers, rubbing her hands up and down her arms. "You aren't kidding. And I didn't even bring anything to warm us up," she adds with a knowing wink.

"That's okay. I'm getting used to it."

"So, don't you work?"

I should've known that this woman was the type not to pull any punches, but wow! She just dives right in.

"Ummm, not outside the home. I homeschool Emmy, so..." I trail off, hoping she'll let this thread die.

"Well that doesn't make you money, does it?"

I laugh uneasily. "No, but we have a little in savings." And that's true. She doesn't have to know all the sordid details about how I came by that money or that what's left of it is hidden beneath the false bottom that I tore out and sewed back up in the floor of my suitcase.

Jordan eyes me as she nods. Not really suspiciously, but more...curiously. "Where's the princess's papa?"

Oh, God! Is this what the whole morning's going to be like?

"I, uh, I don't really talk about it in front of Emmy," I reply in a low voice. That's also true. In some ways, Emmy is an extremely perceptive child and she's never really pushed me on the details of her father. I think in some strange way, she knows that she's better off *not* knowing.

"Got it," she concedes amicably. "Well then let's whisper about your hot plumber. So is there something going on between you two or what?"

"Of course not. Why do you ask?"

Jordan gives me a withering look. "I might be a lush, but I'm not stupid. I pay attention to things that interest me. And, honey, *that boy* interests me." Her smile is genuine. She doesn't seem the least bit put out that he might be interested in *me*.

According to her, that is.

I don't really see it, although I can't say that the idea doesn't give me a little thrill. I can only imagine what it might be like to be the object of something other than his frowns and his quiet, brooding ways.

"Why have you two never, um, dated then?"

I'm remembering Jason's comment about her being the town "bicycle."

She sighs loudly. "No matter how much I might try to drag him out of his shell...and his clothes..." she adds with an impish wrinkle of her nose, "he keeps to himself. I know the guy's broken and all, but I was beginning to think he was gay."

I think of what I know of Cole so far. Nothing, not one single thing, makes me think he's anything other than 100% darkly delectable, manly-man straight.

"But you don't think so now?"

She waves me off with her hand. "Nah, I don't think I ever really did. I think it was just easier to understand than his rejection." Her comment, unexpectedly insightful, takes me by surprise.

"Oh," I say flatly, not knowing what else *to* say.

Jordan's face takes on an uncharacteristic seriousness. "I've got more baggage than *I* can handle. I wouldn't blame anyone else for keeping their distance. Still hurts, though."

"Why would you say that?"

She stares hard at her fingers where they pull and tug and twist a loose string along the sofa cushion. It's the first time I've seen her anything less than comfortable, confident and slightly inebriated, I think.

"My husband left me three years ago. But not before he screwed half the town and told everybody about the problems I had trying to get pregnant. He was a real son-of-a-bitch. I'll be the first to admit that he hurt me and that I haven't been the same since. It's just…it's just…so humiliating," she confesses a bit tearfully. I'm so shocked by her story and by her softer side that I just sit here staring at her. Thankfully she hasn't looked up at me. After a loud sniff and a shake of her head, as if ridding her mind of bad memories, Jordan finally raises her glistening brown eyes to mine and smiles. "That's when I started drinking. Haven't looked back since."

I've never seen someone wear alcoholism more proudly, but in a way, I guess she's earned her weakness. Besides, who am I to judge? We all heal and cope (or avoid coping, in this case) in different ways. I have enough problems without chastising this wounded woman for the choices she's made since her husband turned on her.

"So now you can see why it's my mission to get in that man's pants," she says, nodding her head toward the bathroom.

"Ummm," I hedge.

No, I don't see the connection at all.

She shrugs. "You'd get it if you drank more," she declares with a grin. "But I'm glad you don't. That little girl needs you."

This is the moment that I decide I like Jordan Bailey. Very much. Even if she is damaged and headed down a dangerous path with her drinking. Sometimes I think broken people gravitate toward one another, like our shattered pieces connect on a level that unscarred people never know.

I glance toward the bathroom, thinking of the man inside, holding my daughter so rapt. Maybe that's why I'm so irrefutably drawn to him. He may be the most broken one of all.

TWELVE

Cole

SHE'S GETTING UNDER my skin. I've thought about Eden from the second I left her with a fixed faucet and running water. I've thought about her being there all by herself, about the possibility that Jason might come over to check on her, especially after Jordan tells him what happened. And that eats at me. I hate to admit how much it bothers me to think of him being in her house, of him being close to her. Of any man, really.

Even though I don't want the strings, even though I don't want the feelings, in some way I feel like Eden is already mine. Or at least that she should be. And what's mine, no man touches. Or at least, if he tries, he doesn't get to talk about it for a few days while he heals.

It makes no sense, of course. I have no claim on her. No right to care even. But I do. God in heaven, how I do!

That's why, although I shouldn't–shouldn't care, shouldn't get involved, shouldn't make things worse–I email my agent and ask him to send me a no-contract phone as soon as possible. As inadvisable as it is, I want her to have a way to reach me. And only me.

THIRTEEN

Eden

IT'S ONLY BEEN two days since I've seen Cole, yet it feels like forever. I'm like a junkie, jonesing for her next fix. What is wrong with me? I never get like this. Over anybody, much less a man! I've had too many bad experiences. I have too much baggage. I don't even *want* to want someone this way.

And yet here I am. Wanting. And loving it in a perverse way. The anticipation, the sensations, the exhilaration–they're as addictive as Cole himself is turning out to be. My worry, however, is that they're as *destructive* as an addiction.

I can't let it get to that point. I have to protect Emmy, first and foremost. And even though I feel like Cole could be good and...safe somehow, if the tide shifts, I have to be ready and willing to bail. Emmy comes first. Always. She has to.

The knock on the door pulls me from my troublesome thoughts. I glance at Emmy on the floor. She's in the beginning stages of another drawing. She probably doesn't even know I'm in the room. She loses herself when she has a crayon in her hand. I'm glad she has that respite from the world around her and the ugliness it can sometimes show.

I get up and walk to the door. As I near it, I don't even have to stretch up on my toes to peek through the glass at the top. My heart is already pattering at the dirty blond crown I can plainly see. I know who's outside. Every nerve in my body is screaming his name.

I slip off the chain and unlock the deadbolt, swinging the door open to Cole. His longish hair is framing his face and, despite the cold, he's wearing only a sweatshirt and jeans. But I forget all about that when I look up. The moment I meet his intense cerulean eyes, I'm stuck. Trapped. Drowning in a sea of blue.

Neither of us says anything. The thump of my daughter running up to me and slamming to a stop against my thigh jars me back to reality. I glance down.

Her thumb is in her mouth, but she's already smiling around it. Cautiously, she eases just far enough away from me to still be able to hold on, but also be able to reach Cole's hand. She curls her fingers around his and tugs him toward us.

His eyes flicker back up to mine as he steps forward. Still caught in that blue gaze of his, I don't retreat. We just stand in the doorway, almost chest to chest, his handsome face staring down into mine. Up close, I can count every long eyelash that frames his bright eyes, number every light brown whisker that dots his lean cheeks. He's the perfect combination of beautiful and manly.

"May I come in?" he asks, his voice sending a chill skittering down my spine. I can feel Emmy pulling him in, pulling him closer to me. I don't back down. Something in me craves his closeness. Wants more of it.

I tip my chin up, my lips tingling with an unspoken desire for him to touch them, caress them. Devour them. "Of course," I reply, yet neither of us moves.

For several long seconds, we are rooted to this spot, the attraction between us as perceptible and vibrant as a living thing.

But then he moves to one side to step around me, letting Emmy drag him to the living room so she can show him her drawing. She picks it up and holds it out to him. He takes the paper gently from her fingers. It looks so small when it's held in his big hands. He could easily crumple it, probably crush it into dust, yet he doesn't. He holds it delicately, as though it's the most precious thing in the world.

I was so lost in thought before Cole arrived, I wasn't really watching what Emmy was drawing, but from Cole's elbow I can plainly see that it's her attempt at capturing them. She's holding his hand and her shoes are at least five sizes too big. I'm guessing it's from the day she went to fetch him for me when I was stuck in the tub, holding off a flood.

Cole squats down in front of her, turning the paper back to face her. "Is this me?" he asks, pointing to the tall man with pale yellowish-brown hair. Emmy nods, toying with the hem of her Hermione T-shirt. "This is really good." Cole's expression shows that he's impressed and that he's not just being kind.

I'm proud, of course. Emmy does a great job when she takes her time. She often adds details that surprise me. Every doctor she's had since we left has encouraged her to draw as a means of therapy. Thankfully, she seems to really enjoy it.

Cole starts to hand the picture back to Emmy, but she pushes it back toward him. "Is this for me?"

She nods.

"Thank you. I know just where I'll put it."

He stands, holding the paper in one hand while he smiles down at Emmy. I can see the moment she becomes uncomfortable with his quiet attention. She lowers her eyes and edges toward me, eventually leaning her forehead against my side.

When Cole's gaze leaves Emmy and lifts to mine, there's a sadness in it, a grief that nearly staggers me. I can only imagine that he's reminded of his loss every time he looks at my daughter.

"Cole, I..." I don't even know what to say. I probably shouldn't bring it up. For all I know, I'm not supposed to even know about his loss. But I feel the need to say *something*, to offer some sort of comfort, even though I know that there is none. I don't think there *is* comfort for a parent who has lost a child.

As always, his frown reappears, like he's burying deep any small sign of emotion. Or maybe just burying his pain. I might never know.

"I brought you something," he begins. I've been so wrapped up in his consuming presence, I'd forgotten to even wonder why he might be here. Cole reaches into his pocket and brings out a cell phone. An iPhone to be exact. "I wanted you to have something for emergencies. My number's already in it."

I don't have the heart to tell him that I have a phone. I have a child. It would be totally irresponsible for me not to have a way to at least call 911. This, however, is a nice phone. A *real* phone. The kind I used to have when I was still at my aunt's.

The thought heralds an onslaught of rapid-fire images and emotions that make my heart feel like it stopped in my chest.

"It's just a phone," Cole says.

I drag my eyes away from the flat, rectangular screen. "What?"

His frown deepens. "It's just a phone. It won't bite."

"Oh. Right. I know. I just...sorry. I was just thinking."

"You don't have to use it to call me. I just wanted you to have it in case of emergency. The winters here are–"

"Brutal, I know," I finish for him, shaking off the chill that has settled over me. "I really appreciate it. You didn't have to do this."

He shrugs. "I know."

I don't know what comes over me. Maybe it's the need to know something about this enigmatic man while he's standing here in my living room, feeling charitable.

"Why did you?"

"Why did I what?"

"Why did you get me a phone?"

"I told you. I–"

"I know what you told me, but we aren't your responsibility."

His lips thin in aggravation. "I didn't say you were. I was just trying to help. I can see that I made a mistake."

When he sets the phone on the coffee table and starts to turn away, I stop him with a hand to his forearm. I feel his response to my touch–the rippling of muscle under my fingertips. "Wait! That's not what I–"

"I shouldn't have come."

"Cole, stop! Please. I didn't mean it like that. I just...I don't want you worrying about us. It seems like you...like you've got enough to worry about without us adding to it."

His eyes are like a turbulent sea. "What's that supposed to mean?"

I sigh, exasperated with myself and the mess I've made of things. "I just mean...*God!* I don't know what I mean. I just know that I didn't mean it the way it sounded. I...I'm grateful for the gift. Thank you. I just...I hate that you went to so much trouble for us. Jordan...Jordan said you don't drive and I...I..."

His expression turns stony and cold. "People say all sorts of things about me."

"So you *do* drive?"

The further tightening of his features answers my question. "Use the phone if you need it. Toss it in the garbage if you don't."

He pulls away and heads for the door in long, angry strides. I'm left to either watch him leave again or chase after him.

This time I chase after him. "Cole, wait."

He stops with his hand on the knob, his face in profile to me. I can see the firm set of his jaw and the little muscle that twitches rhythmically there.

"Yes?"

I walk right up to him, winding my fingers around his arm again and hauling myself up on my toes. I press my lips to his cool cheek. "Thank you," I whisper against his skin.

I start to back away when he turns to look at me. His mouth is within an inch of mine and I stop dead, frozen by the magnetism that exists between us.

I see his piercing eyes fall to my lips. I know I should move away, but I don't. I'm not sure I can, even though the muscles in my calves are trembling as they hold me up.

Cole's arm is wedged between my heavy breasts and I have the intense urge to press into him, to ease the ache that's getting stronger with each passing day. As though he can sense it, he lists toward me. Just a little. The tiniest of sways. But it's enough. It's enough to fan the flame of our attraction.

I jump when a harsh knock breaks the spell. Neither of us moves for a few more seconds, hesitant to let this go. Whatever "this" is.

At the second knock, I drop back down onto my heels. Cole clears his throat and steps aside so I can answer the door, but his eyes are still on me. I can feel them, like velvety fingers, keeping me wound up. Disconcerted.

It's with one shaking hand that I reach for the knob and pull open the door. Jason is standing on my porch, smiling down at me.

"Jason. Hi," I say, sounding as breathless as I feel.

"Eden," he says with a nod, his smile widening. "Can I come in?"

"Oh, uh, of course," I stammer, standing back to allow him to enter. I know the moment he spots Cole. His body language changes completely. He stiffens and his smile turns cold. He tries to hide it, but only a complete fool wouldn't be able to see it.

"Hiya, Cole. Didn't know you were here," he says as if there is no tension in the room.

"Jason," Cole nods. "What brings you by?"

Conveniently, Jason holds up a white slip of paper he's carrying. "Brought the receipt for the items you bought at the store. Jordan forgot it when she bagged it all. I told her I'd bring it on out, but you weren't at your place or across the street, so I thought I'd drop it off with Eden. You know, since you were fixing things here."

I guess that makes sense, but still, it seems like an awful lot of trouble for a receipt. "Thanks," Cole says coolly, reaching for the paper. He folds it up and sticks it in his jeans pocket.

"Were you on your way out?" Jason asks Cole innocently enough, pointing back over his shoulder at the door.

Unruffled, Cole simply says, "As a matter of fact I was." Jason moves farther into the living room as Cole approaches the door again. "Call if you need me," he says. Then, with one long look, he's gone, leaving an empty space in the room that ten Jasons couldn't fill. I feel oddly...bereft, a sensation that's becoming more pronounced every time I'm around my handsome landlord and then he leaves.

"I thought you didn't have a phone," Jason reminds after the door is closed and the room is quiet again.

"He brought me one," I confess, not following him into the living room.

His eyebrows shoot up. "He did? Well, looks like you're bringing him out of his shell."

I shrug. I don't know what to say to that, although his observation makes me happy.

"The guy needs all the friends he can get. Nobody really wants to have anything to do with him, so..."

I know what he's doing. I know what he's getting at. And it infuriates me. I don't let him see that, though. "I'm glad I can be different then."

"You are *definitely* different," Jason says, his genuine (if a bit shark-like) smile returning. His gaze skims me appreciatively.

As if sensing my discomfort, Emmy jumps up from her place on the floor and runs to me, wrapping her arms around my waist and looking up at me with her big, shiny green eyes.

"Well, thanks for bringing that by for Cole. Emmy and I were just about to get into her lessons for the day."

His expression sobers, but he still seems pleasant enough. "I'll see myself out then." When he passes me, much closer than what I'd have liked, he stops and bends toward my ear. "If you need help, you'd be better off calling me. I don't think you want to put much faith in Cole. Not with a history like his."

I frown. I want to ask questions. I'm sure *he knew* I would want to ask questions. But I'm not falling into his trap. "I guess you should leave me your number then."

That seems to satisfy him quite a bit. He takes out his wallet and removes one of several crisp business cards. They read JASON BAILEY. OWNER. BAILEY'S QUICK STOP. BAILEY'S PROPERTY MANAGEMENT. BAILEY'S IMPORTS.

What *doesn't* he do in this town?

"Call me anytime. I mean it."

He gives the underside of my chin a quick brush with his hooked forefinger, like we're *that* familiar, and then reaches for the knob. I wait with bated breath for him to disappear, unlike with Cole, who I have to resist the urge to beg to stay. And when the door is closed behind Jason, I can't help noticing the relief I feel. Nothing like the empty, yearning sensation I get when Cole goes.

With Jason gone, Emmy happily returns to her spot on the floor. I drift to the chair and sit down, lost in deep thought. What is Cole doing to me? How can I be so taken with someone I hardly know? What is it about him that pulls me in, that has taken such a hold on me and won't let go?

What. Is it. About. Cole?

I don't know how many minutes have passed–ten, twenty, sixty?– when an insistent fist bangs on the door. Two sharp knocks. My heart is thumping heavily in my chest when I get up to go answer it. But that's nothing compared to the wild galloping that commences when I open it to find Cole staring at me with hunger in his eyes.

Cole.

He came back.

And he's going to kiss me.

I can feel it like static, stimulating every fine hair on my body.

And then he drags me into his arms and puts an end to my curiosity.

His lips. I knew they'd taste like heaven. And they do. They're the perfect mixture of firm and soft, and they move over mine with a power I always knew him capable of. It prowls in him, just beneath the surface, like a caged animal. Right now, the animal is barely contained. I feel it in the way his lips urge mine apart, in the way his tongue tangles and dominates mine, sending shockwaves of thrill all the way through to my core. I feel it in the way his hand threads into my hair to hold me still for his plundering.

He's capturing me.

And I'm captured.

He wants me.

And I'm all his.

And I love it. I love it all. More than I ever thought I could.

When we're both panting breathlessly, Cole raises his head and spears me with a blue gaze hotter than the tip of a flame. As I watch, he licks his lips, as if savoring the taste of me. Saliva pours into my mouth, making me crave the fresh mint of his tongue more than ever. Now that I know what it's like, I won't be able to get enough.

"Eden," he says in his incredible voice, staring down at me with his incredible eyes.

"Yes?" I all but sway, hypnotized by the spell he's cast over me.

He could ask me anything right now, anything at all, and I'd agree to it. I'm putty in his hands.

"Get out of my head. Please. I don't want you there." His words are soft. Sincere. Heartbreaking.

But before devastation sets in, I realize exactly what he said. What it means. And I'm thrilled.

I'm in his head.

FOURTEEN

Eden

WHEN IT STARTED snowing this morning, I was braced for a foot of snow that would preclude us being able to dig out until spring. That's the kind of thing I'd heard about Maine, but so far, that doesn't seem very accurate. The big, fat, beautiful flakes have been falling all day, but the roads are still clear and it appears that life is going on as usual in Miller's Pond.

I woke Emmy up early so we could take the car to Bailey's and get some shut-in supplies–food, matches, some candles, two more blankets and a variety of fun-yet-not-necessary things like marshmallows and a board game. Now, I feel like all that was a bit premature. It seems that this snow is going to peter out before it can bombard us with two-foot snowdrifts that trap us inside.

"Can we go to the beach today, Momma? And then have hot chocolate when we come back? With extra marshmallows?"

"It's too cold, Emmy. You'll–"

"Pleeease! I'll bundle up. I promise. I wanna build a snowman on the beach!"

"There's not enough snow yet to build a good snowman, sweetpea."

"Then a little snowman. Pleeease!"

I bought her a snowsuit and boots when I sent the lease back to Jason. Living up north, I knew the lure of building a snowman would be too much for Emmy to resist without driving me completely insane.

"Thermals first. Two pairs of socks and–" She's racing toward her bedroom before I can even finish. "And a toboggan, young lady!" I yell so she can hear me above her excited thumping and bumping.

Ten minutes later, she runs, albeit slower, back out into the living room, looking like the Michelin Man's firstborn. All I can see is her eyes, nose and mouth. Everything else is covered.

She stops in front of me for inspection, her emerald eyes flashing brightly from the flushed oval of her face. I peek into the neck of her jacket to make sure the thermals are there, which they are. Then I pull down one sock to make sure another elastic band is hiding underneath, which it is.

"Good girl," I tell her with a pat to her padded butt. "Let me get my boots and jacket."

She's all but dancing from foot to foot by the time I get her feet in boots and then get my coat and boots on. We strike out across the street and down toward the beach. When we pass the cabin I know now to be Cole's, a little chill races down my spine that has nothing to do with the temperature or the falling snow. It's a beautiful place, really. Not too big, but nicely appointed. The logs are dark brown and the front is mostly stone except for the six tall windows that surround the front door. There's a big wraparound porch with rockers on one side of it and a swing on the other. It looks like there are blue cushions on them, but all the seats are now piled with a few inches of puffy, white snow.

I see the smoke curling from the stone chimney as we walk by. That doesn't necessarily mean he's home, but I wonder if he's in there, if he's curled up in front of the fire. I wonder if he thinks about our kiss as often as I do, if he ever looks for me when he's working across the street. I wonder all kinds of things, things I have no way of knowing. I have no way of knowing because I haven't seen Cole since the day he told me to get out of his head.

"Come on, Mom," Emmy calls loudly. By the look on her face, she's getting irritated because I'm not moving as quickly as she'd like.

"Look at you, in such a hurry. Bet I can beat you there," I tell her, starting to trot toward her. With a squeal, she turns and takes off down the sidewalk like a puffy pink streak. She giggles and runs the rest of the short distance to the snow-covered beach.

I stop for a second to admire the beauty. The beach looks as though it's been misted with white confetti and fluffy balls of cotton. The pristine blanket melts away where sea meets sand, the surf lapping away at the frosty treat. Beyond that, the ocean spreads out like a blue field under the ominous sky, snowflakes falling to the roiling surface and then disappearing as if by magic. It's quiet and pure and peaceful. I think to myself that it's breathtaking, but I quickly realize that it's not nearly as breathtaking as the man I see huddled on the beach a short distance ahead.

Building a sandcastle.

My heart aches even as it soars at seeing him. The pain he must feel...to be here, on yet another Sunday, in the freezing cold, building his sandcastle.

I know it's Cole. Little of him other than his fiery-red bare hands is visible behind the cold-weather gear, but I know it's him. I can feel it. I can feel the grief rolling off him in waves bigger than the ocean that serves as his backdrop.

I know his loss is something I can't even fathom, but I am more curious than ever as to why he so regularly, so dogmatically erects these castles. Rain or shine, warm or cold, it seems he makes his monument no matter what.

Before I can stop her, Emmy is darting off down the beach toward him. He's not as far away this time, so she reaches him before I can stop her.

His back is to us again, so he doesn't see her standing behind him. He probably didn't hear her either, the crashing waves coupled with the howling wind nearly deafening. I approach her and take her hand, holding my finger to my lips when she looks up at me. Not that she would say anything, but I want her to know that *I'm* being quiet, too. I feel like our presence encroaches on something deeply personal and intensely special, and I don't want to intrude upon that.

The castle appears to be complete. It has six spires and turrets again, a hillside full of snowy trees and a mote protecting it all. There must've been some debris that had washed up because this one even has a drawbridge. I can't imagine what time he must've come out here to finish it by lunch.

Before I can turn away, I see Cole stand. I stop, not wanting to be rude, but he still doesn't see us. With Emmy's hand in mine, we start to back away. That's when I see Cole bend down and swipe up a handful of sand. He stares at it for a few seconds and then gently dumps the granules into his pants pocket, patting it afterward. Almost as though he's reassuring himself that it's there.

Part of me wants to scramble away. I feel as though I'm witnessing something that no one should witness, something that is so private that *seeing it* steals away the soul of it. But another part of me can't move. I'm so utterly broken *for him,* I feel like I lost something as well. I want nothing more than to go to him and wrap my arms around his big, strong shoulders and take some of the load from them. I know *without knowing* that they bear too much.

Before I can decide whether to run or stay, Cole turns and catches sight of Emmy's pink suit. He goes completely still, looking at her as though he's seen a ghost rather than the little girl he's seen several times before. His face is as pale as the snow around him under his two-day scruff and wind-kissed cheeks.

I mouth the words *I'm sorry* and I scoop Emmy up into my arms and go back the way we came. I carry her past the place where we entered the beach and we play there for nearly two hours. I don't see Cole again. Even though I look for him almost as often as I breathe.

⌘⌘⌘⌘

Emmy and I are debating what to have for supper–she wants Spaghettios and I want her to have something healthy–when the knock sounds at the door. The wings of a thousand butterflies beat the walls of my stomach when I think about what happened the last time there was a knock at the door. I can almost taste the minty sweetness of Cole's tongue in my mouth. Heat and want and anticipation pour through me, and my hands shake all the way to the door.

I don't look out the glass; I simply make an assumption.

And it's the wrong one.

Jason is smiling down at me when I open the door. I have to work hard to keep the disappointment from showing on my face or registering in my voice.

"Jason! What brings you out in this weather?"

He holds up a white paper bag that looks heavy. "I brought soup. Thought you might like a little chowder for dinner. It's perfect on a snowy night."

Shit.

I plaster on a smile. "Oh, well...how thoughtful. Thank you." I start to take the bag from him, but he holds it aloft.

"Let me fix it. You have to layer it with crackers juuust right or it ruins the flavor."

Soup that has to be layered? Is he really using that as an excuse to come and eat dinner with me?

"Well, uh, Emmy and I were just getting ready to..." What? Eat? Yes, we were. And now he's here with food. That's not a good excuse. And I'm a terrible liar. So I just give up. Seems like I'm stuck for the moment. "We were just deciding on what to eat, so your timing is perfect. Come in," I say mildly, standing back so he can enter.

From the back of the couch, her favorite perch, Emmy eyes Jason suspiciously. Her thumb isn't in her mouth. Yet.

"Hiya, sweetie," he says amicably enough. He doesn't try too hard to get her to talk or to get close to her, which I appreciate. I'd have no choice but to get stern with him–and *fast*–if he did that.

Jason walks into the kitchen like he's been here a thousand times. He slips off his coat and tosses it over a chair at the table and then takes bowls from the cabinet, bowls which have probably been in the same spot for years. He whistles as he spoons out soup into each bowl, covers it with toppings from the bag, and then more soup on top. "Gotta let them sit for a few minutes. Why don't you fix us something to drink?"

"Oh, sorry." The whole situation makes me slightly uncomfortable, like being in the kitchen with a boy who's too touchy.

I squeeze past Jason to reach for glasses. He doesn't bother moving to give me room, but rather leans back just enough to brush up against me as I stretch, ribbing me with his elbow. "This is nice, right?"

I smile, but say nothing, already thinking to myself that I'll have to curtail this situation, even if it makes him mad. I'd really rather not do that, but...he's leaving me no choice.

"I have milk or sweet tea. Or water," I announce.

"Sweet tea? You *are* from the south." I don't answer, just keep smiling. That's my plan for the night–just keep smiling until this is over. Then I can figure out how to avoid him in the future. "I'll have milk."

I pour each of us a glass of milk and set the table. He hasn't said he's staying to eat and I haven't asked, but at this point, I think it's pretty much implied.

Supper passes smoothly for the most part. Jason is like an oven, only rather than self-cleaning, he's self-entertaining. All I have to do is smile and nod and he takes care of the rest. His favorite topic of conversation is anything that involves him. And he's well-versed in the subject, his stories flowing endlessly from one accomplishment or anecdote to another. All centering around himself.

Emmy actually eats most of her soup. She hardly looks up, but at least she isn't sucking her thumb. I see her slide her eyes toward Jason often, though, like she's making sure he's not going to reach out and grab her.

Sadly, I feel the same way, almost. When she finishes eating, she turns her pleading eyes to me and I tip my head toward the living room, silently excusing her from further torture.

I wait for Jason to take a breath before interrupting. "I hate to cut this short, but I don't have anything for dessert. I really need to get Emmy ready for bed anyway."

Jason checks his watch. "This early?"

"She's a little girl. She likes to play when she takes a bath. Not be rushed."

"Oh, I know how you women are with your baths," he says, unperturbed.

I resist the urge to roll my eyes at his insinuation. Like he's got *sooo* much experience with the ladies.

I laugh, although for the most part, it lacks any actual humor. "We sure do."

"Sure you don't want me to stay and clean up while you're tending to her? I'd be happy to."

"That's nice of you, but I'll take care of it. Not that much to do anyway."

"Well, I can at least take my dishes to the sink," he says, standing.

I put my hand on his forearm. "Nope. I insist. You brought the food. The least I can do is clean up."

He grins. "Oh, so you're one of *those* types of women."

"And what type is that?"

"The type who likes to be equal. In everything."

The light in his eyes, the suggestive tone...they send apprehension skittering down my spine. I clear my throat and slide around the other end of the table toward the door. "Well, thank you again for the soup. Emmy and I really appreciate it."

Jason grabs his jacket and throws it over his shoulder. I'm sure it's meant to be a rakish gesture, but it just creeps me out. *He* just creeps me out, actually.

"I'll come back by to check on you tomorrow. Supposed to drop into the single digits tonight and I notice that you don't even have a fire going," he says, tipping his head toward the empty fireplace.

"I wasn't sure it was functional and I forgot to ask."

"It's functional. Cole keeps the chimney swept. But you probably don't even have any wood. I can bring you some and–"

"Don't go to any more trouble on my account. We'll be fine. I'll give you a call in a couple of days just to let you know we're fine."

If that's what it takes–the promise of calling him–to get him off my back, I'm happy to do it.

"Okay, okay, Ms. Independent," he teases.

I open the door for him. "Thanks again, Jason."

"It was my pleasure." Again, his tone…and the way he emphasizes the word "pleasure"…ack!

I barely wait for him to clear the jamb before I close the door. I slump against the cool wood, glad that he's finally gone. My relief is shortlived, however, when I hear the sick *raarrr raarrr raarrr* of his engine struggling to turn over. "No, no, no," I mutter, hoping against hope that he's not having car trouble.

But when I hear the thud of a slamming door and the clomp of stomping feet, I know I'm not getting my wish. I'm expecting the knock when I hear it this time. With a sigh, I open the door, plastering another smile on my face.

At least Jason has the good sense to look sheepish. "My truck won't start. I'm low on gas. My guess is that the water in it froze."

"Really? That quickly?"

He shrugs. "It happens." I say nothing. He says nothing. We just stare at each other until finally he asks, "Can I come in?"

"Of course," I say, biting back my exasperation. "Do you need to use the phone to call someone?"

"There's only one tow service in town and they're probably gone. And that leaves only Jordan. I hate to get her out after dark, though."

I grit my teeth. "I can take you before I put Emmy in the bath tub."

"No, I'd hate for you to get stuck out in this weather. It'll warm up in the morning, if–"

That's enough to piss me off. "I'm sorry, but you can't stay here, Jason. I have a child and she needs a quiet, predictable environment."

"It would just be for one night. I could sleep on the couch."

Could? Could?? What the hell else other option did you think I'd entertain?

"I'm sorry, but you'll have to make other arrangements."

My tone is stern and I'd be willing to bet my expression has lost a lot of its feigned pleasantness.

"Okay, okay. I understand," he says amiably. "Can I at least wait inside until Jordan gets here?"

Whether or not he's *trying* to make me feel like a douche, I don't know, but I do. I'm not *that* coldhearted. "Of course you can."

I tell Emmy to play in her room and I clean up the kitchen as Jason makes calls. Evidently the towing service really *is* closed, and he calls Jordan three times, all with no answer. "She's probably drunk already," he says by way of explanation. He sits with his phone dangling between his knees for a couple of minutes, as though he's waiting for me to make him an offer. I'm thinking to myself that hell will have to freeze over first. Finally, he takes up his phone again. His sigh is dramatic and loud. "I guess I could try Jep. Maybe he can give me a ride."

Jep answers and agrees to come and get Jason, much to my relief. "He'll be here in fifteen."

My smile is genuine this time. "Good." I don't add what I'm *thinking,* which is that he can't get here soon enough.

FIFTEEN

Eden

THE SNOW STARTS again the next morning. This one is different. It looks different, feels different. It's just...different. There's a stillness in the air that reminds me of the calm before a storm. It doesn't help that the weatherman keeps talking about the Nor'easter we'll get if the jet stream dips down and the moisture stays put and blah, blah, blah. I don't pay too much attention because Emmy and I are stocked up and ready. It doesn't matter to me either way. As long as Jason gets his truck and doesn't try to wiggle his way in here again, I'm good.

It's late in the evening, long past dark, when Jason arrives. He's in the passenger seat of the same truck that picked him up the other night. I should probably go out and speak to him, but I don't want to. I'd rather pretend I didn't see. Even though I did. And only because I was staring at the house across the street, wondering if Cole is there.

I haven't seen him since the beach, and even though that was only yesterday, I want to see him. Again. And again. It makes no sense, of course, but that doesn't change the facts. I think about him so much, think about his life and his past, the way he looks at me and the way it felt when he kissed me. He said that I was in his head. Well, he's in mine, too. In my head, under my skin. He's everywhere. Even when he's nowhere.

I smother a growl when I hear a knock at the door. Emmy looks up from her perch on the back of the couch, her green eyes wary. She doesn't like visits from Jason either.

"Who is it, Momma?" she loud whispers.

I put my finger over my lips. "Jason," I answer quietly.

"Don't let him in!"

"I'll try not to, but I can't be rude."

"Yes, you can." She grins impishly.

"I *can*, but I *shouldn't*. Smarty-pants."

I ruffle her hair as I pass and she smoothes it right back down. I fix my pleasant expression in place and open the door, but not fully.

"Ms. Independent," he says, trying to be cute.

"Jason," I respond mildly.

"Just letting you know I'm here to get the truck. Brought some gas to put in the tank. I'm pretty sure that's the problem." I say nothing because I'm aggravated. If it's *not* the problem then his vehicle is going to be stuck here until he gets someone who knows what the hell they're doing to come and fix it or pick it up. "I would've come sooner, but I had to wait on Jep to bring me. Jordan's over at Cole's, drinking. Don't know how long she's been over there. Maybe since yesterday."

My heart stutters in my chest. Almost like it stopped completely for a few seconds while I digested his words. Jordan is at Cole's? Drinking? Together? Since last night?

I don't know why, but I wouldn't have pegged Cole as much of a drinker. Then again, I thought he wasn't interested in Jordan either. It appears that I was wrong on both counts.

Sickeningly wrong.

"Oh, uh, okay. Well, I just hope it starts."

"Me, too. I don't like being without a vehicle. I can't bring my favorite girls soup." His smile is so presumptuous I want to slap him. That might be a bit of a drastic overreaction, but I'm not in the mood for his audacity.

"We're doing fine, but I'm sure you need it to get around."

"I was thinking that if you and Emmy would like to, I'd–"

"Sorry, Jason, you'll have to excuse me." And I shut the door in his face.

Suddenly, his unwanted attention is just too much. On top of my rising distress over Cole and Jordan being together, and the swimmy feeling in my stomach, my patience is at an end.

Inexplicably, I feel near tears. I thought Cole and I had a connection, something real. Something that was as rare for him as it has been for me. But if he's drinking and playing with Jordan, he's not the man I thought he was.

And the disappointment is crushing.

I didn't realize I had put so much hope, so much emotion into the brief and innocent run-ins I've had with Cole. I mean, why would I? Why am I so desperate to get to know him? Why *him?*

I've gone my whole life without the need–or really the desire–to have a man around. I've taken care of myself, taken care of Emmy. What is it about Cole that has changed all that? Why, all of a sudden, does it make me so happy to think of Emmy having his hands to help her build sandcastles on the beach? To hold her when she's afraid, to comfort her when she has one of her nightmares? Why now? Why him?

I don't know. I have no answers. No way of getting answers either. I only know that some part of me was hoping, wishing. Wanting. But it seems I'm better off without hoping, wishing *and* wanting.

⌘⌘⌘⌘

The house is getting chillier by the hour. Without Emmy asleep in my arms, I'd be cold. Colder than usual in here. I glare at the empty fireplace. The cottage has oil heat, so I didn't give the fireplace much thought, knowing that we'd have heat as long as I kept the oil tank out back full. Which it is. According to the guy who came to check it right after we moved in, there was still twenty-one inches of oil in it. I guess that's his non-technical way of checking–measuring the contents with a long dip-stick–rather than doing some complicated math.

It's almost eleven when I finally carry Emmy to her bed. I turned on her electric blanket earlier to make sure it was nice and warm for her. She doesn't even move when I lay her down and pull the heated covers up over her. She sleeps like a baby. Most of the time.

I'm going through the cottage, turning off lights, when I hear a knock at the door. It's loud and heavy, almost thump-like. My first thought is that it might be Jason. His persistence seems to know no bounds.

I creep to the window beside the door, prepared to peek through one corner to determine who it is before I answer it, when I hear a voice. It's deep and familiar, and it sends a tingle of awareness down my spine.

"Eden?"

It's Cole.

My heart lurches. It's late. Something must be wrong.

I wrench open the door to find him leaning against the doorjamb with his head hanging down. My first thought is that he's hurt.

"Cole, are you okay? What's wrong?"

I look him over, using the light coming from my open bedroom door to check for blood on his clothing. I see none, which only calms me minimally.

"You," he says quietly.

"Pardon?"

He raises his head and pins me with his potent stare. "You. You're what's wrong. I can't stop thinking about you."

I don't know what to say to that and he doesn't give me much time to think before he slides his hands into the hair at my nape, his thumbs holding my face still, and crushes my mouth with his.

I welcome it, welcome *him*. I'm not even going to deny it. I crave him like I crave sunshine and air and water and love. His scent, his taste, they weave a sensual spell around me, flooding my blood with heat and need.

He tilts his head and deepens the kiss, his tongue playing alongside mine, promising delights that I've never known and never had much interest in.

Until now.

Until Cole.

When he pushes inside, I don't resist. I'm lost in all that he's making me feel and my brain is turned completely off. I hear the slam of the door as he kicks it shut and that's the last thought to register until I feel his hands at my breast.

My nipples are painful points and I moan into Cole's mouth when he pinches one between his fingers, rolling it through the material of my lacy bra and single-knit sweater.

"I need to be inside you," he groans, his other hand falling to my butt and squeezing, pulling my lower body into his. I feel the long, hard ridge of his erection and moisture floods my panties. "I can't think. I can't eat. I can't even grieve anymore. It's all about you. Everything is about you."

It's as he speaks that I smell the alcohol. It serves as a bucket of cold water in my face. Apparently Jason was right. He's been with Jordan. Drinking.

I push at his chest. "Cole, wait."

His hands are everywhere, teasing and taunting, awakening feelings I doubted I'd ever feel at the hands of a man. But I have to ask him about Jordan. I have to know before this can go any further.

"Cole, please."

"Please what? Please take off my clothes?" he says in his throaty voice, his hands tugging at the hem of my sweater. I push them away, but they come right back. "Please touch me? Please taste me? Because I will. I'll touch you until you can't think. I'll taste you until you beg me to let you come."

Part of me thrills at his words, but part of me needs room, needs time. Needs him to stop for just a minute. Another man and another voice is standing between us, touching me in the same ways, but scaring me rather than pleasuring me.

"Cole, stop. I need to talk to you."

"I don't want to talk. I want to feel. I *need* to feel."

He's not listening to me and the scent of alcohol seems to be getting stronger and stronger, dredging up memories I've tried for years to bury.

"Cole, please," I plead, pushing at his hands, trying to keep my composure. My chin is trembling and I feel the icy fingers of panic clutching at my heart.

"'Please.' I love that word on your lips," he confesses, still not grasping the hysteria that I'm spiraling toward.

"Cole, stop! I mean it!" The more insistent I become, the more it seems to provoke him. "Cole."

"Eden," he whispers, the slight slur to the word taking me back in time.

I have to get away. He has to stop touching me. I can't breathe, but it's not in a good way.

I sink my fingernails into the backs of his hands, dragging them away from me. "Stop!" My words ring through the room, shattering the silence that falls between us when he finally lifts his head. I feel on the verge of a full-on panic now and I can't hold back the tears. "Get out of my house!"

He looks stricken, but also confused. Now I can see the dazed way his eyes stare into mine. He's drunk. This isn't the Cole I thought I knew. The Cole I knew would never do something like this. But maybe I didn't really know him at all. Maybe the Cole I thought I knew was nothing more than a product of my imagination.

My breath is coming in big, heavy sobs and I'm shaking. The fragile wall that I'd built separating my past from my present is eroding, melting away like the grasp I have on my composure. Memories are colliding with my five senses and suddenly the man in front of me is the same one who still haunts me, who still terrorizes my dreams.

"Eden," he begins, but I cut him off.

"Get out, Cole." When he doesn't move right away, just stands staring at me, I shout, "Get out!"

I double over, wrapping my arms around my middle in an effort to still my jittering insides. I see Cole's snowy boots receding as he backs toward the door. I don't move until the cold wind hits my face as he exits. But then I crumble to my knees and sob until I fall into a dreamless sleep.

SIXTEEN

Eden

I FOCUS ON Emmy's voice as she reads to me. This is part of her schooling. She learns best if I can make it fun for her. I guess most kids probably do. It's one of the most magical parts of my day, too. Her intelligence and animation never cease to make my heart swell with pride.

I watch her little mouth form the words, words far beyond the reading level of other children her age. I watch her little fingers turn the pages, faster and faster as she gets older. I watch her little eyes follow the sentences, sparkling with delight as the story progresses. This little girl, this little miracle, is my whole world. Has been since the day she was born. She saved me from...well, she just saved me. Plain and simple.

I've always applied myself so fully, so deeply to loving her, to protecting and caring for her, so much so that nothing else mattered. And while I'm still applying myself to those same things, right now it doesn't seem to be very effective in quieting the ache that's been emanating from my heart since I opened my eyes this morning.

Cole.

My insides squeeze painfully at just the thought of his name passing through my mind. It drags with it the fright and disappointment from last night.

How could I be so wrapped up in a man I hardly know? Why would I allow that to happen when he's obviously got a metric ton of issues?

It's the same question over and over again–Why him? Why him? Why him?

I'm getting no closer to an answer.

The snow is pouring outside, burying us deeper and deeper in a wintery wonderland. Before, I was sort of looking forward to it in some strange way–being snowed in. But now, I just feel suffocated.

It's almost eight when the power goes out. I bathe Emmy by candlelight with the last of the hot water. She laughs and plays, thinking the whole ordeal is great fun. It's when I get her out to dry her that I'm reminded how wise she is for her years sometimes.

"Why are you sad, Momma?" she asks, cupping my cheek with her tiny hand.

"I'm not sad, sweetpea. I'm just trying to hurry so that my daughter doesn't turn into an ice sculpture right in front of me."

This does nothing to eliminate the worry I find in her eyes. It breaks my heart to see anything other than child-like love and awe and carefree happiness there. Her eyes have seen too much in her short life; I don't want to add to her scars by letting her see too many of mine.

"Are you scared?"

I close my eyes and lean into her warm palm. "No, baby. Are you?"

"I'm only scared of leaving you."

"Well then you shouldn't be afraid. You won't ever have to leave me."

"But what if I do? You'll be sad and no one will make you happy anymore."

"You'll always be here to make me happy, sweetie. And you're all I'll ever need."

I need to get past this Cole thing and get back to just Emmy and me against the world. We never needed anybody before. We don't need to start now.

Once Emmy is dry, I start stuffing her quickly into her clothes.

"Do you think he's still sad because he doesn't have a little girl anymore?" she asks, holding onto my shoulder as she steps into her panties.

I don't have to ask who she's talking about, but I'm very curious to know why she's thinking about him. It seems that Cole has a hold on this household.

"He'll probably always be sad, but that's not her fault. That just means that he loved her sooo much."

Emmy grins at me. "You make him stop being sad."

"Why do you say that?"

"He looks at you different, Momma. He wants to kiss you. I can tell." She giggles, all little girl now. "Momma and Cole sittin' in a tree, k-i-s-s-i-n-g," she sings.

"I don't think Momma and Cole will be kissing any time soon," I tell her as I pull her pajama top over her head.

"But you want to."

"No, I don't."

She giggles again. "Maybe if you kiss him, you'll be happy, too."

"I thought boy kisses were gross," I say, reminding her of her opinion of the stronger sex thus far in life.

"Not for big girls. For big girls, they're magic."

I sweep her up into my arms and she throws her arms around my neck. "The only magical kisses I know of are these." I rain kisses all over her face and hair until she lets the subject drop.

I hope, unlike me, she'll just be able to put it from her mind. Put *him* from her mind.

⌘⌘⌘⌘⌘

I envy Emmy's ability to go straight to sleep. I pray it means that, despite all her worries and questions, her mind is for the most part worry-free. Unlike mine, which is keeping me wide awake. I'm still sitting in the dark, staring at the empty fireplace, covered in a blanket, thinking. That's why I hear the soft knock.

Had I been anywhere other than a few feet from the door, I'd never have heard it.

My stomach clenches and I turn toward the offending sound, debating whether to answer it or pretend I'm already in bed. I tiptoe to the door, pressing my ear to it so that I can hear if my late-night visitor leaves. I hear a subtle scraping sound, as though a rough palm is rubbing the wood between us.

"Eden," comes the sandpaper voice. I don't know how he would expect me to hear him. Maybe he doesn't. Maybe he knows he shouldn't be here and he's regretting coming.

Or maybe he's sober tonight. And maybe this is the Cole I thought I knew.

"Please be awake." There's a quiet desperation to his plea. It punches through the door and into my chest like a fist. "I need to talk to you."

I shouldn't even consider opening the door. I should write him off as a lost cause and move on with my life. Go back to the way I was before I met him. But there's a part of me that wants him to make this right, wants him to clear things up. Tell me I was wrong. Tell me *he* was wrong. To promise he'll never do that again.

Something in me wants that badly. So, so badly.

It's that part which shushes all the other voices and pushes my hand to reach for the lock.

I crack the door and peek out just enough to see Cole pulling his palm away–the soft rasping I heard. His eyes find mine and, even in the dark, I can see the cornucopia of emotions in them. Right now, they aren't hooded. Right now, they aren't hiding his thoughts from me. Right now, they're open.

He's open.

And that's why I let him in.

I step back and he slides past me, not moving beyond the entryway. I close the door, crossing my arms over my chest as we stand watching each other.

"I know it's late, but I wanted to talk to you. Alone."

"Well, here I am. Talk," I say, unable to keep all the bitterness from my tone.

Cole runs his hands through his chin-length hair, pushing dark blond strands away from his face. Thick stubble shadows his cheeks. He looks haggard, unkempt. Like he hasn't slept since I saw him last. And maybe he hasn't.

It's only fair, I think childishly, since I haven't slept much either.

He drops his hands like he just realized something, the familiar frown finally marring his smooth brow. "It's cold in here."

"It's cold everywhere."

He turns to look back over his shoulder. "There's no fire."

"No."

I don't add the *Duh* that I'm so waspishly thinking. I think the reason I'm inordinately aggravated is that I'm so glad he's here, so happy that he's sober and back to the Cole that I was growing so fond of. I shouldn't feel this way. I should still be mad. But I'm not. Not really. Not nearly as mad as I am relieved that he came back.

That he feels enough for me that he would experience regret over what happened.

"May I?" he asks, indicating the empty fireplace.

"I don't have any wood."

"I'll be right back."

He exits into the cold night and I wish for a second that I'd told him no. Just to keep him from walking out that door again. I'm beginning to hate it when he leaves. Things...this house...*life* feels better when he's near.

Which is pure craziness.

Within five minutes, Cole is back, carrying an armful of wood–some big pieces, some little–through my door. "I had some for across the street," he explains, making his way into the living room. He sets his load in front of the fireplace and deftly builds a fire. It's lit and already starting to crackle within just a few minutes.

"You must've done that a lot," I comment, curling up on the end of the sofa nearest the fire. I can already feel myself relaxing.

Cole shrugs. "Once or twice." The curve to his lips is like chocolate for the eyes. It's sweet and darkly sexy at the same time. Much like Cole himself.

Watching the flames, Cole stands, strips off his coat and lays it across the chair. Rather than taking a seat, though, he just returns to the fire, staring down into it like he can see the future. Or maybe the past.

He's not too close. But he's close *enough*. My whole being reacts to him. Pleasure, excitement, contentment, and curiosity are all swimming through my blood in equal measure.

The flicker of the fire highlights the angles and planes of his face–square chin, straight nose, high cheekbones, bold brow. He's magnificent. It's the one thing that never changes.

"I was seventeen when I met Brooke. She was fifteen. We were just kids. Stupid kids," he begins, his voice a soothing vibration in the quiet. "I got a football scholarship to Texas Christian. That probably should've been the end of us, but she kept coming to visit on the weekends. I think she didn't want to break up because I was her big-time college boyfriend. I think *I* didn't break up because I was a guy. I could have my highschool sweetheart and the college girls, too, and no one would be the wiser. And that's pretty much how it went. Until she got pregnant." The silence is broken only by the hiss and spit of sap from the burning wood. "I married her. Because that's what good guys from Texas do. At first it wasn't too bad. She kept me on track with school. I graduated in three years. The coaches backed me when I told them I wanted to go out in the draft. Got picked second round. It was like a dream come true for me." His tone is almost wistful as he speaks. "So, we packed up and moved out here to New England so I could play pro football. We set up house there once we found the perfect place to raise our little girl. Her name was Charity." His voice cracks when he speaks it aloud.

A lump of emotion clogs my throat. I know what's coming. I know that no matter how perfect, how beautiful his life once was, the dream ended in tragedy.

"She was the most beautiful thing I'd ever seen. Emmy looks so much like her it hurts. Black hair, big green eyes and she had this perfect little mouth. Like a cupid's bow." In profile, I can see Cole's lips quirk at the memory. It only lasts for a few seconds, though. Soon, they're pulled down at the corners again. "I spent every minute I could with her until football practice started, but then I had to work. After that, my life was all about the game. Nobody tells you that it can consume you if you're not careful. They don't tell you about the pitfalls. They don't warn you about all the attention and all the parties and celebrating. The fans and the groupies. And I was too young to know. Or to care, really."

Heavy. The air feels so heavy with dread that I could probably cut it if I had a knife.

"I'd practice during the week, but on the weekends, it was a whole other world. Drinking, parties, private jets. But I was with my teammates, so it was work. Teambuilding. At least that's what I told myself. It got to where I rarely ever saw my family. I felt guilty. Guilty as hell. That's why I started bringing Brooke and Charity up here. We'd play house for a few days, build sandcastles, cook burgers and that would buy me some time until I felt bad again." He pauses and a small smile tugs at his lips, briefly. Like before. "When it was good, it was really good, though. Brooke and I got along. And Charity...I could never have asked for something more wonderful. We'd stay on the beach for hours building sandcastles. She loved it. And before we left, she'd stuff sand in my pocket. Every time. She said it was so we could take some of the happy with us."

I close my eyes, emotion welling within me. Now it all makes sense. And my poor heart feels like it might collapse.

When I open my eyes to focus on Cole, I see that his lids are closed. Closed against the pain, against the memory. Or maybe he's savoring those happy times. Happy times that ended so, so badly.

I get up, hesitating for less than a heartbeat before I step closer to him, drawn by an irresistible force. A force named Cole. He continues as though I never moved, as though he'd lost in the past.

"I wasted so much time. On alcohol and parties. On people who never mattered. Time I could've been spending with her. It..." Cole sighs and shakes his head like he's shaking off a bad thought. "I haven't touched a drop since she died. Not one. Until last night." Another pause. "Until you."

I don't know what to say to that. I feel like I should defend myself, but I don't know how. I don't know what I've done or even if it's really my fault that he fell off the wagon.

"When Jordan told me that Jason didn't come home the night he came here...when I saw his truck parked here in the morning...Jesus! I wanted to hurt somebody. Jason mostly. The thought of him putting his hands on you...his mouth..." Cole closes his eyes as though the vision is physically painful. "I haven't felt anything in a long time. *Anything*. Except grief and loss. And that's the way I wanted it. I felt like it was…it was…*penance* almost. Like I owed that to my little girl. Never to be happy again since she couldn't be here. But then I met you." When he turns, his eyes melt into mine, his lips twisting into a wry smile. There's no humor there. Like he said he didn't want me in his head, I get the feeling that he doesn't exactly welcome what's between us. "You make me feel all sorts of things. Too many things. Things I never wanted to feel. But you just wouldn't stop. You just. Wouldn't. Stop."

I take a deep breath. "I-it's not like I've done this on purpose, Cole," I say, becoming angry. Why is he making this out to be a bad thing? And *my fault*, no less? "I didn't come here looking for anyone either. I just wanted–"

My words are cut off by his finger coming to rest against my lips. "You didn't have to *do* anything. You just had to show up. With your big gray eyes and that lush mouth. God, that mouth! I thought I'd go crazy if I couldn't kiss you. Just once. But then once wasn't enough." His expression turns dire. "I was furious. With you. With myself. So I went and got some Wild Turkey from Bailey's. Jordan must've taken that as a green light because she showed up later with more. I didn't say no. I should never have even started. But I was so…God!" He runs his hands through his hair again, his eyes fierce.

My stomach sinks. "So she did stay? Jordan, I mean?"

"Just for a little while, but then I made her leave."

"S-so there's nothing between you?" I ask hesitantly. I want him to say no so badly.

He looks at me like I've grown a second head. "Me and Jordan? God no! She's sweet, but she's...just no."

I shrug. "I didn't know."

"No, you wouldn't know that you're the only woman I'm interested in. You wouldn't know that you're the only woman I've been interested in in a very long time. That's why I was so angry about Jason." He takes a deep breath, his eyes pleading. "Please tell me that there's nothing between you two."

My heart is pounding so hard I wonder if he can hear it. It's thumping in my ears and vibrating in all my fingertips. "No, there's absolutely nothing going on between me and Jason."

He looks visibly relieved. No less intense, of course, but definitely relieved. "I don't think I could stand it if there was. I couldn't...just thinking about it...Shit!"

"Well, there's not, so don't give it another thought."

"It was making me crazy. *You* are making me crazy." I know I shouldn't thrill at his words, but I do. I do because, in his own way, Cole's been making me crazy, too. "Do you think you can ever forgive me for what I did last night? If I could take it back, I would. You don't know how much I regret it, Eden. I–"

It's my turn to shush him with a finger to his lips. "Let's just forget about it, okay?"

He nods.

"It will never happen again. You have my word."

"I believe you, Cole."

And I do. *This* is the man I thought him to be. *This* is the man I had hoped was underneath the broken and brooding man on the beach and across the street. *This* is a man that could change everything for me.

We stand in silence, practically nose to nose, for at least two full minutes. I realize as I stare up into his ocean blue eyes that I could drown in them and die a happy woman.

When his gaze flickers down to my lips, I wet them automatically, every part of me yearning for his kiss. "I don't have anything to give you, Eden. I'm broken. More than I ever thought I could be. But you can have what's left of me. If you want it. You can have what little I have to give."

"That's all I want, Cole. That's all I want."

SEVENTEEN

Cole

OUR EYES ARE still locked as I tilt my head and draw closer to her. I watch her lids flutter shut just before mine, before my lips meet hers. When they do, it takes every ounce of my willpower not to go crazy. The taste of her...*sweet Jesus!* It's the most delicious thing that has ever touched my tongue. As I sweep along the inside of her mouth, I have to fight harder and harder to go slow. Every fiber, every nerve, every muscle wants to strip her down and ravage her. Lick every surface, test every opening, taste every juice.

I can't remember wanting something this badly. Not once. Everything about her sings to me. Her eyes, her smile, her laugh, her body. I want to lose myself in her. And I am. I'm not thinking of anything other than

Eden right now. And the reprieve from my usual pain is almost overwhelming.

I feel her hands come tentatively to rest on my chest. My pecs flex in response to her cool touch. I run my fingers into her silky hair and hold her head still as I dive deeper into her mouth, wishing I was already inside her.

When her palms trail from my chest down to my stomach, my cock fills with blood so fast it's almost painful. I groan into her mouth and she digs in with her fingernails.

I jerk my head up, feeling like I'm about to lose control. "Eden, you can't do things like that."

"Things like what?" she asks, her eyes wide and innocent, yet dark and sexy.

"Touch me like that. It's…it's been a long time."

I feel the huff of her breath against my chin as she stretches up to brush her mouth against mine. "It has for me, too."

She runs her hands around my waist and presses her lips to my throat. I feel the plush mounds of her breasts rubbing against me and I grit my teeth to keep from doing something stupid. I feel like a bomb, getting ready to explode and take out a damn city block.

"Eden, I'm serious."

"I am, too. I don't want you to hold back with me."

"But I don't want to hurt you."

"You won't hurt me."

"I-I don't have any protection. I wasn't planning to…"

"I haven't been with anybody in a long time. I'm clean," she tells me.

"Me, too. It's been a while."

"And I have an IUD."

That one short sentence...holy God! I feel it like a punch to the gut. Just the thought of being inside her slick heat with nothing between us, just the idea of shooting come way up inside her, of spilling every last ounce of myself into her, is nearly my undoing.

"Eden, give me this one time and I'll make it up to you. I promise. Next time, I'll go slow. But tonight..."

I barely hear her breathy *Okay* before I let go. She said not to hold back, but if she hadn't, after telling me that she has an IUD, I probably would've had to leave and come back later. It has to be all or nothing. Those are my only two speeds right now.

I wind my arms around her and crush her to me from her lips to her knees. I feel every softly rounded contour of her body against mine as I lay her down on the rug in front of the fire. I think to myself that I'll take my time and enjoy every inch of her after this. But right now, I have to get inside her.

I reach for the button and zipper of her jeans and flick them open quickly. Our tongues tangle in the most delicious way and I can feel her heat all the way through the denim of my own pants. My cock is throbbing for her. My whole being is concentrated on her–the way she smells, the way she tastes, the way she feels underneath me.

I pull away just long enough to drag her jeans and panties down her legs. I lean back to look at her, the skin between her spread legs glistening, all pink and wet, in the firelight. My mouth waters reflexively and I bend to run my tongue into her crease.

I only meant to have a quick taste, just because wondering about it has been driving me nuts, but my throbbing dick gets put on hold the instant her flavor hits my tongue.

She's as sweet here as she is inside her mouth. Sweet and soft and silky. For a few seconds, I forget everything except how she tastes. She's like a mind-altering drug. An aphrodisiac. Intoxicating. Addictive. Suddenly driven to taste more, to taste all that she has to give, I find myself sliding my hands under her, gripping her plump ass and holding her to my mouth, like I'm drinking from a cup of sugar water.

I slip one thumb inside her, the wetness of her coating it and making my cock jump against my zipper. I pump it into her, anxious to feel more, taste more, take more. I push her legs wide and eat, like a starving man might eat.

I set her hips down and run two fingers up inside her, feeling the tight clench of her body. I growl against her as I reach for my own zipper, knowing that if I don't get into her now, something embarrassing might happen.

With my cock out, I stretch out full length on Eden, taking her lips in a kiss that sets my blood on fire. I wedge my hips between her spread legs and cage her upper body with my forearms to take some of my weight off her. I hear her sharp breathing and I tremble with the effort it takes not to slam my body into hers.

The head of my dick finds her entrance with an unerring precision, like I've been here before. Or maybe that I'm meant to be here. Like I know her body already.

I slip in a couple of inches and meet resistance as her body stretches to accommodate me. "Oh God, Eden. You're so tight. So tight..."

At this point, I don't know how I'm holding out. I must be stronger than I thought. And it's a good thing, or else I might not have felt her hands grabbing at my shoulders. Because they aren't holding me to her. They're pushing me away.

That's when I realize that the little sounds she's making aren't sounds of pleasure anymore. They're sounds of fear.

I jerk away from her like she burned me, memories of her reaction last night rushing back, all too clear.

I lift my head to look down at Eden. Her eyes are wide and afraid, full of tears. She's staring at me like I'm a stranger and she's stiff as a board beneath me.

"Eden, did I hurt you? God, I'm so sorry."

Her breathing is erratic and her voice trembles when she answers. "Y-you didn't. I-I'm sorry, Cole. I just... I can't do this. Not yet. I...I don't..." She starts to cry, soft sobs that rip through my heart. What did I do?

"I swear, I didn't mean to hurt you. I...I...God, I'm such an asshole!"

When I lever myself completely off her, she scoots away, drawing her legs up to her chest protectively. "Can you go? Cole, please. We can talk tomorrow, but right now...just please. Please go."

"Of course," I tell her. What else would I say? I feel like shit and I don't even know what I did. That's arguably the worst part. "Eden, I–"

"It's not you, it's me, Cole."

I straighten my clothes and roll to my feet, reaching to take my jacket form the chair. I can't take my eyes off her. Something about the fear in her, the vulnerability that I feel blowing off her like cold air, slices through me. Through skin and muscle and bone. And goes right into my heart.

More than anything, I want to pull her into my arms and hold her, to tell her that whatever it is, it'll be okay. But she doesn't want that. I can see it in the white of her knuckles, in the stiffness of her back. In the tightness of her face. She's freaked out and she just wants me out of here.

As I start past her, I pause. I want to bend down and kiss her so that this can end on a good note, but I don't. I get the feeling nothing can salvage this night. I just don't know why.

She doesn't say another word to me as I go to leave, not even as I close the door behind me.

EIGHTEEN

Eden

MY HEART IS slamming around in my chest like an eight-ounce pinball. I can hardly breathe and memories assail me like demons in the air, running at me from every direction. I tell myself over and over that it's in the past, that he can't hurt me anymore. I tell myself that Cole is different. But his words...they resonated within me. Like a scream reverberating through an empty cave. Through the hallway of time.

I don't bother dressing. I simply roll onto my side and curl up into the tightest ball that my body will make. I close my eyes and concentrate on the heat of the flames. I picture it like comforting hands, reaching out to gently touch my face. I picture them warming me, chasing away the cold, soothing away my fears. And the darkness. And the demons.

I don't know how long I stay this way before I finally doze off. An hour. Three. A week. A lifetime.

When I wake, it's with a start. I'm flat on my stomach, face turned toward the dwindling fire, and my pulse is pounding. As though someone spoke the future right into my ear to rouse me, I have the crystal clear realization that I just let something amazing slip through my fingers. All because of something awful in my past. How long can I let Ryan haunt me? How long can I let him decide my future? How long can I be a prisoner of yesterday? And how many tomorrows will suffer because of it?

I think of my daughter, sleeping soundly in her bed. I think of her concerns of late, her fear that my happiness is her burden to bear. No child should feel that responsibility. And certainly not a child who already has the weight of bad memories pressing on her thin shoulders.

Cole could be good. Good for me, good for us. I feel it. All the way down to my bones. He's broken, yes, but not twisted-broken. Not like Ryan was. Not even broken like I am. He's the good kind of broken, the honorable kind of broken.

And I pushed him away because of fear. Because I got out of the moment and into my own head. I let myself fall into the darkness, into the chasm where all the monsters lurk. And they chased away my one shot at normal, at happy. At love, even. Maybe. At the very least *the hope* of love.

❄❄❄❄

The demons from my past haunt me. Last night, they ran rampant through my dreams, turning them into nightmares that left me in a puddle of my own cold sweat. They whispered to me from every corner today. They've done that for years. They tell me that I'm not normal, that I'm damaged goods and that no one will ever want me. And, for the most part, I've believed them.

Until now.

Until Cole.

All day, I've watched for him. I saw him inside the house across the street earlier and I've watched for him to come out. He never did. At dark, the lights came on inside and they're still on now.

I move into the living room, away from the window. Away from Cole. But I don't leave him behind. I bring him with me. I dwell on him as I sit, staring into the fire that I've nursed since he built it. Somehow I've equated it to what burns between us, as though if I let the fire die, so will the attraction. The possibility. The hope.

The hope of Cole.

I've never been so drawn to another person. Never wanted someone this way. And I do. God, how I want him! Before he uttered those words, before he caged me with his arms, I was lost. Ecstatically, euphorically lost.

But I let a monster ruin it. A monster that now lives only within the confines of my head because he's hundreds of miles away. All I've ever wanted was to be normal, to be happy and healthy and *whole*, and part of me believes that I could be all of that with Cole. That he's the one who's destined to drag me out of the past. Only I don't think he's the type to drag me if I resist. He stopped the instant he felt me resisting him last night. And it hurt him. I could see it. He was so kind about it, but I could see the confusion and the hurt.

What if that completely ruined it? What if he doesn't want to try again? What if now *he* thinks I'm damaged goods and wants nothing to do with me? What if I don't get another chance? What if I've looked into his beautifully intense blue eyes for the last time?

I envision my life ahead as more of the same. I love my daughter and I live for her, but this thing with Cole…feeling like a part of something else, one half of a whole…I never realized it could be this way. That I could feel this way.

But that could be over. I could go the rest of my life and never feel this way again. Never get butterflies of excitement. Never melt with a look. Never burn with a touch. Never crave with such intensity. All because I was afraid. I let someone who can't hurt me anymore hurt me. And he'll keep on hurting me if I don't get over this.

Now.

I look around me, at the way the fingers of light stretch into the dark shadows around the room. Or is it the dark shadows encroaching on the light? It mimics the power struggle within me. My past–black nothingness, lurking, stalking, mocking. My present– warm, golden, promising. Alive.

Without even stopping to think about what I'm doing, I shove my feet into boots, creep in to check on Emmy and then head straight for the door. I don't even grab a coat. I just lurch out into the cold, snowy night and head for the street.

I clomp through the drifts, oblivious to the wind whipping at my hair and the flakes wetting my cheeks. I have one thing in mind–Cole. I need him. I need him to come back. I need him to make me forget rather than remember. I need him to replace the ugly with the beautiful.

I march up the steps and knock on the door. He might answer. He might not. But I'm not leaving until he does. Because I need him. And I think he needs me.

I jump when the door jerks open. I wasn't expecting such a rapid response.

For a few seconds, I'm struck speechless by the heat in his wildly blue eyes. They're the most amazing color, and the way they hold me...the way he looks at me...it's like he's touching me. Through and through.

Cole shakes his hair back. He has great hair. Sexy hair. The longish locks lay like a hairdresser fixed them and then messed them up just the right amount. The bangs hang nearly to his chin, effortlessly framing his gorgeous face.

My heart stutters in my chest when I take in his naked torso and his low-slung jeans. Rather than taking the risk of saying something stupid, I just bend and grab the boots by the door and hand them to Cole. I hold my breath as I wait. What if he's not interested since I freaked out? What if he starts asking me questions that I have no answers for? What if this is all a huge mistake?

I bring myself up short. There's no turning back now. There's just not. Not for me.

Cole's brow furrows, an expression that I'm learning to love. I think for a second that he's going to resist, or tell me to get lost, but he doesn't. Instead, he wordlessly takes the boots from my hands and drops them on the porch. My heart sinks for a second, thinking that's as far as this is going to go, but then, with his eyes on mine, he steps into them.

Hesitantly, I reach for his hand and tug. My stomach flips over when his fingers curl around mine and he reaches back with his other hand to close the door behind him.

I waste no time crossing the street again. My determination is still at fever pitch, but now my nerves are kicking in and I'm jittery, which makes my steps even more hurried.

"Eden, what's wrong?" Cole finally asks when we're nearing my front door.

On the porch, I turn to face him. I look up and up and up until I meet his fathomless midnight eyes. "Last night I woke and you were gone," I explain. "It felt wrong. So wrong. And today..."

Unmoving, he stands watching me, his big hand still gripping mine, his frown still firmly in place. "I couldn't sleep last night. At all. That's why I'm working tonight," he finally confesses.

My soul sighs in relief. Maybe he can overlook my crazy. Maybe he can love me despite my issues. Maybe he's the one. And maybe this is the first step.

And the second step is to get closer. To him. So I do. I move in and don't stop until my chest is brushing his. I rest my palms against his cool, flat stomach. I feel the jerk of his muscles. Then I feel the answering twitch of my own. "I need you, Cole," I whisper. "I need you to touch me again, to kiss me again." I hear his sharp intake of breath. "I need *you*. Please." I rise onto my toes to kiss his chin.

As gently as the wind tosses the falling snow into a swirl of white mist around us, Cole sweeps me off my feet. Slowly, he carries me up the steps and inside. He pauses only to kick off his boots, his eyes never once leaving mine. They hold me as securely as his strong arms do.

When we are once more in front of the fire, mere inches from the exact place where we stood last night, he sets me on my feet. "I will love every inch of you until you tell me to stop," he declares. It's as much a sensual promise as it is a pledge that he won't do a single thing that I'm not comfortable with. What I don't tell him, what I'll *show him* instead, is that I won't stop him this time. I need this more than he does.

With his intense stare focused on me, Cole tips his head toward the hall. "Emmy?" he asks.

"Asleep," I answer. "She sleeps like a rock."

Cole reaches for my hands and brings my knuckles to his mouth. He drags his lips back and forth over them, a tiny grin teasing a dimple out of his cheek. "We'll be quiet anyway." Slowly, he stretches my arms above my head, curling his fingers in the hem of my shirt, the backs of his cool fingers brushing my belly. "So. So. Quiet." He punctuates each word with a soft kiss to my lips before his hands begin to inch the material up my body.

He tugs my sweater over my head and then tosses it on the couch without looking. It's like he's as hesitant to take his eyes off me as I am to take my eyes off him. This moment…it's so fragile, it seems. I'm almost afraid to look away. To break the spell. To forget even one second of it. Of how he looks, how he feels.

Cole traces the lacy edge of my bra with his fingertip. He follows it all the way to the strap and up to my shoulder. Chills break out across my chest when he eases the strip down my arm until it hangs loosely at my elbow. I feel the cup of my bra slip down to my nipple and catch on the rigid peak. I stand perfectly still, breathing as quietly and steadily as I can even though my insides are a quivering mess.

With excruciating deliberateness, he repeats the movement with the other side until my breasts are nearly bared to him. Tantalizingly half-covered.

Still, Cole watches me as he leans closer, our eyes locked until he passes out of my vision. A fraction of a second later, I feel his lips at my ear. "So beautiful," he whispers, tracing the shell with the tip of his tongue as he teases my aching nipples with the backs of his fingers.

He brushes his lips and flicks his tongue along my jaw until he reaches my mouth. He hovers at the edge of my lips, close enough to kiss me, yet not. He licks the corner and I open reflexively, hungry for the taste of him on my own tongue. But he doesn't come in. He must know what he's doing to me, though, because I feel the huff of warm air and the light rumble of his laugh, followed by a soft, "Be patient."

I close my eyes as Cole kisses his way down my throat, across my collarbone and then down to the swell of my breast. I feel his warm breath. I anticipate his touch, his firm touch, so much that it makes my hands tremble.

I arch my back the tiniest bit, a silent plea for him to take what I'm offering. But still, he won't. He simply skims his open mouth back and forth over my throbbing nipples, taunting them with his moist breath. Taunting but never taking.

I feel his hands move around my ribs, skating lightly over my skin as he goes. With a flick that's as quick and soft as a butterfly kiss, his fingers unhook my bra.

When he straightens away from me, I feel it. I feel it in the loss of his body heat, in the loss of this crazy magnetism that's between us. And when he inhales, I feel it in the air, like his slow drawing of breath created a vacuum, a bubble where only he and I exist.

I open my eyes when the quiet becomes too still. Cole's gaze is trained on my chest, even as his hands come to the straps at my elbows, slowly dragging them down my arms, inch by excruciating inch. I have to bite my tongue to keep from moaning when my nipples pop free of the lace and Cole's breath hisses through his teeth. "Damn, you're gorgeous," he breathes, his pupils swelling as he drinks me in. Truthfully, I've never felt more beautiful than I do right now, with his eyes blatantly loving what they see.

Cole lets my bra drop to the floor. In slow, slow motion, he reaches for my breasts, cupping them, weighing them, feathering the peaks with the pads of his thumbs. My nipples pucker prettily for him and he exhales on a breathy groan. He closes his eyes for a second. Time seems to stop. But when he opens them again, they're on mine, intense as ever. Hotter than the fire behind me.

"Perfect," he says softly, bending his head to swirl his tongue around my tingling flesh.

I let my head fall back, threading my fingers into his hair to hold him to me. "That feels so good," I murmur, squeezing my legs together, intensifying the delicious throb taking place between them.

"I've never seen anything more beautiful," he says against me. "Lush. Round. And your nipples...Jesus! They fit perfectly in my mouth. They beg for my tongue to lick. My lips to suck. For my teeth to bite." The last is said on something like a growl. It reverberates through my chest and furls my nipples even tighter. "Mmmm!" he mutters, scraping his teeth lightly over me and causing my insides to spasm.

How embarrassing would it be to have an orgasm at this point in the night? How embarrassing, but how amazing. No other person has ever brought me pleasure before. Just me. Me and my imagination. Me and my fantasies of a man who might change everything. A man like Cole. And this time, in real life, I might not be able to stop my body from reacting.

Cole makes hungry sounds as he devours my breasts. I'm arched so deeply into him, it's a wonder my whole breast isn't in his mouth. But I want it to be. I want him to consume me. To eat me alive, leave nothing but the bones.

His fingers find their way to my waistband, effortlessly unbuttoning and unzipping my jeans as his mouth works to unravel me. He drops to his knee in front of me, his tongue still flicking my left nipple as he drags my pants and panties down my legs.

When I feel them at my feet, I step out of them and kick them to the side. The air circulates between my legs, cooling my hot, wet flesh. Stimulating me. Torturing me. The muscles within me ripple and squeeze, telling me I'm getting closer.

"Christ Almighty!" Cole moans as he abandons my nipple for the flat plane of my stomach. "I can smell you. So sweet it makes my mouth water."

Lava gushes to my core, and the closer Cole gets to it, the harder it becomes to remain upright. But Cole fixes that. As though he can't wait another second, he pulls me down to my knees and lays me on my back in front of the fire.

Then his mouth is on me again. Crushing my lips, sucking my tongue, laving my nipples, testing my bellybutton. And when his hands reach between my legs and press them wide, I'm breathless with anticipation. This time, I'm here with only Cole. There are no memories, no ghosts. No tragedies and no pain. Only the now. Only the beautiful now.

He moans into me when his tongue finds my crease. He laps and licks, his fingers teasing and taunting as they advance and retreat within me. Never too deep, never enough to satisfy. Only to torment. Sweet, sweet torment.

Even though he's not trying to push me over the edge, I can't stop my body from reacting. It feels too good, I want him too much.

When the first surge of climax washes through me, it steals my breath. It's slow and deep and so, so pleasurable that I can do little more than hold on until it passes. Until it releases me from its spell.

Only it's not over.

"God, yes!" Cole murmurs against me, his fingers and tongue vying for the center of me, battling it out in the most delicious trade-off imaginable. With every thrust and wriggle, with every lick and nibble, another swell breaks over me, tightening my stomach and arching my back. My thighs clamp rhythmically around his head and my fingers curl viciously into the rug. My ears are ringing with the sounds of his fervor and my ecstasy, and I don't want to hear anything else.

Before the last of the spasms can wane, Cole is kissing his way up my body, dragging the flavor of me into my mouth, swirling it around my tongue with the tip of his. And then he's pushing into me. Slowly, unceasingly. Giving me time to stretch for him, to welcome him, to move with him.

When he starts to withdraw, I wind my legs around his hips to keep him close. He thrusts back into me, even deeper, even thicker.

Back and forth, back and forth, he eases out and then rams back in. Never enough to really hurt me, but enough that I feel a delightful sting, a delectable stretch. I can't help wondering how much of him is left

I urge him on with my heels and he lifts his head to look down into my face. His expression is almost pained and there's a fine sheen of perspiration glistening on his forehead.

"I made you a promise. And I don't want to give you any reason to tell me to stop. But dammit, Eden, I can only take so much."

He flexes his hips, almost as though a beast is riding his back and he's trying with all his might to keep it at bay. To save me from it. Or save me from *him*.

Only I don't want to be saved this time. I'm not afraid. I see no one, I *feel* no one but Cole.

And now I want to feel *all of him.*

I push at his shoulders until he leans up off me, a frown knitting his brow. I keep pushing until I can wiggle out from under him and then I press hard, urging him onto his back. With a desperation I don't quite understand, I climb onto him, positioning my body over his. Our eyes meet, his backlit with a fire that burns brighter than the flames behind his head. He's beautiful and intense and I can feel his want like a physical heat, brushing my cheeks, kissing my lips, caressing my body.

My nipples pucker at the first touch of his wide head at my entrance. Cole groans and squeezes his eyes shut. I feel powerful and sensual and more womanly, more *normal* than I've felt a day in my life.

I lower myself onto him, just a little, before pulling back. I feel the smile play with my lips. I feel the desire coil inside me.

Cole's eyes flick open, as though he can feel it, too. He reaches up and grabs my breasts, rolling the nipples between his fingers, pulling and pinching them. I throw my head back on a gasp, moisture flooding the place where we are connected. And then, with one arm snaked around my waist and his mouth at my breast, Cole pulls me down onto him as he juts his hips upward.

And I am impaled.

I am melting over Cole.

He is driving into me.

A loud moan escapes my lips and then his hand is at the back of my head, forcing my face toward his own where he swallows the sounds of my submission, the sounds of my body being completely overtaken by his. I am on top, but I am not in control. At this moment, he owns me. Possesses me. And I'm gladly giving up all that I am to him.

With his mouth devouring mine, his fingers tempting and teasing, Cole moves me on him. Faster and faster, harder and harder. Higher and higher.

Until I'm at the top again. Falling over the edge. Flying through the air like a thousand tiny birds.

I'm aware only of him rolling me over, onto my back, and then his weight and heat is covering me. He never stops kissing me. Never stops thrilling me. Never stops riding me until I feel the heavy throb of his cock as it starts to pulse. Heat sprays into me and I wrap my limbs around him, holding him to me, holding him inside me. I want all that he has to give. Every word, every sound, every ounce. I want it all.

"So perfect," he whispers as his movements slow and become blissfully lethargic. "So perfect."

Those are the words that usher me into a peacefully exhausted slumber, tucked in the arms of the man who turned this girl into a woman. A normal woman.

NINETEEN

Eden

I WAKE TO the most amazing smell–bacon, one of my favorite foods.

I turn onto my side, my body tender and weak in the best possible way. I smile. I can't seem to help myself.

My eyes search for Cole. I know he's still here. I can feel it in my chest, in my soul, like a warm breeze.

I smile even bigger when I find him. Cole is standing in front of the stove, bathed only in candlelight and the faint bluish glow from the gas burner. He's naked except for the strings of an apron tied around his waist. For the most part, that's all I notice. I can't take my eyes off his incredible butt. God, it's amazing! Firm and narrow, the cheeks rounded just the right amount, the dents on either side pure, masculine perfection.

I hear the pop and sizzle of hot grease, and I push myself into a sitting position and rest back on my heels. I'm not sure what I'm hungrier for right now—the bacon or the man cooking it.

My body heats as though I'm close to the stove, as though I'm close to Cole. All I have to do is look at him and…

I groan. It's unintentional. Practically pulled out of me when I squeeze my legs together to quell the throb of desire that pulses in my sex.

Cole's head whips around and his eyes fix on me. I see the dark, fiery look in them. He's hungry, too.

He turns back around, stabbing strips of bacon from the pan and setting them on a paper towel to drain. He cuts off the eye and brings the whole plate, paper towel and all, into the living room.

I smile when I see his front covered by an apron. A tented apron at the moment. A blush stings my cheeks. I can't believe something that size fits inside me.

Another squeeze at the memory of what it felt like to have him buried so deep, his body slamming mercilessly into mine.

"If you don't stop that, all this bacon will go to waste and we'll starve to death," he warns in his silk-and-gravel voice. Just listening to him talk could get me all worked up.

I try to curb my enthusiasm. "What's with the apron?" I ask, taking the proffered plate.

"Didn't want my junk splattered with hot grease. Can you blame me?"

His expression looks horrified. I laugh.

"No, I suppose not. I didn't even think of that, actually."

"That's because it wasn't *your* junk in peril," he explains, taking off the apron and tossing it over the chair before he sits down beside me and takes a strip of bacon.

He snaps off half the piece in his mouth before offering me the other end. My lips part willingly, trembling only slightly when I see his eyes focus on them as he chews.

I wish he wouldn't look at me that way.

I also wish he'd never stop.

It makes me a little self-conscious. But it also makes me a melty, gooey mess, which I love.

We watch each other as we chew the salty meat. Cole reaches for another strip, this time trailing the crispy end around my nipple. I inhale sharply, glad that I wasn't swallowing or else I'd have choked on bacon bits.

His eyes follow his movements and they get all dark and voracious again. I feel like *I'm* on the menu. And I wouldn't want it any other way.

"Do you like my bacon?" I ask breathily, grinning behind my rising passion.

"Your bacon is the most delicious bacon I've ever tasted. I could get addicted to it if I'm not careful."

"By all means," I reply, fighting back a groan when Cole swipes my salty nipple with his finger and brings it to his mouth. "There's plenty more where that came from."

"Are you sure? Because I have a huge...appetite." As he speaks, he brings the piece of bacon to my mouth and I let him lay it on my tongue.

As I close my lips around the flat slice, Cole reaches between my legs and slides a single finger from his other hand into me. The flavor on my tongue, the slight pressure of his touch...the combination dances over my senses, one accentuating the other.

Cole's gaze is riveted to mine, searing into me like his finger. In and out, in and out, his pace never quickens even as he snaps off the bacon and puts the rest of it into his own mouth.

The moment is instantly shattered by a familiar, high-pitched scream–*Nooo!* The single word is shrill with terror.

Panic skitters through me. I grab my sweater from the couch as I pass, throwing it over my head as I race down the hall. I find Emmy in her bed, stiff as a board and thrashing her head back and forth on her pillow. It's as though she can't move her body, only her head. That's how I know what she's dreaming of.

I draw her into my arms, holding her against my chest. "You're safe, Emmy. You're safe, baby. It's just me. It's just momma."

I rock her back and forth until she relaxes. It's almost instantaneous, as it always is. Once my words penetrate her fear, once they break the hold of her nightmare, she goes limp as a rag. Always.

Her scream fades into soft sobs and quiet murmurings. I've never been able to understand them. Maybe it's the way she calms herself. Maybe it's something she's telling herself to ground her in reality. I don't know. I'll probably never know. I've asked her about it before, but she never remembers saying anything.

But she does. She always does.

I don't let her go until her breathing is deep and even, until I know she's drifted back into a peaceful sleep in the safety of my arms. Even after I lay her gently back onto her mattress and cover her chilly little arms with the blanket, I don't leave her side for a long time. It's not until I see the first fingers of snowy light filtering through a crack in Emmy's curtain that I remember Cole waiting for me in the next room.

He's sitting in the chair, fully dressed, watching the hallway with a fathomless expression. When his eyes click up to mine, I stop and we watch each other again. It seems we do that a lot—watch each other, wordlessly. Thinking. Wondering. Imagining.

I walk to the couch and sit facing him, curling my legs up under me. Before I can turn to stare into the fire, Cole speaks. His voice is quiet, yet as intense as a shout. "Are you going to tell me about it?" he asks.

This time, I *do* turn to look into the flames. I study the way they lick at the blackened logs. I ponder the way they consume with such beauty.

I don't have to ask what Cole means; I already know. It's the only thing he *can* mean. It's in the air—the haunting voices of our past, the rattling chains of our bonds. The arterial spray of our wounds.

I consider not telling him. I've never told *anyone*, after all. It's been my own personal albatross, my own personal hell. But I'll tell him. I know it before I even really make the decision. I know it as surely as I know that the soft velvety material of the couch tickles my bare feet when I wiggle my toes. I don't know why, but I feel like it's important that I do. And, for once, I don't question it to death. I just go with it.

"It's hard to know who to trust," I begin with a sigh. Cole doesn't assure me that I can trust him. He doesn't beg me to divulge all my secrets. He doesn't try to convince me to spill my guts. He simply waits. Silently. Rock steady. In true Cole form.

I drag my gaze from the fascinating fire in front of me to the fascinating man across from me. I meet his eyes. I examine them. I dissect them. I search for an agenda, for some plan he might have to hurt me, to hurt Emmy. I find none. I find nothing more than a gentle yet cautious curiosity. It's his peace within the moment, it's his unspoken patience, his unshakable steadiness that carves out the dread and replaces it with resolve. Maybe it's just time to share my load with another human being. Maybe it's just time to let someone else take the weight, even if it's only for a few minutes.

"But I'm going to trust you." Still, he says nothing. He only watches me. Within the silence, though, there's a solidness, as though the very air whispered to me that Cole is a rock and that I can lean on him as much as I need to. He can take it. Although he's broken, he's still strong enough to bear it.

"My parents left for Papua New Guinea when I was fifteen. They were both involved in *Doctors Without Borders* before I was born. I wasn't planned. I ended up being a surprise that they weren't particularly thrilled about. I changed their lives in ways they didn't want changed. They were never mean to me, but they weren't able to hide it either. They gave up the fight eventually and left me with my Aunt Lucy so they could do *one more tour*. Or at least that's what they said. They sent cards for Christmas and for my birthday every year, but that was it. I haven't seen them since I was fifteen years old."

Cole's eyes drop to my lap where I'm rubbing circles on my thigh with my index finger. A nervous habit. I'm sure he's figured that out. I can feel all the emotions, all the fear and…aloneness that I've fought to overcome creeping back in, like the memories themselves have life. Or that they can steal it.

Cole's expression is unreadable. I should expect no more. He hides what he's feeling well. Until he wants it to show.

"Anyway, Lucy is a lawyer. Ambitious. Controlling. Cold. It didn't really surprise anybody when she married Ryan, a guy ten years younger. She was thirty-five, he was twenty-five. He was an on again/off again underwear model who looked really good in a tux. She was loaded and bought him whatever he wanted. That dynamic worked for them."

I drop my eyes when I feel the frown tug my eyebrows together. It happens whenever I think about this part. Whenever I have to acknowledge that maybe my parents knew. Although I hope they didn't. Just *the idea* that they might've known steals my breath for just a few seconds. The sense of betrayal is *that* intense. I have to concentrate on inhaling, exhaling, inhaling, exhaling, willing myself to calm.

I clear my throat. "I don't know if Mom and Dad knew about them. I like to think they didn't, but...I could never be sure."

I pause again, wondering if I've made a mistake by going back, back to a time that nearly killed me.

"Eden, you don't have to do this. I shouldn't have asked," Cole says quietly, drawing my eyes back to his. His face is still handsomely inscrutable. It's probably better that way.

"I want to." And I do. Although it's hard to think about and talk about this time in my life, I feel like I *need* to tell him. Like he needs to know this about me. About us. It's like it *has to* come out. And maybe that's good. It has eaten away at my insides for too long. "Ryan drank a lot. Always smelled like alcohol. He was up at all hours. Slept at weird times. He was the party boy. The arm candy. The trophy husband. And he was okay with that. I guess I should've known that it took a certain kind of man to live that kind of life. I just had no idea *what kind* of man."

I take a deep breath and try to relax my tense muscles. I remind myself that I survived. That Emmy and I both did. And that we are safe. That calms me somewhat, but my stomach is still in a tight knot as the first words roll off my lips.

"The first night he came to my room, he said he'd heard me scream and thought I was having a nightmare. I didn't remember screaming, but I couldn't say for sure that I didn't. I thought it was kind of sweet when he pushed me over and climbed in bed beside me. I'd never had someone who actually cared enough to check on me when I had a nightmare." I hate the sadness in my voice. I hate that what I had thought was an act of kindness ended up being something awful and dirty, and that it devastated a young girl who only wanted to be loved. And to not be alone.

"But then it started happening more. He'd tell me that he heard me scream, even when I didn't remember having a nightmare. But then one night, I realized what was happening. I didn't want to believe it. I wanted him to be someone in my life who cared about me. But he didn't. He only wanted me for...other reasons."

I'm staggered by a wave of nausea as, out of the blue, the sweetly alcoholic smell of Ryan's breath assails me. It's as though he's kneeling beside me, whispering all the things he plans to do to me. Just like he used to. Just like I hated.

I focus on reality, on the scent of logs burning only a couple of feet away, and the subtle soapy aroma of the man across from me. All that is here in the present. Where the past can't hurt me.

"The first time it happened, he'd crawled in bed with me and I'd fallen back asleep. I don't know how long he waited, or how long I'd been asleep, but I woke to his hand under my nightgown, slipping into my panties." My throat is tight, like a strong hand is curled around my neck, something that happened a time or two when Ryan was drunk. I struggle to swallow, to find my strength. To push the words through to my mouth, out past my lips, into the air where they're free. "I stayed perfectly still for a few seconds. I didn't know what to do. I think I even thought maybe he was dreaming. Or that I was. Only I wasn't. And neither was he. The instant I reached for his hand, the minute I was going to ask him to stop, he rolled me onto my back and pinned my arms to my side. He was so strong and...he was so heavy...I-I couldn't move. I-I..." I lean forward, fighting the burn in my lungs, the burn in my eyes.

He's not here. He can't find me. These are just memories. Memories can't hurt me. Not anymore.

Cole says nothing, and I'm afraid to look up at him. I'm afraid of what I'll see.

"I remember my heart was beating so fast, looking up into his face. He looked scarier than he did in the daylight. He wasn't a gorgeous older guy anymore. He was...real. Like the way he usually looked was a mask and I was just seeing his real face. 'Don't scream,' he said. 'It'll only make it worse.' So I didn't. I-I didn't scream. I d-didn't do anything. I just laid there and let him touch me. And the only other words he said to me were that I was tight. 'God, Eden. You're so tight'."

My voice breaks as I think about the night my innocence was taken. How frightened, how shattered, how disillusioned I was. It was as though Ryan tore away my childhood and all of life's possibilities with a few words and one sharp thrust.

"Jesus! Is that why...when I said that...? Is that why you...?" he asks, referring to my freak-out the night before.

I nod, squeezing my eyes shut, forcing myself to continue. I just want to get this over with. I just want to let it out and then put it behind me again.

"He came to me every night for a week. I thought maybe he would get tired of it, tired of me. But he didn't. Each night, he would come earlier. He would pull the blankets off the bed, take off all my clothes and kiss me everywhere. Touch me everywhere. And if I started to struggle, he would stop and hold my arms at my sides. Like a threat. He didn't have to say a word. That said it all."

Anger begins to surface. I'm relieved to feel it. It's easier to hide behind anger than drown in misery that can't be changed. It saved me once before. It'll save me again.

I dry my face, wipe away the tears I wasn't even aware of shedding, and I press on. This isn't the hardest part. If I fall apart now, I'll never make it to the end.

"When that week was over, I knew I had to tell Lucy. I thought she would help me. She *had to help me*. When I came home from school that Monday, I waited for her. I didn't know she was working late. Ryan brought takeout, like he was this caring, doting uncle. We watched a movie. He even made popcorn. It was so...*normal* in the sickest, most twisted way in the world. But it was always there underneath–the knowledge of what was coming. Like a clock ticking away the minutes. Or a bomb counting down to explosion. I was so afraid to go to bed, I fell asleep on the couch that night. I didn't wake up until he was carrying me up the stairs.

"I pretended to be asleep, but that didn't stop him. I didn't fight him. I knew it would be no use. I just wanted it to be over so I could go to sleep. And then tell Lucy in the morning. Only there was no need." I pause, reliving that sinking moment like it happened only seconds ago rather than years. "I didn't see her standing in the doorway until Ryan rolled me over onto my stomach. I don't know how long she'd been watching. Or how many nights she'd stood in that doorway. I think probably most of them."

My heart squeezes painfully at the memory of how hopeless that moment felt. I'd never felt so alone, so afraid. But I had no idea how much worse it would get.

"I guess once I saw her, she stopped trying to pretend that she didn't know. Or that she didn't enjoy it. I remember watching her walk to the bed that night. Her eyes on mine. I thought for just a second that she was going to stop him. I hoped against hope that she would. Prayed that she would. Only she didn't. She just stood at the end of the bed, looking up at me for a long time before she started undressing."

Bile rises in the back of my throat like acid, bubbling up from a corroded wound, long hidden and neglected. "Lucy had it all. Had her act together. Or so everyone thought. But no one knew. Not really. As smart as she was, though, even *she* didn't stop to think about birth control. That or Ryan lied to her. I'm not sure which. Either way, I think he *wanted* me to get pregnant. Sometimes after he'd…" I trail off. I can't even force the words past my lips. "Afterward, he would push it all back up in me and tell me to stay curled up on my side. He'd wrap his arms around me to make sure I stayed still." A small whimper moves into my chest and I force it back down. "And if that *was* what he was after, he got it. It worked. I found out four weeks later that I was pregnant. Not quite sixteen years old and pregnant by my guardian's husband."

I continue, trying to be matter-of-fact. And probably not succeeding.

"Lucy didn't say much other than that she was pulling me out of school. She said Ryan could homeschool me since we were there together all day. I hadn't been there that long, so I had no friends that I could go to, I couldn't reach my parents. I was just stuck. I kept thinking to myself that as soon as I had the baby, I'd run away. I knew I couldn't make it until after that. At the time, I didn't even want the baby. I thought maybe they'd keep it and let me go. Not even look for me. And if they wouldn't, I was going to kill myself. I even had it planned out, just in case. But that was before I met Emmy."

Even in the midst of such painful, humiliating memories, I feel a peace come over me just speaking her name. Emmy saved my life. "The minute I saw her, I knew I could never leave her. That I could never live without her. Somehow, she became my whole world the moment she drew breath. She became my reason for living, for surviving. But they knew that. Lucy and Ryan, they both knew. They knew all they had to do was threaten me with her–threaten to take her away, threaten to hurt her, threaten to have me declared an unfit mother–and I'd do whatever they wanted. And so they got their way. They got a sex toy when they were bored with their underground parties and I kept my mouth shut as long as they left Emmy alone. They knew I'd do anything for her. I'd die for her. I'd be a slave for her. I'd give up everything I am for her. She was the only reason I stayed and they knew it. They knew I wouldn't risk not being able to care for her. Or losing her to Ryan, if he ever chose to try to take her. I was just a kid, all alone with a child of my own. A kid with nothing."

I gulp, my mouth dry as a bone. My heart races at a sickening pace as I prepare myself for the rest of the story. For the worst part. For the part that scares me the most.

Finally, I glance up at Cole. I wonder if he can see the blood and the tissue as someone tears into my chest with a butcher knife, ripping tendon from muscle, flesh from bone. Because that's what it feels like is happening. Every time I think about it, I'm shredded, all the way to my soul.

Cole shakes his head. "No. Don't tell me…"

I say nothing. Then, as though he senses what comes next, he lunges from the chair and walks to the fireplace. He spreads his arms wide and palms the mantle, leaning against it so that his head hangs down between them. I hear his breathing in the quiet. It's heavy, labored. Angry.

So I finish. I've come too far to stop now. "Not much changed for four long years. During the day, Emmy was all mine. I cared for her, clung to her, protected her. I fed her, bathed her, put her to bed. But the nights…the nights belonged to Ryan and Lucy. I got numb to it eventually. I lived for the days. I'd get a few hours sleep after they left me and then I'd spend every second I could with Emmy. But the nights… I drifted through them like a zombie. But I had Emmy. That's all that mattered. She was clothed and well-fed, she had toys and parks and playgrounds, and as long as she was okay, I was okay. Until the one day that she wasn't."

I *feel* the tears now, hot and urgent, burning. My heart pounds against my sternum, demanding release. Like the memories themselves are alive within me. An alien clawing toward the freedom of open air.

"I was only asleep for a few minutes. Emmy had been sick and I'd been up with her for two nights straight. She was watching cartoons when I drifted off on the couch. When I woke, she was gone. I went all through the house looking for her. I even checked in the backyard, thinking she might've gone out to play on her swingset. But she wasn't there. And neither was Ryan." My words are coming faster, my breath more frantic. My voice hardly sounds like my own. It sounds shrill and shaky. "I don't even remember climbing the stairs. I only remember praying that she was okay, that he didn't have her. That's when I heard her scream. It sounded exactly like the one you just heard."

I close my eyes. I have to force myself to calm down, to remember that she's safe. That we are hidden away where no one can find us. Not even Ryan.

"He had taken off her pants and her panties and w-was holding her down, t-t-trying–"

"Stop!" Cole snaps. "Please stop." His voice is tortured, as tortured as I feel.

I drop my face into my hands and I let the sobs come. Deep, gut-wrenching, painful. They come from a part of my soul that I haven't visited since it happened. I can't. For Emmy's sake, I can't. The anger overwhelms me. The fear incapacitates me. But Emmy needs me, so I have to be better than that. I have to be stronger.

"When Lucy saw what I did to Ryan's face, when she heard what *he* was doing when I found him, she took me to town the next day, gave me five hundred thousand dollars and told me to disappear. She didn't like that Ryan wanted me so much. Wanted Emmy. It wasn't fun anymore. At least not for her. But that was fine with me. Anything to get away. And so we did. Emmy and I disappeared. That was two years ago."

Cole turns to me, a mixture of rage and heartbreak on his face. I see it clearly despite the tears flooding my eyes. As always, he watches me for a bit first, but then, he walks to stand before me. Slowly, he kneels, taking my hands in his. He stares down at them as though they might speak to him at any moment. Purposefully, he brings each finger to his lips, kissing them one by one. When he's finished, he lifts his eyes to mine.

"Eden, I..." he begins. His voice is low. Gruff.

He doesn't finish his sentence. Instead, he pulls me onto the floor in front of him and draws me into his arms. He holds me this way–both of us on our knees, my cheek pressed to his chest, his lips pressed to my head–for so long that I know the rhythm of his heart better than my own. Mine starts to follow it, matching the pace, beat for beat.

We breathe together, beat together, hurt together, closer now than we were even when his body was buried deep inside mine. Right now, we are the same. We are two broken people, finding strength in each other's remaining pieces. We've both lost so much, paid so dearly for what we have left, for what we were allowed to keep. Maybe, just maybe, it's enough to make a whole. Our pieces. Together.

It's minutes, hours, days later when Cole speaks again. "Is that why she doesn't talk?"

I nod against him. "Selective mutism. She hasn't talked to anyone except me since the day I pulled Ryan off her." My voice is a whisper in the quiet, like the patter of rain in the halls of a mausoleum.

"And the nightmares?"

"They're getting less and less. She pulls out of them more quickly, too. She's still sucking her thumb, though. Something she only started doing again after Ryan. The doctors say that with time and safety and normalcy, she'll heal."

There's another long pause. I hear the steady thump of Cole's heart, the even wisp of his breathing. And then I hear his eerily cold, "If I ever lay eyes on him, I'll rip his throat out."

I squeeze my eyes shut against the notion of seeing Ryan again. "He can never find us. Never. I can't risk Emmy. I can't risk him trying to take her away."

"I would never let that happen. He'd have to kill me first."

His tone is ferocious, but it doesn't scare me. It makes me feel as safe as the strong arms that haven't let me go since I told him.

"Momma?" comes a sleepy voice.

Cole freezes, like we're two young lovers caught making out under the bleachers by the principal. "Shit," he hisses softly into my hair.

I disentangle myself from Cole's arms and turn toward Emmy. I don't want to jerk away guiltily, like we were doing something wrong. We are simply kneeling on the floor, hugging. No harm, no foul. My daughter has just never seen good, healthy affection between a man and a woman before. She might be surprised or confused. I'm just glad we weren't doing anything else.

Nice, Eden. Nice. Good, solid parenting.

"Come here, baby," I tell her, holding my arms open. She rubs her eyes sleepily as she trots across the living room and launches herself into them. She's up a little earlier than usual, probably because of her nightmare.

I can feel her craning her neck around me to look at Cole, who has backed away a few feet. He has an innate feel for not making her uncomfortable, an intuitiveness that must come from having been a father once upon a time.

"Are you hungry, monkey?" I ask, stroking Emmy's silky hair.

I feel her nod.

Just then, I hear a click and the lamps come back on. "The power's back on!" I tell Emmy. "Are you a magician?" I ask, tickling my fingers up her side. She flinches and I hear a tiny giggle, but she's still draped over my shoulder. Probably watching the mesmerizing man behind me. "Cole came to fix us breakfast. How about we get your belly full and then go make a snowman out in the yard. Sound good?" Emmy pushes away from me, her bright eyes shining happily into mine. She nods again.

She looks past me to Cole. She doesn't have to say a word to convey her thoughts perfectly. Her expression and body language say it all. Her eyebrows are raised, her eyes are wide and she's practically vibrating with excitement.

I glance over my shoulder at Cole, who is now sitting on the edge of the chair. "I think that means hurry," I loud whisper.

He stands, a smile playing with the edges of his gorgeous lips. "Who likes French toast?" Emmy raises her hand enthusiastically. "Can you show me where your bread is?" he asks. He's not pushing her to talk, which is good, but he's engaging her in a casual manner, which is also good.

Maybe Cole will just be *good*. For both of us. Only time will tell. And time is something we have plenty of.

TWENTY

Cole

I EXPERIENCE A collision of emotion when Emmy steps cautiously out of her mother's arms and walks toward me. At first, every feeling is the soft kind, the kind that decent people feel toward a child. But when she puts her thumb in her mouth, knowing what causes her to do it brings on a fresh stab of rage. It cuts through my sternum and goes straight into my heart like a sharp spear. In this moment, if I could find him, I would gladly rip apart the man who did this to her. I'd tear him limb from filthy, disgusting limb.

But then another shift happens. When Emmy reaches me, she curls her tiny fingers around mine and pulls me with her toward the kitchen. Rage is immediately forgotten, replaced by the soothing comfort that this little girl brings to the battered parts of my soul. Looking down at her, it's almost like having Charity back. At least a little bit. And I can't help thinking that maybe I can do right by Emmy, that I can somehow make up for what happened with my own daughter by saving someone else's. But it will never undo what I did. It will never bring back the life I stole.

I'm aware of Eden's soft gaze on us as we walk together into the kitchen. It's a warm feeling, as though her happiness and security shine out from her like rays of heat from the sun. I glance back over my shoulder when Emmy steps in front of me and points up to a cabinet. Eden's smiling, like I expected she might be, but even from here I can see the tears in her eyes. It makes me realize that I never want to see any pain or sadness in them. Never again. Only contentment. Or desire. Or love.

Turning back to the task at hand, I open the cabinet and pull out the bread before squatting down in front of Emmy. She takes a step back, but just one. I figure that's probably something like progress.

"Do you wanna help? Be my mini sous chef?"

She looks shyly from me to her mother and back again. She doesn't answer; she just takes off running toward Eden. She tugs on Eden's hand until she bends so that Emmy can whisper in her ear, and then she races back to me.

"When Emmy and I cook together, we always listen to music," Eden explains as she flips on the television and finds a music station.

"Then let's get to it," I say to Emmy, slapping my hands together and then holding them open. "Can I put you up here so you can help me better?" I ask.

At first Emmy just looks at me, her little lips pursed around her thumb. Music begins playing softly in the background as she watches me. I'm just about to make an excuse to let her off the hook when she slips her thumb out of her mouth and spreads her arms.

Something burns in my chest when I reach for her, cupping her gently beneath her arms and hefting her up onto the countertop. She's light as a feather. So small and delicate. Fragile. How could anyone even *think* of hurting her?

I push the thoughts away. They don't belong here with us. Not today.

Emmy doesn't smile until she looks back at her mom. And when she does, her grin is enough to melt the coldest of hearts. I guess as long as she can see her, she feels safe.

I glance back at Eden again. She's dancing for her daughter, head bouncing, eyes closed. When she opens them and finds me watching her, she blushes ten shades of red. After a few seconds she starts laughing, though, and then I hear an answering giggle closer to me.

Emmy's eyes are lit up as she watches her mother. It hurts to see it, but more in a good way this time. It makes me incredibly sad, but not the hopeless kind of sad I've felt for so long. More like the feeling that I wish my own daughter could be here, enjoying a breakfast like this. But this little girl needs it as much as mine did. And at least I can be here for her.

TWENTY-ONE

Eden

I FEEL LIKE acting silly. I'm happier right now than I've been in a long time. Maybe ever. My parents were never the fun kind. Their work was always more important than me. Giving me attention was never a priority.

Then, when they sent me to Lucy's, I got all kinds of attention, only it was attention that no girl ever dreams of having. I promised when I had Emmy that she'd never know the kind of childhood that I had. She'd have all my love and attention, and she'd never doubt how precious she is to me. I promised myself that we'd laugh and act silly and enjoy every day. I swore to myself that she'd have a million good memories of her childhood to compete with her horrible ones. And today will be one of those good memories for her. Since Ryan, she hasn't let a man touch her, even in the most casual way, not even the doctors.

Until now.

Until Cole.

She seems to sense something in him. Brokenness? Gentleness? Sadness? Safety? I don't know, but it puts her at ease with him in a way she hasn't shown anyone in two years.

But today, Emmy's happy. Her smile is music to my soul like the song playing behind me is music to my ears. And Cole...watching him interact with her, seeing the expression on his face when he looks at her...this day couldn't be more perfect. And it's only just begun.

It started with talk of the worst time of my life. Maybe it will end with laughter from the best.

"Come on, Emmy. Dance like you do in your car seat," I call across the room to my daughter. I raise my arms and pump them to the beat like I've seen her do so often.

Emmy shakes her head, her eyes flickering quickly to me then to Cole and back to me again.

Cole notices. "You mean like this?" he asks, shaking his hips and shoulders. Even though he's goofing off for Emmy's sake, I can see that he has rhythm, and for some reason that is a huge turn-on for me. It makes me think of his rhythm in other activities, thoughts of which have no business being in my head when my child is near. But still, all in all, I just feel warm and happy. And...hopeful.

Grinning over at Cole, Emmy raises her hands, just a little, and thumps them to the beat. "Go, Emmy! Go, Emmy!" Cole cheers when she starts to wiggle her shoulders. Her face is lit up like the fourth of July and I've never seen a more wonderful sight. Even as gorgeous as the man at her side is, seeing her make this small bit of progress is breathtakingly beautiful.

From the living room, I direct Cole in supply procurement as he gathers a bowl and fork, takes eggs, butter and milk from the fridge, grabs cinnamon from the cabinet and gets a skillet from under the stove.

He moves like he's comfortable in a kitchen. I guess he has to be. I mean, he's a bachelor. It's that or starve.

"Think I can crack this egg with one hand?" he asks Emmy. She watches with wide eyes as he does exactly that. I can tell she's impressed, but not nearly as much as when he dances his way to the trashcan to throw the empty shell away. She watches his every move, a smile playing with the corners of her lips the whole time. It occurs to me that she probably finds him just as incredible as I do.

As she whisks the milk and egg mixture, Cole turns to me. When his eyes fix on mine again, they make me feel breathless. He's impossibly handsome anyway, but when he's like this–so relaxed and playful, taking such care with my daughter–I think to myself that there can't be a more attractive man on the planet. There just can't.

"Come on, mom," Cole says, holding out his hand to me. "Help us make dancin' French toast."

So I do. And it's the best French toast I've ever had.

⌘⌘⌘⌘

We decide to make the snowman in Cole's small yard. It didn't take much to convince Emmy of the benefits of it, especially once Cole told her that he had carrots at his house and that the snowman would be devastated if he had no nose. She practically dragged me all the way to his place after that. The snowman *must not be* noselessly devastated!

Now, we're sitting in *his* kitchen, looking out at the snowman in his back yard while he makes us hot chocolate to cap off the grilled cheese and soup we just ate. Emmy is watching cartoons on his enormous TV, playing with her toes through her socks, eyes glued to the screen.

"So, why did you *really* want the snowman in your yard?" I ask. That question has been bugging me all day. Cole seemed very determined to bring us here, to have the snowman *here.*

His eyes flicker to Emmy and then back to me. As always, even after such a brief reprieve from them, I'm struck by the bright blue intensity of his gaze. I think I can *literally* feel it when he looks at me. No kidding.

"Is it so terrible that I wanted you here? That I wanted to see you playing in my yard, sitting at my table, watching your daughter from my kitchen?"

His words warm me better than the crackling fire that's blazing in his huge fireplace. "I guess that's not *too* terrible," I deflect, lowering my eyes so he won't see how much pleasure his words bring me.

Cole reaches out and hooks a finger under my chin, lifting until my eyes are back on his, unable to escape. "I'd keep you here if I could. I'd memorize you in every room of this house. It would never be empty again. It would smell like you, feel like you. It would hold *you.*"

I can't help the smile that breaks out across my face. "Well, in that case, we'd better get started. Do I get a tour of all these rooms I'm staying in?"

"I'd love to show you around." His smile is heart-stopping. God, I almost wish he wouldn't do that. Especially when I'm not expecting it. It makes my lungs shut down completely. But it fires other organs up to the point of being bothersome. Hot and bothersome.

Cole turns off the stove and sets the saucepan of cocoa onto a cool eye. "Would you like to see the other rooms, Emmy?" he asks, taking my hand and leading me into the living room where she is. She's stretched out on the couch now, her head resting against one of the pillows. Her eyes are sleepy when she looks back at him and smiles, shaking her head. She promptly dismisses him by turning her attention back to her cartoons.

"Gotta admire that kind of focus," he says wryly, pulling me with him toward a door on the other side of the room.

The cabin is laid out with the living room and kitchen being basically one big, open room with floor-to-ceiling windows facing the ocean. There's a rock fireplace on the right wall of the space and a couple of doors on the left. Two hallways frame the kitchen, but I'm guessing we'll get to those in a minute.

Behind the first door is an office. It looks well-used yet orderly, and I'm guessing Cole does most of his business from in here. I walk around the chunky, mahogany desk, trailing my fingers along the edge. It suits him. It's rich and masculine, it's color dark and sensual. It's Cole. Down to a T.

When I round the desk, I look up to find Cole watching me. His eyes are the same intense electric blue as always, but they're not so unreadable right now. Right now, they're hungry. The way he's looking at me...it's like he's starving to death and I'm his favorite meal.

The thought sends a chill racing through me. It lands with a delicious thud right between my legs.

I almost groan. But I don't. I hold it in.

Being alone with Cole again (even though we aren't totally alone) after being so close to him all day and not really being able to touch him (even though I wanted to so, so badly) is making me feel bold and a little dangerous. I stand in front of his chair, brushing my fingers back and forth over the slick wooden surface.

I drop my voice low, the blare of the cartoons easily keeping my words from entering the living room. "So, Mr. Danzer, after you've memorized me in *this* room, what will you imagine doing with me?"

No sooner than the words are out of my mouth, Cole's pupils explode, swallowing up every bit of his blue irises. "Oh, so that's how you're going to play." His voice...*God*, it is *scrumptious*.

"Who's playing?"

One dark blond brow shoots up as he steps closer to the desk. He doesn't stop until only the expanse of mahogany separates us. "I'd imagine you as my personal assistant, dressed in a slim skirt that stops just above your knees and a silky blouse that buttons up to about right here," he says, reaching across the desk to press his finger to the space right between my breasts. I feel his touch like a bolt of electricity shooting through me.

Damn, maybe I shouldn't have started this, I think when I feel moist heat gather in my panties.

"That's very...specific," I say breathily, wishing he wouldn't take his finger away. But he does.

"You'd be wearing high heels and black stockings and your hair would be held up with a pencil." His words draw me into a scenario. I can all but feel the brush of the skirt against my thighs as I walk into this office to find him sitting behind his big desk.

"Would I be bringing you coffee?" I ask, getting into the vision.

"I don't give a damn *what* you'd be bringing me. As long as *you* bring it, because I'd meet you at the door and I'd close it behind you. Your big, gray eyes would get all wide and innocent like they do sometimes, and you'd back slowly toward the desk. When you felt it brush that beautiful ass, you'd stop. And when I reached you, you'd stop me with a hand to my chest, telling me not to mess up your lipstick. I'd laugh, and then I'd turn you around and bend you over the desk. I'd ease that skirt up and find nothing underneath. Not a damn stitch of underwear. Because you're a dirty little vixen that way." His grin is enough to melt all my clothes off. Right here, right now. I'm practically panting as I wait for him to continue. "I'd drop to my knees and I'd kiss those creamy thighs. That pretty ass. That sweet pussy. I wouldn't stop kissing...and licking...and touching...until you came for me. And then I'd stand up and *eeease* into you. Again. And again. Until you came a second time, until all that sweetness was dripping down your legs. Then I'd push your skirt down. And I'd turn you around. You'd slap me, but then I'd kiss you and smear your lipstick anyway. You wouldn't complain. Because you'd love it. *You'd* love it and *I'd* love it."

I'm so turned on, I think I'd be grateful if a good, stiff wind would blow between my legs. I clear my throat, realizing I'm way out of my depth in this game that I so pluckily started. I don't even know what to say, because everything I want to say is totally off limits with my daughter in the next room. I settle for, "Well, I guess I'll have to buy a skirt the next time I go to Ashbrook."

Cole gives me that smile again. It nearly stops my heart, I think, which is not a good thing. At this point, I need all the oxygen to my brain that I can get. All my bloodflow seems to be diverting to...other places. "In that case, let me show you the other rooms, too. You might have a list."

Excitement twitters through me. This man might be dangerous after all.

TWENTY-TWO

Cole

I AM SO hard right now, I could probably drive a nail through a cement block with the tip of my dick. I've taken Eden into nearly every room in my house and spun her an explicit, erotic tale about the things I'd like to do to her in each one. With each scenario, she's only gotten more excited. I can see it in the flush of her skin. I can feel it in the flutter of her hand in mine. And I can sense it in the rapid way she breathes, in the throaty way she asks questions when she plays along.

Hot damn! I never would've expected such a sexual creature to be hiding behind those amazing gray eyes. It's like a bonus–for a woman to be such a good mother, such a decent person, such a pleasure to be around, but to have a dirty-girl streak, too.

Jackpot.

I pull Eden behind me into the second guest room's bathroom. "It's so spacious," she mutters in her low, husky voice. I know she's trying to be quiet so she doesn't wake Emmy, who fell asleep two rooms ago, but it's sexy as all hell. I don't even think she realizes how she sounds, how she could ask me to do *anything* in that voice and I'd do it.

"What was that?" I ask, flattening her against the short wall, out of sight of the door. Just in case.

I feel her shallow breathing. I see the sensual slant of her eyes. She's on fire right now. Just like me.

"I said it's so. Spacious," she repeats, her eyes falling to my lips as she annunciates.

"There are so many things I'd like to hear you say right now. In that voice," I confess, my mouth mere inches from hers.

"Like what?" she asks, all sex and innocence, spicy and sweet.

"Say 'cock'."

Her cheeks flush, but she doesn't look away. "Cock," she says softly.

I bend my knees enough that I can press my hips into hers. Her gasp of pleasure is nearly my undoing.

"Are you wet right now?"

"Yes."

"You are?"

"God, yes!"

"Show me."

Her eyes widen the tiniest bit. I know what she's thinking. "But Emmy..."

"One finger. Show me with one finger."

She debates for less than a second before she reaches between us, her knuckles brushing my stiff dick, and slides her hand into her pants.

"Go deep," I tell her, loving the way her lids get all heavy and her lips part like she's about to moan. I know the instant she does it. I know when she pushes her finger inside. Her breath brushes my cheek in a quick puff. I figure she's about as close to coming as I can stand her being without doing something I'll regret. "Now let me taste."

"Ohmygod," she groans quietly, gently taking her hand from her pants and hesitantly raising it between us. When she stops, I reach for her wrist. Without taking my eyes off hers, I bring it to my mouth and slide her moist finger across my tongue, licking it from base to tip.

"You taste better than ice cream, Eden Taylor," I tell her. And then I give in to the urge to kiss her. It's quick and violent and full of all the insane things that she makes me feel. And then I let her go. Because that's the responsible thing to do. Her kid's in the house, for chrissake.

Reluctantly, I release her mouth and rest my forehead against hers. "Damn you, woman! Damn you for making me feel this way."

"I'm pretty sure this is all *your* fault, Mr. Danzer."

When I raise my head, she's smiling up at me. I've never wanted something, *anything, anyone,* so much in all my life as I want *this woman* right now.

I push away from the wall and take her hand again. "Come on. If we don't get this over with, your daughter's liable to get an education that she's too young for."

Her smile tells me she knows I'm kidding.

Mostly.

The last stop on the tour is the master suite. It takes up the majority of the west side of the house. I stop at the double doors and gesture for her to go first. I just stand back and observe.

It's as I watch her walk through the room, touching the ice blue comforter, dragging her fingers along the edge of the dresser, that the reality of having her here, of feeling the crazy way I do about her, hits me. She belongs here. With me. In this room. In this house. In my life.

"This is amazing," she whispers in awe when she reaches the floor-to-ceiling windows across from the bed. They're framed by nothing and filled with the snowy beach beyond.

Most people find the beach soothing–the waves, the horizon, the endless stretch of sand. But I don't care about most people. I care about this woman. And for some reason, it pleases me that she's reacting this way.

I don't approach her. For some reason, this moment has taken on a different feel. It's not sexual, despite the things we've done and talked about doing. This moment is real. The jarring kind of real. The earth-quaking kind of real. And I feel it in numb places that I never thought would be able to feel again.

She turns abruptly and pins me with those incredible eyes of hers. "What are you thinking? Right now?"

I start toward her, loving the way she looks both nervous and excited the closer I get. Her face is so expressive. I doubt she could hide what she was feeling if she tried. I've known from day one that she was attracted to me. I love that I can read her so easily.

Even though I can see how she feels, written right there on her face, I still don't tell her what I was really thinking.

"I love that, even though you're a good mother and a lady right down to the way that you fold your napkin in your lap, you took a naughty tour of my house and said 'cock' in the guest bath. You realize that officially makes you every man's dream woman, right?"

"Are you saying you dream about me?"

"More often than you know."

"Care to tell me about some of those dreams?"

"I think I just did, but I'd be happy to show you later if you're *that* interested."

"Oh, I'm interested alright."

I'm so close I'm practically pressing her back to the cold glass of the window. It would take so little for me to get her out of her pants and wrap those luscious legs around my waist. Just a flick here and a zip there.

"You're dangerous. Did you know that?" I tell her.

"Funny, I was just thinking that same thing about you a few minutes ago."

"Stay with me, Eden," I say impulsively. I'm not even sure what I mean, what I'm asking of her.

Again, her transparent eyes tell me what she's going to say before she says it. "I can't. Emmy…"

"She can stay, too, of course. I meant *both of you.*"

"She needs her room, her things. She needs that stability. We move so much, it's the only thing I can give her on a consistent basis. Other than me. I, uh, I guess you'll just have to come to me," she adds with a sexy twist of her lips.

I smile down into her face. "Wild horses couldn't keep me away."

TWENTY-THREE

Eden

THE LITTLE COTTAGE we've called home for almost three months feels empty tonight. Cole got a call from Jason about a renter who lost hot water, so Emmy and I came on home while he went to fix it. He didn't know how long he'd be, so we didn't make any set plans to see each other or talk to each other later. Maybe that's the reason I feel off.

Emmy seemed to notice the quiet when we first got here, but she's lying on the living room floor, coloring happily now. We played a game and read a story, so determined was I that she not notice his absence. Or my reaction to it. Whatever else happens in my life, it's imperative that Emmy not be affected by it. And the melancholy I'm fighting has me wondering if having Cole in our lives was such a good idea.

It's too late now, though, and the thought of giving him up is becoming increasingly distasteful.

I'm sitting quietly in the chair, watching my daughter draw and listening to her hum, when she throws down her crayon and climbs to her feet. She races the short distance to me and throws herself into my arms. She puts her little hands on either of my cheeks and squeezes, giving me "fish face" as she loves to do.

She's smiling at me when she observes, "You laughed a lot today, Momma."

"I did?"

"Uh-huh." The expression on her face is that of someone who has uncovered a wonderful secret. "You like him, don't you?"

Hmmm. How to answer that carefully…

"I think he's very nice. Don't you?"

She nods enthusiastically. "He makes good French toast. And he dances funny."

She wrinkles her nose and I do the same, nodding in agreement. "He does, doesn't he?"

Emmy giggles. "But I like it."

"I do, too."

"He makes you happy, right?"

"*You* make me happy," I skirt.

"But he could make you happy if I'm not here, right?"

"Nothing could make me happy if you weren't here. I love you too much, doodle bug."

Her smile melts into a disappointed face. "But you'd try, right?"

I try not to make a big deal of her odd questions and her concern with my happiness. I figure it *has to have* something to do with her emotional scars from what happened. I don't even pretend to know the way a child's mind works, but it worries me when she starts this stuff.

"Emmy, why do you worry about me being happy without you?"

"Because I might not always be here."

"What makes you think that?"

She shrugs, letting her hands fall away from my face to rest on my chest. "Sometimes angels go to heaven. And you said I'm an angel."

"You're *my* angel, but that doesn't mean you'll go to heaven anytime soon. Most of the time, God lets mommas and daddys keep their angels for a long, long time."

As she ponders this, she pooches her lips out over and over, like she's kissing. "But Mr. Danzer didn't get to keep *his* angel."

"No. But you shouldn't let that worry you, sweetie. I'm here. I'll keep you safe."

I know I shouldn't make promises I can't keep, but as long as I'm alive and able, I *will* keep her safe. And I'm hoping my promise will ease her mind. Emmy has enough to deal with in her life without worrying about death and what will happen to her mother if she were to die.

Just letting that thought drift through my mind is enough to clog my throat and tie my stomach in knots.

I push aside my rising emotion and send a comically suspicious sidelong glance at my daughter. "Is this a stall tactic? Are you trying to get out of taking a bath?"

"No," she answers. And I don't think for a second that this had anything to do with her bath, but I need to take her mind off it.

I dance my fingers down her sides, eliciting a squeal. "Are you *suuure*?"

"I'm suuure!" she laughs, trying to wiggle away from my tickling fingers.

"I didn't hear you."

"I'm sure!" she says again through her smiling lips.

"I guess the only way to prove it is to get this little body in the tub. Let's go, little miss," I say, scooping her up into my arms. "And then…ice cream!"

Her eyes widen. I try not to let her eat after her bath, and I control her sugar intake as much as I can, but tonight…well, tonight I think maybe ice cream is a good idea.

⌘⌘⌘⌘

I didn't hear from Cole last night. Now, it's time for Emmy's bath *again*, yet I *still* haven't heard from him. I've picked up the cell phone at least a dozen times, thinking I'd text him, just to see if he got the water heater fixed. But I don't. I've spent the last twenty-four hours telling myself that maybe it's for the best if I *don't* hear from him again. I can't decide if it's a good thing or a bad thing for Emmy.

On the one hand, she seems to really like him. From that first day on the beach, she seems as taken with him, as inexplicably drawn to him as I am. Only in a different way, of course. Even though she hasn't talked in front of him other than to call to me that first morning, she's opening up around him, and that makes my heart soar with happiness. Plus, she seems to be fixated on me being happy with someone in life. Maybe that's a natural concern for a child, but I think she's a bit young to be getting started with thoughts like that.

But despite those positives, I worry that if she gets too attached to him and things don't work out between us, she'll be crushed. And she's been hurt enough by the men in her life. I don't want to risk scarring her further.

Maybe if Cole *does* call me back, I should have a talk with him about boundaries. Maybe I should have a talk with *myself* about boundaries.

After her bath, Emmy reads two of her favorite stories to me before her bedtime. As I watch her lips move and her eyes scan, as I listen to the brilliant way her young mind works, I pray that I won't do anything to hurt her, intentionally or not. Children shouldn't know hurt and fear the way she's known them. Maybe that's enough to last her a lifetime. Maybe the rest will be smooth sailing.

When she's asleep, though, without her presence to distract me, the night drags on. I try to watch television, but nothing interests me. I find myself glancing outside repeatedly, looking *for what* I don't know.

Well, yes I do. It's not a *what*; it's a *who*.

Cole. When I'm not actively thinking about something else, he's on my mind. I click off the television and go to the kitchen for some water, my eyes automatically drawn to the house diagonal from mine. I wonder if he stays there at night. He was obviously staying there the night I went to get him. How many other nights has he spent there? Is he there now? If he is, why hasn't he come over? Why haven't I heard from him?

My endless spool of unanswered questions is enough to give me a headache, so I grab two Tylenol and take up a book that I bought from Jordan's limited selection a couple of weeks back. I do my best to lose myself in it and let the heat from the fireplace sooth away my tension.

I wake up nearly two hours later, my book open and resting on my chest, the fire nearly died down. I'm almost grateful for the prospect of sleep. Trying not to think about Cole has been as frustrating as it's been exhausting.

I stoke the fire, cut off the lights and head for bed. I must fall immediately to sleep, because it seems like a dream when I feel soft-yet-firm lips brush mine and a cool hand skates up the inside of my thigh.

I drift in that place between dream and reality for a few more seconds, enjoying the warm, liquid feel in my stomach and the ache that has started between my legs.

But when cold air hits me as the covers are drawn slowly away from my body, I come groggily awake.

"Am I dreaming?" I say aloud.

"No, but I might be," a sandpaper voice says.

Cole.

My heart speeds up to twice its normal pace and excitement races through me, waking me fully.

"Breaking and entering, huh?" I tease playfully, happier than I care to admit that he's here. Finally. It seems like I've waited forever.

"I didn't break anything, but I sure do plan to enter. Several times, actually."

I grin, listening to the rustle of his clothes coming off in the dark.

"This is illegal, you know. To come into a tenant's home unannounced."

I hear the springs creak and feel the mattress dip as Cole sets his knee and one hand on the end of the bed. He slides his hands up my legs, parting them as he goes. I feel the scrape of his stubble at one point, up near my groin, and a wicked stab of want gushes through me.

I feel his weight settle on me, pinning me beneath his naked heat. He answers just before his lips take mine.

"So sue me."

❋❋❋❋

"Are you upset that I came?" Cole asks as he kisses a trail from my chin to my ear, his body still completely sheathed within mine.

"Not at all."

"Good." I hear the smile in his voice. "I missed you too much to stay away a second night."

"Why did you stay away at all?"

"It was late by the time I got the water heater apart last night and then today I had to catch a ride with Jordan to Ashbrook for some parts that they didn't have here. By the time I got it finished up, I knew you'd be right in the middle of getting Emmy ready for bed. I didn't want to intrude, so I waited. But this was it. Maximum wait time. I'd have busted down your door if it had been two minutes longer," he confesses with a lusty growl.

"Is that right, Mr. Testosterone?"

"Hell yeah, that's right," he says, flexing his hips and causing me to gasp at the hardness that's already starting to take shape inside me. "Are you complaining about my testosterone?"

He swivels his hips, rubbing me in just the right spot. "God, no," I moan quietly, tilting my pelvis to capture him more fully.

"Because I can leave if I'm bothering you." He fastens his mouth on one nipple as he withdraws and then pushes all the way back into me, deep enough to rock my hips back.

"You're bothering me alright," I tell him breathlessly, "but I wouldn't have it any other way."

"Good, because I'm thinking that as long as you're here, you're stuck with me."

I don't get to worry over that comment because Cole leans back and pulls me up into a sitting position, held in his arms, impaled on his length. But when I'm lying bonelessly beside him an hour later, I can think of little else.

⌘⌘⌘⌘

As much as I'd love to wake up beside Cole, I'm afraid that Emmy will rise early again, a fluke thing, and find us in bed together. I don't think she's ready for that, no matter how much she likes Cole or thinks he makes me happy.

But in the wee hours, Cole, seemingly almost as in tune with Emmy's welfare as I am, gives me a long, passionate kiss and announces that he's leaving.

"I probably shouldn't be here when Emmy gets up."

I don't argue, because it's exactly what I was thinking.

I sit up to watch him dress, shafts of moonlight pouring through the curtains he insisted on opening. *I want to see you,* he'd said. *I want to see your face when you come. I want to see your beautiful legs spread and I want to watch my cock slide in and out of you. I don't ever want to forget what that looks like.*

How was I going to say no to that? And now I'm getting the benefit. I can see his muscles flex as he pulls on his pants, like titanium machinery gliding smoothly under flawless skin. And I can see his face, partly shadowed, when he looks at me. That look that says he could stay here and make love to me forever and never get tired. That look that says he wants me more than he wants to eat. That look that says he wants... more. Only I don't know exactly what "more" is for him.

"Will I see you later?" I ask.

"How about dinner tonight? I'll cook."

"I promised Emmy I'd take her to Bailey's for a cheeseburger tonight. She did well on her math test and that's what she wanted as a reward, so..."

"Can I come?"

I hide the smile that wants to light up my face. "I suppose we could put up with your incessant chatter for another night." I see his wry expression. "What are you up to now? I mean, is the house across the street finished? Or will you be working on something else?"

"I'll be back across the street tomorrow," he responds vaguely.

"And today?"

I see his pause. I see his hesitation. I've overstepped.

"Today, I'll be at the beach."

It's Sunday.

"Building a sandcastle?"

He nods once, his brow furrowing like it's done so often since I've known him. The thing is, I haven't seen him frown much in the last few days.

"We, um, we could come and help if you want. Or if you'd rather do it by yourself..." I let the sentence trail off, flabbergasted at my audacity. What the hell is wrong with me? It's like I own him, like he can't spend a minute without me or have a day that's unaccounted for.

"Thanks, but–"

"Oh, God! I'm so sorry! Listen to me! I sound like a controlling fruitcake. Just forget I said anything," I plead, covering my face with my hands. How. Humiliating. If he ever wondered whether I've had any kind of normal relationship in the past, I'm sure he has his answer now.

Cole pulls my hands from my face. His expression is kind, but inscrutable. "Don't apologize. I want to be with you. But," he adds, his smile small, "this is just something that's...it's just something that I have to do on my own."

"I understand, Cole. Truly I do. I don't know why I even offered." I shake my head.

"Because you're caring and fun and you want to be with me, too."

I neither confirm nor deny his assumption, but he's right. I *do* want to be with him.

"I'll pick you up at six. And wear something formal. You've never been to Bailey's at night."

For a split second, I wonder if he's serious. "You're kidding, right?"

His laugh is a short bark. "Of course I'm kidding. Have you *seen* Bailey's? You don't even have to have *teeth* to get served in there."

"Good point," I concede. "I just wanted to make sure."

Cole leans into me where I'm sitting on the bed. "If it were up to me, you could come naked. You'd be the best dressed person there. But there's Emmy. And the police, of course. It probably wouldn't end like I'd want it to–with you riding my cock at the bar."

I screw up my face. "Is that what you think about when you ask me to dinner at Bailey's?"

"Don't look at me like that. If you weren't so delectable, so irresistible, so damned addictive, I wouldn't think about you all the time like I do. It's your own fault."

He bends his head to nip at my breast with his teeth. "If you're leaving, you'd better stop right there," I warn.

His sigh is long and loud. "Fine. I guess I'm going. I had a good reason, right?" he teases.

"Emmy."

"Right right. A *very* good reason."

I grin as he pecks me hard on the mouth and walks away like I took his favorite toy.

I think to myself after I hear the front door shut and snap locked that he's not the only one who's addicted.

TWENTY-FOUR

Cole

MAYBE COMING TO Bailey's was a mistake. I expected the whispers and the long, odd looks, but I never expected to feel so...possessive. I find myself glaring at any man who stares at Eden for more than ten seconds. And there are a lot of them. Bailey's is the only place to eat in the whole town. It has a pretty big crowd on the weekends.

It doesn't help that my mood was a little testy to begin with. I didn't really want to leave Eden's this morning. I wanted to stay, to play with her beautiful breasts, to lick her satiny skin, to reach deep inside her body with mine and drag out moans and gasps from her unwilling lungs. That constant want left me distracted when I went to the beach.

After that, I came home and showered, torn between thoughts of what Eden's body would look like all wet and soapy, and the asshole that I am for finding some amount of happiness when my own daughter can't.

All in all, it left my mood a little sour before we even arrived at Bailey's. And now I'm having to contend with all the locals drooling over my beautiful date.

"Are you okay?" Eden asks as we take a seat at one of the few booths available in Bailey's.

"Of course. Why?"

She watches me suspiciously, her hazel gray eyes searching mine for answers that I'm unwilling to give. "Just curious."

I open the menu and pretend to peruse it. I've got the whole thing memorized and I already know what I want. I just need a few minutes to collect myself, to conceal the growing agitation that must be reflected on my face.

"Hiya, sweetie," Jordan slurs when she approaches the table to take our order. She leans down to hug Eden. "I've been meaning to get out to your place, but it looks like you've been plenty busy without *my* company," she says loudly as she nods in my direction.

I scowl at her.

"Oh come on, Cole! You know there's no keeping secrets in this town. *Everything* comes out eventually."

I grit my teeth.

"Maybe people should just mind their own business," I say mildly, holding her brown eyes until her smile dies.

"Well," Jordan says, clearing her throat and turning to Eden. "What can I get you two tonight?"

Eden orders Emmy's meal and then her own. After I order and Jordan leaves, she announces, "Emmy and I are going to check out the jukebox." She says it with a smile, but I can see the tightness in her face.

She doesn't give me time to respond, just gets up, waits for Emmy to slide out and then they walk off.

I'm screwing this up. I know I am. But damn! I feel kind of crazy today. I'm used to feeling one of two emotions–pain or numbness. Not all this other stuff.

I watch Eden as she walks away. Her ass looks amazing in the jeans she's wearing and her pink sweater fits her upper body to perfection. Nearly every head turns as she passes. Even the women look, although they're probably either jealous because she's so incredibly beautiful or appreciative of her relationship with her daughter. It's plain to see that she adores Emmy and that she's a good mother. It's there in the way Emmy looks up at her and the way Eden never lets go of her hand.

The longer I watch her, the more I realize that she's the perfect woman. And the more I think about it, the more it eats at me that everyone else wants her, too.

She avoids my eyes as she walks back to the booth, making me feel even more like a shitheel for ruining her night out with Emmy.

I wait until they're both situated back in the booth and Emmy is coloring before I speak. "I'm sorry," I tell her quietly.

That draws her stormy eyes back to mine. "For what?"

She's not playing dumb. She's asking me what's been up my ass.

I sigh. "I've never been jealous before."

Her brows draw together. "Jealous? Of what?"

"Of all these men looking at you."

She glances around. "What men looking at me?"

"You really don't see it, do you?"

"See what?" She's genuinely perplexed.

"See the way your hair pours down your back like a waterfall made of ink. See the way your eyes sparkle when you look at Emmy. See the way your laugh makes other people smile. See the way everybody wants you."

Pink spots bloom on her cheeks and she looks away from me, shy all of a sudden.

"Or the way you blush when someone tells you you're beautiful."

"Well, if *that's* what's wrong with you, then maybe you shouldn't apologize," she teases with a grin.

"Yes, I should. You don't deserve my mood. And neither does Emmy."

Eden glances over at her daughter, who is coloring pretty damn well for someone her age. Eden looks back at me and shrugs. "We're okay now that *you're* okay."

"I'm trying to be."

She smiles. "Now you know how I feel when Jordan is so *friendly* with you."

I scoff. "Please. There's not a woman in a ten state radius that holds a candle to you."

I can tell my comment pleases her. "You're gonna give me a big head."

I tilt my head and consider her. "Nah. You're not the type to get conceited."

"Oh really? Then what type *am I*?"

I pause, debating how truthful to be. In the end, I tell her exactly what I'm thinking. "The perfect type."

Her smile widens and her cheeks turn pinker, and just like that, I feel more relaxed than I have all day.

"You two going to be able to eat around all that flirting and smiling?" Jordan asks when she returns with a tray of our food. "If not, princess and I will eat it, won't we, little Emmy?" She winks at Emmy and Emmy leans her head against Eden's arm to hide her face. "That must be a 'no'."

"Emmy would share her food *with me*, wouldn't you, Emmy?" I ask of the little girl who looks so much like mine. She grins shyly and nods. "Jordan's out of luck, isn't she?" She grins bigger and nods more vigorously. I wink at her and am gratified by a tiny giggle. She's not talking to me yet, but I figure the fact that she's smiling and not sucking her thumb is progress. And I'll take every little small bit of progress I can get.

⌘⌘⌘⌘

I'm studying the picture Emmy drew for me after dinner when Eden quietly reappears in the living room doorway. The level of detail in the sandcastle and in the flowers is probably pretty advanced for a child her age. But that's not what strikes me most about the picture. What knocks the breath out of me is that she seems to have caught the emptiness I felt there today.

"What's wrong? Don't you like refrigerator pictures?" asks Eden.

"I like them just fine." I turn my attention back to the drawing, once again bothered by something that was eating at me earlier. When I was at the beach.

Eden comes to sit beside me on the couch, curling her legs under her and tucking her hands between her knees to warm them. I inhale the clean smell of her shampoo and the lightly sweet perfume or body lotion that she wears. Whatever it is, the scent suits her perfectly.

"Seriously, what's the matter? You look like you just saw a ghost."

My smile is more bitter than anything. "That's the problem. Only reverse."

"The reverse? What's that mean?"

I sigh and let the paper drift out of my fingers to settle silently on the wooden coffee table in front of me. Like letting go of a memory and watching it drift off into nothingness. Only I don't want to do that.

"Everybody in this town thinks I'm crazy," I begin. "Did you know that?" She doesn't respond. She doesn't need to. The answer is right there in her expressive eyes. They tell me more than what she'd be comfortable with sometimes, I think. "I'm not surprised. It's probably a juicy topic of conversation in a place like this. If gossip had headlines, I'm sure they'd read, 'Ex Football Pro Talks to Dead Daughter On Beach'." I pause, gathering my thoughts, choosing my words carefully as I toy with one edge of Emmy's picture. My fingers are drawn to it over and over. "I'm not crazy, Eden. I *wanted* to see Charity. I *wanted* to hear her voice. I wanted it so badly that I *could* see her. And hear her. But I knew she wasn't really there. Not even in ghost form. It was just my way of keeping her alive. Of never forgetting even one small detail about her, like the way her voice sounded."

I take a deep breath and rub my hand over my face, forcing myself to sit back and let go of the paper. "It was always strongest at the beach. Making those sandcastles. Until today." I close my eyes. My chest feels tight just thinking about this. About losing Charity.

Eden's voice is whisper quiet. "What do you mean?"

I don't look at her. I can't. "I didn't hear her today. Didn't see her. I wanted to. I did everything right. Just like I always do. The flowers. The castle. The pocketful of sand. But she wasn't there. In my mind, she just wasn't there."

"Why? What happened?"

I roll my head on the cushion and look at Eden. Her features are as beautiful as ever in the flickering firelight. I'm glad she's kept it going. I don't know why, but I am. It seems to be...*symbolic* somehow.

I study her. As always, her eyes tell the tale. There's trepidation in them. Dread. "You happened. Emmy happened."

"Cole, I–"

I interrupt because I need to get this out. Now that the guilt is eating me alive. "I wasn't looking for anybody, Eden. I wasn't trying to move on or get over her, to find something more in life. I was content in my misery." I pause. "I had no intention of pursuing you, even though I felt like I'd been hit with a sledgehammer when I saw you on the beach that day. But still, I wasn't going to do anything about it. Only I couldn't stay away."

"Cole, I never–"

"I know, I know. I didn't either. But I did. You did. *We* did. And now...*today*, all I could think about was you. How I didn't want to leave you this morning. How anxious I was to see you again at dinner. To see you with Emmy. To see her smile and maybe hear her voice. Just once. And because I took you with me, there was no room for *my* daughter."

I sound bitter. Resentful. I don't mean to. It just came out that way. I should apologize. But I feel like that would be an even bigger betrayal to Charity.

I'm filled with dread as I wait for Eden to respond. I wouldn't be surprised if she told me to leave.

"Cole, did you consider that maybe you're just finding some healthy middle ground?"

I turn to look at her. She doesn't appear mad or hurt. She just seems...calm. She sounds calm, too. Calm and practical.

"How can forgetting my dead daughter ever be healthy?"

"You're not forgetting her. You're sitting here talking about her. You went to the beach today to honor her memory. That's not forgetting her. But Cole, I doubt it's a healthy coping mechanism to imagine seeing and hearing her. Don't you think that maybe *this* is the healthy way to grieve? To think of her, talk about her. Visit places she loved."

I study Eden. Why am I angry right now? Is it because I feel like she's trying to replace my daughter with her own? Or is it because she and Emmy are disrupting the delicate balance I had between living and grieving? Or am I just mad at myself?

Eden reaches for my hand, laces her fingers through mine. I jerk slightly, my first instinct to pull away because of what I'm thinking, how I'm feeling. But she won't let me. She just tightens her grip. Like she's tightened her grip on *me*.

"She wouldn't blame you for being happy, you know."

And there it is.

The guilt.

This is what's eating at me—guilt. The guilt of finding someone, of moving on when I had no intention of moving on. Of letting anything other than Charity be the focus of my life.

I pull away and stand, pacing to the other end of the living room. "You wouldn't understand," I tell her coldly. That's how I feel—cold.

"I've never been through what you've been through, Cole, no, but that doesn't mean that I don't understand. She was *your child*. She would want you to be happy.

She would never want you to sacrifice your life to somehow memorialize her. Accidents happen. Even if she were here, she wouldn't blame you."

"You don't know that." I don't face her. I can't.

"Yes, I do. She was a child. Children are forgiving and resilient. More than anything she would want you to be happy. And to stop blaming yourself for something you couldn't control."

"But I deserve the blame. It's my punishment."

"Cole, you can't carry the weight of an accident. That's insane!"

"Is it?" I spit, whirling toward her. "Is it? I killed her dammit! Is it insane to carry the blame when my daughter died in a drunk driving accident *with me*? *Because of me?* Is it insane to carry the blame when she trusted *me* with her life and I threw it away because of a party? No, that's not insane, Eden. That's *justice.*"

My chest is heaving, my pulse pounding in my ears. I didn't realize how loud, how harsh my voice was getting until the quiet set in. Now the quiet is like death, cold and empty.

"Y-you were driving drunk in the accident that killed her?"

Shame. God, the shame...the remorse...the pain...it's overwhelming. I turn and lean my forehead against the wall, resisting the urge to pound my fist against it. But Emmy...Emmy is sleeping. She doesn't need to be here for this. To witness this–the dissolution of Cole.

"The last time we came up here three years ago, Brooke wanted to come a day early. It was the weekend before Charity's seventh birthday and she wanted to have a surprise party for her. We fought because I wanted to stop by a friend's party first. I ended up agreeing to get Charity here by eight just to shut her up. But I went by my friend's house first anyway. Stayed long enough to have a few drinks. And to be running late." I close my eyes. I can still see my little girl, smiling up at me from the passenger seat. Innocent, trusting. Alive.

"I wasn't drunk, but I wasn't sober either. It started raining about halfway here. I remember Charity telling me that this time, she was going to bring back enough sand in her pockets to give some to all her friends at home. Of all the things she loved about our trips, building sandcastles on the beach with her daddy was her favorite."

I don't have to look back at Eden to know she's crying. I hear her shaky breaths, I hear her quiet sobs. Only a parent would understand the pain that this kind of story means. Even if they've never experienced it, they've feared it. Dreamed about it. Prayed that it never happens to them.

"I was speeding when I saw the truck coming around the corner. He was barely over the line, but I swerved anyway. I was still going too fast when my right tire hit the gravel on the side of the road. I lost control. I couldn't correct the skid. There was a steep bank and we started to roll. The car flipped four times before we hit the tree. Charity's side was impacted the most. She was crushed." I'm shivering. I feel like my teeth are chattering and my insides are trying to jump through my skin. "They said sh-she died instantly."

TWENTY-FIVE

Eden

"OH, GOD!" I mutter brokenly. I don't even know what to say. "Oh God, oh God, oh God." I cover my mouth with my hands. When I look back up at Cole, leaning against the wall, defeated in his devastation, I'm drawn to him. Like I always am. I'm drawn to his pain, to his fury, to his intensity. I get up and cross the room, stopping inches from him. I can feel the heat radiating from him, warming away the chill that's come over me.

"Cole, I'm so sorry." I lay my hand on his broad back.

"Don't," he murmurs miserably. "Please don't."

"You can't punish yourself forever. It was a tragedy, yes. An awful tragedy. But it was still an accident. You would never have hurt her on purpose. Never."

"I'd give anything to be able to tell her that."

"If she were here, she would already know that. Cole, you can't give up on life because she's gone. How does that honor her? To live a sad existence mourning her is just adding another tragedy to the pile. Can't you just continue to love her? Can't you find love and happiness and bring her with you?"

Cole turns to face me, his expression ravaged, and he tells me something I never wanted to hear. "No. I could never do that. I told you I was broken. I told you I didn't have much to give. You just didn't believe me."

"What are you saying?"

His expression doesn't change as he reaches up to cup my cheek. His touch is so light it's almost ethereal. Like a cool breeze or the brush of a cloud. "I could fall in love with you, Eden. I might have already. But it won't ever matter. The judge loved my team. Barely gave me a slap on the wrist. For killing my daughter. But I deserved to be punished. And this is my penance. That will never change."

My heart is hitting my ribs like a battering ram. Did he just tell me he loves me? Or that he *might* love me? And then tell me that we are doomed in the very next breath?

"Won't you at least try?"

"I have been. I've been falling in love. I've been happy, more and more the longer I've known you.

And I've lost her. I've failed her again. And I can't live with that."

"So what does this mean for us?" Do I really want him to spell it out? Do I really want to hear him say the words?

"I'm saying that this can't go on. At least not like it has been. I can't be with you, Eden. Not like you'd want. Not like you deserve. What I've given you, it's all I have to give. There *is* no more."

I feel sick. Physically ill, like someone took a hot poker and jumbled up my guts. Can I be with him knowing that there is no future? Knowing that there isn't a tomorrow? That we will never be more than we are right now?

I don't know.

But can I let him go? Can I walk away? Let *him go*, right this minute? Move on and never look back?

I don't know that I can do that either. I don't know any of the answers. I only know that when he leans into me, when he brushes his lips over my forehead and pulls me into his arms, I *feel like* there's more. I *feel like* this can be more. If I only give him time.

I tilt my head and press my lips to his chin and then to his mouth. Hard. I hold him to me like I don't want to let go. Because I don't. I can't. Not yet. We just need time.

I hear his breathing pick up. I feel his hands grip my arms. It's my only warning. That and the pause. His stillness. His way of telling me that if I'm going to stop him, do it now.

Only I don't. I don't stop him because I don't want to. Instead, I reach under his shirt and I press my palms to his warm skin. And then we're on fire. We are two flames, raging out of control. Licking, burning, engulfing.

I don't know how we get undressed, but suddenly his hot, smooth skin is all I can feel. Against every inch of my body. Sliding, grinding, pressing.

And then the couch meets my thighs. And he's spinning me around. And he's bending me forward. And his hands are in my hair. And his mouth is at my shoulder. And his hips are pressed to mine.

And then he's inside me.

Forceful. Possessive. Undeniable.

He takes. I give.

He asks. I answer.

Finally, I am glass. Splintering. Separating. Reflecting.

A hundred colors. A thousand lights. A million emotions. Flying. Colliding. Swirling.

This is when I know without a doubt that I'm in love with Cole Danzer.

⌘⌘⌘⌘

I'm lying limp against Cole's side. I didn't ask him to stay. He didn't tell me he was leaving. He just picked me up when I couldn't stand anymore and carried me over here to the rug. Our rug.

I trace the letters that dance gracefully up his ribs on his left side. *Always.* I've admired his tattoos many times, but since I've been close enough to ask him about them, I'm always too absorbed with his presence, with his touch to ask. But now I have to know. Even though I'm almost afraid to ask about them, I've come too far to stop now. If I'm to find a way to keep him, I need to know everything. I can't fix it if I don't know about it.

"What does this mean?" I ask quietly, the first word spoken between us since he told me there was nothing else he could give me. I still disagree. I just have to make him see it.

"It's for Charity. She'll always be closest to my heart."

I gulp. Another reiteration of how he will never let me any closer? I don't know, but I have to make him understand that Emmy and I will never replace his daughter. I would never want for us to. But surely he can love us all. Surely.

"You don't need words on your skin for her to be close to you. She's your child. You'll never be without her. Not really. She's a part of you. Just like Emmy is a part of me. Nothing and no one could ever change that."

But that doesn't mean I don't have room to love someone else, too, I add silently, wishing he could read my mind.

I swallow my sigh when he makes no comment. "What about the other side?" I ask, referring to the script I've seen there. *Never.* "What does it mean?"

"Never means a lot of things," he says enigmatically. Another hint at what we will never have? What he can never give?

"What does it mean to you?"

"Never forget. Never again. There are a lot of nevers in my life."

I feel tears sting my eyes. "Am I a never now?"

"I think you always were."

TWENTY-SIX

Eden

THANKSGIVING WENT BY in Miller's Pond practically unnoticed. Emmy and I just had turkey pot pies at the house. But Christmas... Christmas is another matter altogether. I know the instant I open the door at Bailey's that this is a town that loves Christmas.

"Ho ho ho, ya hoser!" Jordan greets merrily from behind the counter. She's wearing a risqué Santa costume that includes a Santa hat, a cleavage-flaunting red top trimmed in white fur, and skin-tight black leather pants. Her wide black belt has a buckle as big as Emmy's head and it's encrusted with flashy faux diamonds. She's very...eye-catching. And very Jordan.

"Hi, Jordan," I call as Emmy and I head for the long bar. I told her we'd get a grilled cheese for lunch and then do our shopping.

The only two empty stools are between a guy named Cody that I've seen here before and an old wino that I'm not sure ever leaves. I put Emmy beside Cody and then I slide onto the stool beside the wino. He's swaying slightly, evidently already obliterated at quarter til twelve on a weekday. The best thing I can say about him is that at least he doesn't stink. Granted, he might actually *bathe* in alcohol, as strongly as he smells of it, but that's better than body odor.

He gives me a bleary smile and then returns his attention to the flat screen mounted on the wall that separates the bar from the kitchen behind it. Cody smiles and nods at me when I turn to help Emmy out of her jacket.

"Ladies."

I smile in return. Emmy leans toward me, slipping her thumb into her mouth. She at least smiles around it, though, when Jordan comes slinking down to take our order. She smells like alcohol, too, but at least she's more functional than the old man beside me.

"You two ready for Christmas?" she asks, leaning a curvy hip against the counter.

"We're running behind, but we'll catch up this week," I explain, thinking that I probably really do need to get up to Ashbrook to get some decorations and buy a few things for Emmy.

"If you need someone to watch the little princess while you do your shopping, just say the word. I'm great with kids." She winks at Emmy. Emmy turns her face into my side.

"I bet you'd make a great mom," Cody says from beside Emmy. His soft blue eyes are fixed appreciatively on Jordan. I've noticed him watching her before. I've heard him say kind and complimentary things before, too. Jordan always waves him off, though. Like she's doing now. It makes me wonder if she's overlooking something good that's right in front of her eyes.

"You must be as drunk as she is, Cody," Jason says as he appears down the bar at the cash register. He opens the till and removes some receipts from under the cash slots. Jordan blanches under her makeup. I've noticed she's reacting less and less flippantly to her brother's cruel teasing. It makes me worry about her. She's had enough abuse from the people in this town, apparently, and the last thing she needs is more from her brother.

"I'm sober enough to see her brother for the asshole he is," Cody rebuts with a grin.

"Don't make me come down there, man," Jason replies amicably.

Cody looks over at me. "He's all bark and not a damn bit of bite."

"I heard that," Jason sing-songs over his shoulder as he disappears again into his office.

"He just doesn't see that all his sister needs is the love of a good man and she'd be right as rain." Cody winks at me and I grin, too. Oh yeah. He's definitely got a thing for Jordan.

Jordan's smile is less bright when she clears her throat and tries to get back to business. "What are we eating, girls?"

I order lunch for Emmy and myself, and before Jordan leaves, Cody stands and tosses some bills onto the bar.

"Thanks for lunch, Jordan. Catch you later."

"Bye, Cody," she says, swiping up the cash and palming his plate. "See you later."

"Count on it," he says, smiling widely at her as he pushes through the door.

Jordan puts his dirty plate in a gray bus-pan and then tallies up his bill at the cash register, pocketing the change he left for tip. After she puts our lunch order ticket on the spinning wheel in the corner of the kitchen window, she comes back to clean up the bar where Cody sat.

As she drops his silverware into his empty glass and begins wiping the bar clean, I speak quietly to her. "I think Cody really has a thing for you, Jordan." I use my best girl-conspirator tone. I just want to feel her out on the situation. Overstepping my bounds would not be a good idea.

She doesn't look up at me and her smile is a sad one. "He just thinks he does. What would a nice guy like that want with someone like me?"

"What do you mean? What's wrong with you? You're beautiful, funny, smart. And you make a heck of a Mrs. Claus," I add, eyeing her outfit.

"I'm nothing any decent man would want to take home. Unless it's just for the night."

This isn't like Jordan. She's usually so ballsy, so confident. It's heartbreaking to see her so...down.

I reach over to put my hand over hers, stilling it and drawing her eyes to me. They're glistening and I realize how near tears she is. My heart breaks even more for her. And I could just strangle her brother *and* her ex for making her this kind of a wreck.

"Jordan, don't sell yourself short. You're worth more than one night and you can't let anyone convince you otherwise. I know it. Cody knows it. Jason knows it, too. He's just too big of a butt to admit it." I'd like to call him something much nastier, but little listening ears preclude me from doing so.

"You really think so?" she asks, her voice wobbly.

"I know so. Why don't you give Cody a call? Just to see. What can it hurt?"

"My pride," she answers. "My heart."

"Both of those are already hurting, though, right?" She shrugs. "But if I'm right... Maybe he could be someone who would make you really happy. Isn't that worth the risk?"

Her eyes search mine for long seconds before she nods grudgingly. "I guess so."

"I know so," I repeat, squeezing her hand before I release it.

As I lean away, I'm filled with hope for my friend. I hardly notice the beautifully-modulated southern voice when it sounds from just over my shoulder. Until I hear the name she mentions.

"Pardon me, but do you know where I might find Cole Danzer? I went by his house and he's not there."

I turn to see to whom the voice belongs and I'm stunned. A gorgeous brunette is standing behind me, casually poised, smiling pleasantly at Jordan. Her hair is as black as mine, only wavy, and her face looks like it should grace the cover of a magazine. She's dressed like she might've just come off the slopes of Aspen with her winter white ski jacket and matching moleskin pants.

"Eden, do you know where he is?" Jordan asks, pulling my attention back to her.

I'm speechless for a few seconds. A lancing pain in the vicinity of my heart tells me that this is not a good thing. That this woman is going to be a game changer for a game I was already in danger of losing.

I don't look back at the woman. I don't want to meet her eyes. I don't want answers to the questions rolling through my mind, like how does she know Cole and who is she to him. Besides, I imagine that I already know.

"I think he was working on the cottage across from mine today," I explain, brushing Emmy's hair back from her face to give myself something peaceful to focus on. She leans her head back against my chest so that she can look behind us at the stranger asking about Cole. I don't. I don't want to look at her.

The gasp I hear, though, draws my gaze anyway. The woman is even paler than she was when she walked in and she's staring at Emmy like she's just seen a ghost.

Just like Cole did the first time he saw her.

216

She places the tips of her trembling fingers over her lips as she watches my daughter. After several tense seconds that feel like hours, she turns her shocked eyes up to mine. Tears are welled in the corners. "Do you know Cole?"

I nod. Yes, I know him. I know his touch, I know his kiss, I know his heartache.

She nods, too. And judging by the pain I see in her eyes, she knows how well I know him, too. "Okay then." I watch her pull herself together. Straighten her spine, raise her chin, wipe one stubborn tear from her cheek. "Thank you."

And with that, she turns and walks gracefully out the way she came.

⌘⌘⌘⌘

I'm numb as I take groceries from the back seat and carry them inside. What feeling I have left in my heart freezes the instant I see the sleek black SUV pull to a stop in the driveway. My eyes meet the woman's, the same woman who came into Bailey's. The same woman who knows Cole. The same woman who I'm pretty sure is his ex-wife. But why is she here? What does she want with *me*?

I smile, pausing with bags dangling from my fingers, the cold wind whipping through my hair. I watch as she climbs out from behind the wheel and makes her way slowly to me, carefully picking her way along the snow-cleared path.

"Eden, right?" she asks, obviously noting Jordan's use of my name earlier.

I nod.

"I'm Brooke Danzer, Cole's wife. Can we talk?"

Cole's wife.

Cole's.

Wife.

Wife. Not ex-wife. Wife. Present tense.

I want to ask why, why we need to talk. I want to tell her that I don't want to. I want to tell her to get lost. I want to tell her Cole is mine and she has no business here.

But I don't.

Because I can't.

He's not mine and I don't know what her business is here. I was so caught up in Cole's story about losing his daughter, I never asked what happened to his wife. I just assumed. I assumed all sorts of things and never confirmed any of them. I just noted that he was alone. Solitary. That he wore no wedding ring and had no connections. And I let the rest go.

Like a stupid child.

I wanted to trust blindly. And so I did.

"Maybe we could go inside?" she asks, shivering noticeably. Her clothes may look nice and probably cost a fortune, but they obviously aren't very weather-worthy. I want to smirk. I want to tell her to go back to wherever she came from.

But I don't.

Because, again, I can't. I have to know. No matter how much it hurts.

"Of course."

I lead her inside, setting the last of the groceries in the kitchen. "Have a seat," I tell her as I busy myself getting Emmy situated in her room with a brand new sketch pad and colored pencils for her to draw with. When I return, Brooke isn't seated, but rather staring out the kitchen window. Toward the house Cole has been working on.

My heart drops into my stomach.

I clear my throat and begin to sift through a bag, pulling out cold items and placing them in the refrigerator. I'm not going to make any overtures. I'll wait for her to get to the point.

"How long have you known Cole?" she asks finally. She turns toward me. I can tell because of the clarity of her voice, but also because the hair on my arms stands up. Like they're reacting to her scrutiny.

"Just a few months."

"How is he?"

I shrug, taking the milk out of a bag and setting it carefully in the fridge. "He's fine, I guess. I didn't know him before, so…"

"Right," is all she says. After a couple of minutes, during which my nerves are about to make my skin bleed, she continues. "Did he tell you about…everything?"

"What's everything?"

"Charity, the accident. Everything that happened."

"He told me that she was killed in a car accident. And that he was driving."

"Did he tell you he'd been drinking?"

I turn and meet her eyes. They're a beautiful lime green color. Stunning, like the rest of her. "Yes, he did."

She nods and looks down at the kitchen table. I turn to put cheese on the shelf. "And did he tell you about us?"

My hand freezes on the cheese. Just for a few seconds. "Some."

"Did he tell you we're still married?"

"No," I manage to whisper, even though my heart is in my throat.

Her laugh is bitter. "I'm not surprised."

"And why is that?"

"He's cheated on me more times than I can count."

I feel like I've been kicked in the chest by someone wearing razor-sharp stilettos.

"I'm sorry to hear that." What else am I supposed to say?

"I've only seen him a handful of times since...since the accident. He just lost it. We both did, I guess. Losing a child..."

I close my eyes and I push the refrigerator door shut. I don't even bother turning to face her. I don't want to see the pain. I can already imagine what it must look like–a mother's face when she talks about the child she lost.

"I couldn't stand to come back here. He couldn't stay away. We just sort of silently agreed to heal however we could, wherever we could. But I never stopped loving him. And I think we're both ready to try again. When I talked to him last week–"

"Last week?" I interrupt, my stomach twisting into a bundle of knots.

"Yes. We've kept in touch, of course. I wanted to make sure he was okay. He's never wanted me to come here, to visit him here, but it's Christmas. And I hate the thought of him spending another Christmas alone, so I thought I'd surprise him."

Oh, he'll be surprised, alright.

Or will he? Is this why he started pulling away? Did it really have anything to do with getting too close to us? Or did he think he was on the verge of getting busted?

The thought makes the room dip and sway behind my closed lids.

"Maybe I shouldn't assume that there's something between you, but if there *is*, I want you to know that I'm not trying to hurt you. Cole is a gorgeous, charismatic man. A woman would have to be blind not to see that. But we have a lot of history together."

I nod, trying hard to swallow past the lump in my throat. "I completely understand."

"I was hoping you would." I hear the tread of her soft-soled shoes as she walks toward the living room. I collect myself and smile as I turn toward her. "It was...it was nice meeting you, Eden. I wish you the best of luck."

"You, too," I say as sincerely as I can. And for the most part I mean it. This woman has lost enough. I won't stand in the way of her attempts to salvage her marriage. Now that I know that there *is* one.

"I'll see myself out."

I wait until I hear her engine start before I go to Emmy's room. She's drawing a turtle, a pretty good one actually. I plaster a bright, excited smile on my face. "Hey, you wanna go do some Christmas shopping in Ashbrook today?"

I have to get out of here. I have to be somewhere that I can't sit and think, that I can't see Cole and his wife from my window. I don't need that visual to add to my torture.

"Yeah!" she exclaims, hopping off her bed and racing for the door.

"Coat, young lady."

She runs with a boot in one hand to get her coat from the hall closet and then runs back to finish putting it on. I fight back tears as I remind myself that Emmy and I have done just fine by ourselves these last two years. We'll be just fine for the next two, as well. And the two after that, and the two after that.

That's my mantra all the way to Ashbrook and all the way home three hours later.

⌘⌘⌘⌘

I've been lying in bed, awake, in the dark, for hours. I didn't want Cole to see lights on if he should happen to pass by. If he should happen to care.

I figure he does. He'll feel guilty most likely. Try to explain so that I won't hate him. That would bother him, I think. Of course, what the hell do I know? It seems that I know very little about the man after all. I keep getting revelation after revelation, very few of them good ones.

And yet, I still love him. I do. In fact, except for this last bomb, I think his brokenness may have made me love him even more. If there's one thing I can relate to, it's brokenness. I've seen it. I've felt it. I've lived it. It's been my constant companion for as long as I can remember. And I didn't think it could get any worse.

I was wrong.

I hold my breath when I hear the soft knock on the front door. I don't move a muscle, as if he'd be able to sense it all the way outside. The minutes tick by like shotgun blasts, each one rattling my nerves. After a couple of minutes, I breathe more easily. Surely he's gone. Surely he left when I didn't answer the door.

But then I hear the scrape of metal on metal. A key, sliding into the lock. I roll over and curl up on my side, pulling the covers up close to my face, watching inconspicuously from mostly-closed lids. From my bedroom, I can see the edge of the front door. I see it swing open and then swing quickly closed. I hear the soft pad of shod feet moving almost silently through the living room. I see the shadow–Cole's big, broad-shouldered shadow–move into the mouth of the hallway and head my way.

I make my breathing as slow and deep as I can, not an easy thing considering how my heart is galloping like a runaway horse. Through the slits of my vision, I see Cole stop in the doorway. He watches me for ninety-four long seconds, each of which I count as I inhale deeply and exhale slowly. With each breath, I can smell the unique scent of his skin–salt and soap. Like the sea and the man have become one. Both big enough to drown in. Both strong enough to carry me away. Both as turbulent as the eye of a hurricane.

"Eden?" he finally whispers in his sensual sandpaper voice. I let my lids drift all the way closed. Just my name on his lips, covered in pain, dripping in regret, is enough to undo me.

But I can't be undone. Brooke is a game-changer. Cole is married. There's nothing else to say.

I barely hear Cole cross to the bed. I hear the friction of material against skin as he kneels on the floor right beside me. I keep my eyes closed, my breathing even, and I wait.

"I hope you can hear me," he whispers. If I were asleep, I'm not sure his low, deep voice would wake me. It's more a rumble than anything. So much so that for a second, I feel it vibrate along my skin, tickling every tiny hair and tingling along every twitching nerve.

"She's not my wife," he begins. My heart trips over itself and my breath catches. Hope floods my soul, and I might've responded to him had he not continued on so quickly. "Not in any way other than legally."

Oh. Is that all?

I will my chin not to tremble the disappointment is so great.

"I loved her the way a kid in high school might love his girlfriend. We were barely together after I went to college, but I was a typical guy. Stupid. Horny. Proud. When she kept coming around, who was I to tell her no? Then she got pregnant. I thought I was doing the right thing by marrying her. But I never loved her. Not the way I should've. Not the way I love you."

Oh, God! My heart! I feel like it was made of glass and it just exploded inside me, shards sticking into the walls of my chest like shrapnel.

"There were other women. She knew it. She knew I was caught up in the world of fame and money and fans. She didn't deserve any of what I did to her. And when Charity...after Charity, I knew it was time to set her free. She deserved better than me. Someone who would love her like she needed to be loved. Someone who could help her heal. Give her more children. Someone other than me." He pauses and I want so badly to open my eyes. But I don't. I know better than to look at him.

"I left and came here. Sent her divorce papers. She never signed them. I didn't really care either way. I gave her a way out. The divorce wasn't for *me*. I never planned on meeting anyone, on having anything more in my life than the misery I deserved. Than an eternity spent mourning my daughter. But then you came along."

I feel the ever-so-slight warmth of Cole's head when he rests it on the mattress right in the curve of my body. He's not touching me. But he doesn't have to. I feel him as if he were.

"Emmy looks so much like Charity, but as beautiful and sweet as she is, she's not the one I couldn't stop thinking about, even from the beginning. It was you. It's always been you."

Another pause. Another deep breath.

"I've been alone for a long time, and not once have I ever felt lonely. Bereft, yes. Angry, hell yes. Bitter, remorseful, hopeless, yes, but never lonely. Not until you. You changed everything. And I was so caught up in you–in the way you respond when I touch you, in the taste of your body, in the sound of your voice–that I didn't think about tomorrow. Or even yesterday as much as I used to. Most days I've thought of you more than Charity. And I wasn't prepared for that. I wasn't prepared for *you*. Because of that, I've handled it all so, so badly."

I hear his shaky breath. I feel his sincerity. I want it to matter. But it can't.

"Please forgive me. I've hurt so many people, but I swear on my life, I never meant to hurt you. I hope you believe that."

Another pause. Cole is quiet, his breathing heavy. I keep mine even, continuing the ruse. I can't let him know I'm awake. I can't have him here, in my bedroom, so close and so sincere, and expect to resist him. I need time. And distance.

I feel him lean back, pull away. I hold perfectly still.

"I'm twenty-nine years old and you changed everything for me. You made me want to laugh and love and live again. You made me feel when I didn't think I could feel *anything* anymore. I just wish I could've been whole when we met. I wish I could've said the right things and done the right things. I wish I could be the type of man you deserve. I wish I could be the kind of man you could love."

I hear him shift and then I feel the feather-light brush of his lips on my forehead, the tip of my nose, the curve of my cheek.

"I know you're awake. And I love you," he says quietly, his mouth near my ear.

I open my eyes and meet his. They're dark and fathomless in the shadowy night. I say nothing. He says nothing. We just stare at one another, memorizing lines and shapes, angles and planes.

And then he stands and walks away.

My heart doesn't start beating again until he closes and locks the door behind him.

TWENTY-SEVEN

Cole

I'M ON THE beach before daylight. I couldn't sleep after I left Eden's. I didn't want to be in the house when Brooke got up. So I came here. This is the one place that's brought me whatever comfort I've been able to find for the last three years.

Until Sunday.

I push back the snow until I see sand. I start this castle like I've started them all–building up the ground, laying the foundation. I bring up the mental image of Charity, picturing her face with so much clarity my chest hurts. I see every tiny detail–every freckle on her nose, every gold speck in her green eyes. I listen for her laugh.

Only it never comes.

I work a pile of sand into a tall turreted structure, right in the center of the mound and I wait for my daughter to arrive. I watch and I listen, glancing around the empty beach over and over again, but still there's no Charity.

I sit back on my haunches, the snow no longer cold to my numb knees and hands, and I close my eyes, trying harder to see and hear my daughter. I mentally flip through a hundred different memories, losing myself in them. But the moment I open my eyes, she's gone.

With a primal growl that the wind carries away, I destroy the castle tower with one brutal swipe of my hands, guilt and pain spewing from my gut like a volcanic eruption, burning in my chest, laying waste to everything it touches.

"Charity!" I yell, glancing up and down the beach in the last-ditch hope that I'll see her, that I can make this right again.

But I don't. I don't see my little girl when my eyes are open. I don't hear her voice when I'm not listening inside my head.

I flatten the cold, wet sand and I try again, smoothing the ground, building the mound, shaping the base of the tower again. I think harder of Charity, of my little girl, and I wait. And I wait. But still, she's nowhere to be found.

Again.

I destroy the structure for the second time before I get to my feet and spin away from the ruins. I head for the hard-packed sand near the surf and I take off at a run parallel to the shoreline. As fast as I can, until my lungs burn and my legs ache, I run. Until I can no longer see or hear or think, I run. And when I can go no farther, I stop and hit my knees, closing my stinging eyes.

That's when I see her. That's when I hear her. That's the only time I can see or hear her now—when I shut out the world around me and exist only inside my head. With her.

She's holding out her arms for me to pick her up, which I do. She lays her head on my shoulder, something she used to do all the time when she was tired.

"Are you sleepy, baby?" I ask her in my mind.

"Yeah," she murmurs heavily. "I think it's time to take my pocketful of sand home, Daddy."

"Don't you want to build a castle today?"

"No, I think I've built enough."

My heart slams to a stop. "But that's your favorite."

"But the other little girl needs you to build one with her."

Oh, Jesus God! What is she saying?

I feel like what's left of my world is collapsing, falling in on top of me. Drowning out sight and sound and air. I can't breathe.

I can't lose my daughter again. I can't let her go again.

"I'll always be with you, Daddy. You don't have to look for me anymore. And you don't have to be sorry. I promise."

One cold tear slips from the corner of my eye to inch its way down my cheek. "But you're the most important thing in the world to me, baby."

"I know, Daddy."

"Do you? Do you really know that?"

She lifts her head and fixes me with her sweet green eyes. "I do. You told me that all the time, remember?"

And I did. When I was with my daughter, I was really with her. She had my heart, my attention, my love. Always. I can only hope she knew how much I loved her. How much I'll always love her.

"Yeah. I remember."

"I didn't forget."

"I didn't forget either." I won't. I can't.

"But you're sad when you remember. And you don't have to be. I don't *want* you to be."

"I can't help it, honey."

"Yes, you can. You have to try."

"But that's not fair to you."

"You've stayed with me long enough. I'm happy, Daddy. Now you just have to be."

"I don't want to be happy without you. It's..." *It's not right,* I was going to say. Because it's not.

"You won't be happy without me. You'll be happy *with me*, too. You don't have to be alone to be with me."

With a smile that lights up her whole face, she winds her arms around my neck and lays her head back on my shoulder.

And then she's gone.

TWENTY-EIGHT

Eden

AS PAINFUL AS the days are, I can tolerate them better than the nights. The nights are the worst. In the quiet, after Emmy has gone to bed, the loneliness sets in. The ache I feel for Cole is as visceral as it is emotional. For three nights, I tossed and turned, reliving every moment we spent together. Every smile we shared, every touch we exchanged. And the pain of loss seems only to be getting worse.

It doesn't help that every night I've heard a soft knock at the front door. It's always later, after Emmy has been asleep for a while. It melts my heart that he considers her in this small way. He never knocks loudly or more than once. It's as though he's giving me every chance to forgive him. Yet I don't.

I can't. At least not enough to let him back into my life. Emmy doesn't need the kind of heartache a man like that could bring. I'd have seen that sooner if I'd known he was married.

But today is another day. And I'm hoping with it will come some peace. Finally some peace.

"Do you like it here, Emmy?" I ask as she sits sprawled in front of her bookcase, deciding which book she wants to read to me later this evening.

"Uh-huh," she mumbles with a nod. She's distracted.

"Would you be happy if we stayed here?"

I don't know what I want her to say. Either answer will hurt, but a "no" might make it easier on me in the long run. I can look back and know that leaving was what I did for my daughter's happiness and wellbeing, that getting away from Cole wasn't an act of cowardice, but a byproduct of doing what's best for my child.

"Yeah. Would you?" She turns to look at me, her eyes finding mine. She's definitely not distracted now.

"I'm happy when you're happy."

"You always say that, but you're happy when Mr. Danzer's around, too." Her lips spread into a mischievous grin that brings out her dimples. "I can tell."

"You can? And just how do you think you can tell, Smartypants?"

"You look at him funny."

"Funny how?"

She giggles. "I don't know. Like you want him to hold your hand."

"I do?"

She nods, still smiling.

"Well, we weren't talking about *me*, now were we?"

She turns back to her search. I'm content to let the subject drop. Maybe it's not the right time to ask.

"Why did he stop coming over?"

She doesn't turn back around when she asks, which I'm grateful for. I don't want to have to worry about my expression.

"Some of his family came to town. He's busy with them."

"Will he come back when they leave?"

"I don't know," I hedge, hating to lie to my daughter. Although I can't be *absolutely positively certain* that he won't. So it's not really a lie.

"Do you want him to?"

"Yes." My answer is reflexive. I want him to more than anything. But he can't. And I can't *let* him. That's all that matters.

"When are you taking me to see Santa?" she asks, giving me a way out of this suddenly uncomfortable subject.

"How about tonight? Jordan said he'd be at Bailey's all week."

Within seconds, Emmy is up on her feet, dancing her way over to where I sit in the chair. She throws her body against mine, winding her arms around my neck and squeezing as hard as she can. "You're the best momma in the world!"

"Only because you're the best daughter in the world," I reply, pressing my face into her shampoo-scented hair.

Emmy pulls back enough to look at me, her nose less than two inches from mine. "I'm glad I'm not the only one that makes you happy anymore. That made me worry."

That made her worry?

She's so mature for her age sometimes that it makes *me* worry.

"You don't ever need to worry about me, babydoll. Ever."

She nods and smiles, but I can tell my words don't affect her at all. Whatever the reason she's been so focused on my happiness lately is still plaguing her. I can see it in the sad way she watches me.

"I love you, Emmaline," I whisper, rubbing my nose against hers.

"Love you, too, Momma." She hops off my lap as quickly as she hopped on. "When can we leave?"

"How about right after supper? I'll call Jordan just to make sure he'll be there."

She bounces and twirls away, singing something about seeing Santa Claus and getting all her wishes this year. Hopefully at least one of us will get all her wishes this year. I'm pretty sure mine are too far gone.

⌘⌘⌘⌘

Emmy wanted to stand in line by herself, just her and the other kids. She isn't sucking her thumb, but of course she hasn't said a word to anyone either.

She's had her list made out to Santa for a week. She brought it with her so that she won't have to tell him if she doesn't feel like talking, which we both know she most likely won't. That was her idea, not mine. She's so self-aware sometimes, like she knows what's better for her, how she's feeling and progressing, than I do.

"She sure is a pretty little girl," Jason says from my left. He hasn't been more than arm's length away since we got here. "And talkative, too." He elbows me and laughs at his own joke. Before my bristling can make its way to my tongue and lash out in the form of a cutting remark, he recovers. Somewhat. "I'm just kidding. I shouldn't have said that. She's just so quiet."

And you're just such an asshole, I add silently. I don't know why I'm surprised that his teasing is mean. That seems to be the way he is with everyone except me. And I can imagine why I'm exempt. Something about the mystery that lies within my panties, I'm sure.

"She talks when she's comfortable," I explain mildly, not even glancing up at him. I'm afraid I won't be able to fight the urge to slap his smug face.

"I'll just have to come around more often so she can get comfortable with me then. Since Cole's not coming around anymore," he adds, slipping his arm around my waist and squeezing.

I grit my teeth and say nothing. I don't know how he knows what's going on between Cole and me, or if he's just taking wild shots in the dark. But it doesn't matter. It's none of his business and I refuse to respond.

"I thought you were pretty fond of your arms," comes an achingly familiar voice from behind us. Jason and I both turn at the same time to find Cole standing less than a foot away. His electric blue eyes are trained on Jason, his expression as cold as his tone.

"Didn't see a 'taken' sign on her, Cole," he says, unaffected.

"I didn't see a 'touch this' sign on her either," Cole replies steadily.

"She can speak for herself. If she doesn't want me around, all she has to do is say so."

"If you'd take the hint, she wouldn't have to," Cole growls.

"I think you're overstepping your bounds a little here, brother," Jason says, taking a step toward Cole.

Cole doesn't budge, and I can see why. He's so tall and he tops Jason by at least three inches. Probably outweighs him, too, by at least thirty pounds of sheer muscle.

I eat him up as I look at him. Just seeing him is like a cool compress to a fevered brow. In the back of my mind, I wonder if I'll compare every man for the rest of my life to this one. To this one handsome, amazing man who walked away with my heart. And then crushed it with his lies.

I feel sadness creep into my chest and tug at my chin. I make my excuses and turn away before either man can see it tremble. "It's almost Emmy's turn," I mutter by way of explanation.

I hurry away, not looking back. No matter how much I want to.

I haven't seen Cole since the night he snuck into my room and poured out his heart beside my bed. Although I'll never forget that night, his words and the emotion I could feel pouring off him, it doesn't change anything. He's married. So I dare not look back at him. It makes it a thousand times harder to hold onto my resolve when I can see his gorgeous face, when I can read his beautiful eyes.

I stand near the front of the line and I focus on my daughter. She looks so grown up, standing in line holding her list between her tiny hands. Outwardly, she looks like a normal, healthy little girl. Eyes can't see the scars she bears. I just hope one day they'll be so faded that she won't know they're there either.

Jordan makes me jump when she appears at my side and throws an arm over my shoulders, but thankfully she's the *only* person who approaches me. I don't look back toward either man. By the time Emmy takes her turn on Santa's lap and we turn to leave afterward, both of them have disappeared.

I know before we even push through the doors that tonight will be particularly rough for me.

❄❄❄❄

A frown knits my brow when we pull into the driveway and I see a black SUV parked there. My first thought is of Brooke and dread pools in my stomach like acid. I get Emmy out, intending to ignore Brooke

Danzer as we pass, but I notice that the vehicle is empty.

That's odd, I note.

I wonder briefly if she got confused and thought she was at the house Cole's working on. But if that's the case, where is she? Did she just walk over there?

I unlock the door to our cottage and push it open to let Emmy inside. I step back out to the end of the porch and glance across the street to see if there are lights on. There aren't. I move to follow my daughter inside. Before I can continue to wonder about what the hell Brooke is doing, I hear a voice that makes my blood run cold.

"Hey there, darlin'. It's been a long time."

My heart jumps up into my throat when I see Ryan. He's squatting down at the edge of the living room, holding Emmy between his knees. Her face is pale as a ghost and her eyes are big and terrified.

"Momma," she whispers in fright.

My throat closes. Oh God, that sound! To hear the fear in her little voice. The tremble. The plea.

"I'm right here, baby. Why don't you come sit with me on the couch?"

She starts to move, but Ryan stops her. That's when her eyes start to water. She's a smart girl. She knows this isn't good.

"Not so fast, little one. Let's talk for a few minutes. I haven't seen you in two years. You've grown. You're such a beautiful girl now," he says, stroking her hair, letting his hand linger a little too long on her back and butt as he continues his touch down her body to then drop away.

"Ryan, let Emmy go to her room. You and I can talk out here."

I don't want to attack him and risk hurting Emmy. And I don't want to say anything that might scare her even further. I'm doing my best to keep my tone and my expression as calm as possible, despite the panic that I can feel clawing at my insides. Panic and rage. The only thing that's keeping me sane right now is the knowledge that whatever I do and say could worsen Emmy's condition. She's been hurt enough. I don't want her to have to live with the vision of her mother killing a man right in front of her. Or maybe watch her mother die if that man gets the better of her.

That's why I have to stay calm. For Emmy. For my sweet, precious daughter.

"She looks just like you," he says, leaning around so he can see Emmy's face. She stands perfectly still, her eyes fixed on mine. I smile at her, hoping to soothe her.

"Yes, she does. Emmy, you go play in your room. Shut the door and don't come out until I come get you, okay?"

Please God, make him let her go. Please make him let her go.

I glance from Emmy to Ryan. I hold his darkly familiar gaze. "Uncle Ryan and I are going to talk for a while. All alone." I emphasize the last, hoping he knows what that means. If I have to pretend to go along with another rape to get my daughter out of this room,

I will. I'd do anything, say anything, withstand anything to keep her safe and unharmed.

Ryan watches me, his eyes narrowing on me then scanning me from head to toe. The slow trip they make back up my body, stopping between my legs and at my chest, makes my skin crawl. It doesn't matter that he's handsome, that he could have practically any woman he wants. He's nothing but a sick degenerate on the inside. A man who rapes children. There is no worse predator in my opinion, no more grotesque offense.

Finally, one side of his mouth pulls up into a leer. "Yes, why don't you run along, little Emmy? Momma and I have *a lot* to talk about. We've got some catching up to do."

When he stands, he rubs his crotch. My stomach turns.

My eyes fall to Emmy. "Don't come out, baby. No matter what you hear, don't come out until I come and get you."

She nods and my body goes nearly limp with relief when she runs down the hall and slams the door to her room. I hear the knob rattle as she twists the lock and I think to myself, *Good girl.*

Now I just have to figure out what to do about Ryan.

"How did you find us?" I ask, moving the short distance to the couch.

"Did you really think Lucy would just let you disappear? You know she's the type to keep her thumb on everyone and everything. Control. She has to have it."

My heart sinks. "She had me followed?"

He nods once. "From the moment you left the house. I'm surprised you didn't expect that. Maybe you're not as smart as I always thought you were," he says.

I guess I *should've* expected it. But I was so scared, so anxious to get away, to get *Emmy* away, that I just left. I didn't look back. Not once. Not even to see if we were being followed.

Ryan comes to sit next to me on the couch. He's so close his thigh brushes mine, rubbing suggestively as he leans back and crosses his arms over his flat stomach. His eyes are on mine and I hold them. I'm not afraid of him. Not for myself. I'm afraid for my daughter, though. If something happens to me, she'll have no one to protect her. No one to defend her from men like this. She'll go to live with them and she'll be abused until she can get away. But by then it will be too late.

"Why wait so long to make your move then?" Please God don't let him tell me that he was waiting for Emmy to get older. More to his liking.

My guts twist at the thought.

"She kept it well-hidden for a long time. But she's not the only one who can manipulate. So here I am. To see you. And *my daughter.*"

My pulse speeds at the way he emphasizes that Emmy is his. She is *biologically* his offspring, but not in any way is she his daughter. Not in the ways that count. She will never be. Not as long as there's breath left in me.

I turn toward Ryan, facing him fully, leaning in a little closer even. I hold his eyes. I speak slowly, clearly. "Do you really think that I wouldn't fight you tooth and nail for her? Do you really think that you'll ever be a part of her life?"

His smile is smug as he see-saws his head. "I figure my chances are pretty good."

"And why would you think that? Have you lost your mind?"

"I can be quite…persuasive, Eden," he says, reaching out to run his finger from my chin down to my cleavage. I want to grab it in my fist and break it. But I don't move. Still, I hold his gaze. I won't be backing down tonight. Tonight or any other night.

"I would rather spend my life on the run for killing you than give you five minutes with *my daughter*." One smoothly-arched brow snaps up. "And if you don't move that finger, you stand a good chance of losing it."

Fire is pouring through me. Rage, built up over years of being an unwilling sex toy, bubbles within my veins. Bitterness that this man has the right to claim my daughter as his own burns inside me.

I feel at once powerful for standing up to him, angry for waiting so long and terrified that this won't work out in my favor somehow.

But it has to.

I have to make it.

Ryan does nothing, says nothing for long seconds. He doesn't move his finger, but he doesn't advance it either.

But then he does.

He moves so quickly I yelp in surprise. He fists his fingers in my shirt and jerks me off the couch, rolling onto me as we both fall to the floor. The jarring impact knocks the breath out of me. I gasp in an effort to get it back, but it doesn't come. With his unrelenting weight on me, my lungs can't expand.

I start to kick and scratch at him, but he easily pins my arms to my sides. Like he used to.

That's when fear settles in. For a few seconds, I'm a scared child again, at the mercy of someone older and stronger. My heart races and my chest burns with the need for oxygen. I tilt my chin up, trying desperately to get even one good breath. But it won't come. Ryan presses down on me with his muscular upper body, making my head feel like it might explode.

I barely hear the knock at the door over the blood pumping behind my ears. But I do. I try to make some sound, but all that comes out is a raspy, wheezing sound. And then Ryan's hand clamps down over my mouth, making it even harder to breathe. I wiggle the best that I can, anything to break free, to gain one inch of purchase with arm or leg, all to no avail. I'm too small. He's too big. Too heavy.

My head starts to swim lightly from hypoxia. The only thing left I can think to do is to sink my teeth into the finger that rests over my lips. So I do. With every ounce of strength in my jaws, I bite down. I feel the give of flesh tearing away from bone. I taste the coppery tang of blood entering my mouth. I hear the satisfying growl of my captor.

And then I see Cole, a furious angel bearing down on Ryan. I see his big hands grab Ryan by the shoulders. I feel the weight lift when he slings him off. I breathe in relief when cool air rushes into my lungs.

I scramble away unsteadily, aware only of the crash of things breaking as I crawl frantically to the other side of the room. I lean into the corner near the door and I watch Cole silently, viciously beat the blood and breath out of Ryan.

He's straddling him, pummeling him with first one fist and then the other. Back and forth, never stopping.

Blood starts to spatter the walls, Cole's shirt and face. Ryan stopped moving several punches ago and his visage is completely unrecognizable. Some part of me relishes what's happening in front of me, but there's another part that realizes this won't end well. As much as I'd like to know Ryan is gone, as little as he deserves to live, this can't happen. It just can't.

"Cole, stop," I say in a hoarse croak. He doesn't even pause. "Cole, stop!" I call louder.

This, he hears.

When he turns his head to look at me, it's as though he's still seeing Ryan. For just a second. Maybe two. He looks murderous. Confused, almost, that he's seeing me. And then his expression softens. It softens into something that makes me want to cry and curl up in his arms and never move.

But then he looks away. Back to Ryan, who is unconscious beneath him. He climbs off him, kicking him once in the ribs for good measure, before he reaches into his pocket for his phone. "I'm calling the police."

And so he does.

As he speaks to the 911 operator, I stand to shaky legs and make my way to Emmy's room. I knock on the door. "Emmy? Unlock the door, sweetpea. I want to come in."

I wait, listening for rustling or crying, afraid of what I might find.

I hear nothing.

I knock again, a little harder this time.

"Emmy, open up, baby, it's Momma."

I wait. I listen. Nothing.

I try the knob. It won't turn. It's definitely locked.

"Emmy, you're scaring me. Please open the door. You're safe now. I promise. Cole is here."

My heart picks up the pace again, my soul coming into the clutches of some nebulous fear. I knock again. Try the knob again.

"Emmy, please. Open the door."

I sense Cole's presence before his arm shoots out past me to try the knob.

"It's locked," I explain unnecessarily. "She locked it when I told her to stay in her room and not come out until I came to get her."

"Emmy, can you open the door please?" he asks, pecking with his knuckles.

No response. I press my ear to the door. No sound. Not one.

"Ohgod ohgod ohgod," I mutter, racing into the bathroom for a hairpin that I can use to pick the lock.

When I return and bend to push it into the tumbler, Cole moves me back with one hand and kicks the door in, startling a shriek out of me.

The first thing I feel when the door flies open is cold air. That's when I see her open window. And my whole world comes crumbling down around me.

TWENTY-NINE

Cole

I SEE IT register on her expressive face–that fear that everything you love, everything you live for is hanging in the balance. In a balance you can't see, in scales you can't find.

Panic clouds her vision. It's there in the way her eyes dart around the room in confusion and circle back to the open window, around the room again and then back to the open window.

"Emmy!" she cries, flitting through the space as though she's missed something. "Emmmmy!" she screams, nearing the window.

A hollow pit opens up in my stomach as I watch her, this woman that I love. She's trying to understand one of life's most terrifying possibilities. But also trying to deny it.

I want to say something, but I know that even if there was something comforting *to say,* it would fall on deaf ears. The only thing that will help Eden right now is to find her daughter.

So that's what I'll do.

"Stay here. I'll find her," I tell her calmly. My voice, my expression, my presence is solid. Steady. But my insides are clamped down, the fear in the air an all too familiar black cloud.

"I'm coming with you," she says, not even meeting my eyes. The devil himself is nipping at her heels. I know that feeling well. And I know there's no use in arguing.

I step out of the hallway and reach for Eden's coat. I hand it to her as she scrambles for her boots. Before we head out the door, I grab the blanket that's folded along the top of the couch. Emmy will need it when we find her.

And we will find her.

I promise myself that much.

We strike out, leaving an unconscious asshole in the middle of Eden's living room floor amidst the wreckage of busted furniture and broken things. He's the least of my worries right now. Hopefully the Sheriff will get there and keep an eye on him until we get back. This is more important.

This is more important than anything.

Eden can't lose Emmy. I know what that does to a person and I can't let that happen to her. Besides that, *I* can't lose Emmy either. She needs me. And I need her. We all need each other.

We walk along the road from house to house, both of us calling to Emmy. The wind is whipping off the ocean, howling through the streets, carrying our voices out to sea before they can get very far. I hear the panic rising in Eden's tone. The way she says Emmy's name is becoming more and more shrill, more and more desperate.

My heart is thudding heavily in my chest and I try to imagine where a little girl might go when a monster from her past pops up on her front porch.

Icy fingers of dread grip me when I think of her love of the beach, when I think of how the empty stretch of dark sand might seem like a safe place to hide to a scared child. A place no one would look for her. I push the thought away. I refuse to consider it as a possibility, even as my feet turn in that direction.

We call her name. Still, there is no answer. No small forms hiding in the shadows or running toward us in the pools of yellow light shed from the street lamps.

"Let's check the house I've been working on," I tell her, steering her toward the sidewalk. "Maybe she hid there." I pray that she did, but some strong sense of foreboding tells me she didn't. Or that if she came here and found it empty, she moved on.

I unlock the door and push it open for Eden. She walks through, shuffling from room to room calling for her daughter as I walk around the outside, repeating her name over and over and over.

"She's not here! She's not here!" Eden whimpers when we meet at the door. She clutches my biceps with shaking fingers as her anxiety rises. "Where could she be? Where would she go?" she asks.

"Maybe she went to my house," I tell her, praying that she did exactly that. That she could find it in the dark. That she was level-headed enough to think that way.

"OhgodOhgodOhgod," Eden mutters, her voice trembling as we start around the curve that leads toward the beach.

We both scan left and right as we walk, calling, calling, calling. My pulse pounds faster as we draw closer to the beach.

Patches of snow still cover long swaths of sand. They gleam silver in the moonlight. Everything else is nearly black in contrast.

Above the gust of the wind, I hear Eden's gasp. I hear her following sob, trailed by the sad song of her daughter's name from her lips. My stomach knots for her. My heart bleeds for Emmy. So much like my own child. So damaged in her own way. She doesn't deserve this. Neither of them does.

We walk quickly along the beach, drawing closer and closer to my cabin. It's when I'm doing a left-to-right sweep that I see the object. It's floating just off the shore, just beyond where the waves begin to break. It bobs in and out of the slice of moonlight that slants across the ocean.

Without thought, I take off at a dead run down the beach toward the water's edge. I focus on the object.

The waves rise and obscure it. Then they break and reveal it. I see a tiny pale hand floating on the surface and I know that it's her.

I throw down the blanket and sprint into the surf. I pay little attention to the fifty-some degree water when it hits my skin. I ignore the clench of my stomach muscles when it creeps under my sweater. I lift my chin when everything inside my chest locks down. Just a little farther and I can grab her.

Just a little farther.

I turn my body to the side and reach out, stretching my arm and my fingers as far as they'll go, grasping at the five little digits that float nearest me. I pinch at one, but my joints are stiff and it slips right out of my grip. I lunge forward, grabbing again before she drifts farther into the deep. This time I squeeze the end of her finger as hard as I can and pull toward me until I can get a better purchase.

A finger. Two fingers. Five fingers. Her arm. As I drag her toward me, every small movement is increasingly difficult. My muscles are sluggish as I finally pull Emmy's cold, limp body into my arms and turn with her. My legs struggle to cut through the undercurrent. They scream as I push them to carry us to shore. But push them I do, step after step.

Closer to shore the waves help force us onto the sand. I fall to my knees, still cradling Emmy's body. I barely hear the crying over my own heartbeat. The world is mute and I can only see Eden when she's kneeling in front of me, reaching for her daughter.

Until I hear her scream.

"Nooooooo!"

Dear reader,

What if you could have a do-over? Would you take it? Would you take your rewrite and see what MORE is? Or would you just want to ride off into the sunset with your happy ending? Let things rest as they are? Well, here, you're in control. You get to choose, but choose carefully because your answer will decide the fate of Cole, Eden and Emmy.

TURN TO PAGE 256, door number one, if you want your happy ending now.

TURN TO PAGE 286 , door number two, if you want MORE (that will lead to a second book).

Or, if you're like me, you'll want both. And by all means, take them.

Door Number One

THIRTY

Eden

"NO! EMMY!" I cry, tears blurring her face as I take her out of Cole's arms and into my own. "Oh God, baby, open your eyes! Look at me!"

She's so cold. Her body feels like ice against mine. Her hands rest limply atop the dark blue of her wet shirt and her feet dangle lifelessly from her legs.

"Emmy, baby, please wake up," I wail. "What am I supposed to do?" I ask Cole, who's staring at me as though he's reliving the worst day of his life.

"Eden, let me help. My cell phone is in my pocket and I'm sure it won't work now, so you need to run ahead to my house. The side door is unlocked. Call 911 immediately. I'll be right behind you. I'm going to start CPR and then I'll bring her on in. Give me five minutes."

"No, I can't leave her. I can't leave her, Cole! She's my little girl. She's my baby. I can't leave her. She has to be okay. She'll be afraid when she wakes up. I can't leave her."

I feel more frantic the longer I talk. I hear my own words. I hear the desperation. The fear. It feeds the terror that's swelling within me, around me. Threatening to drown me. Like the ocean that tried to drown my daughter.

"Eden!" Cole snaps, his fingers gripping my upper arms, digging in. As his eyes bore holes into mine, I see his own anxiety. The alarm. The dread. The hopelessness. Fighting its way to the surface. Wrestling him for control. "We don't have much time. Do what I say and do it quickly. Emmy needs our help. Right. Now."

Without waiting for my agreement, Cole takes my daughter from my straining arms and lays her gently on the dry part of the sand. With wide, burning eyes, I watch him set to work on her–checking her neck for a pulse, listening to her chest for breath sounds, tipping up her chin, plugging her nose, blowing air into her lungs.

Her chest rises and falls, once, twice. He spares me one sharp look and one loud word. "Go!" And then, with the heel of one hand, he's pressing into her chest, pumping life-saving oxygenated blood through my child's gravely still body.

With a sob that's torn ruthlessly from my throat, I clamber to my feet and run as fast as I can to Cole's house. I find the side door and fling it open, not even bothering to close it behind me. I race to the kitchen for the phone. Surely this is where it would be.

I spot it immediately and dial 911. With breakdown fighting me for dominance every step of the way, I speak to the operator, directing rescue workers to this location the best that I can without an actual physical address. She transfers me to an emergency worker who begins questioning me about the circumstances in which we found Emmy. He asks about water and how long she might've been immersed. He asks about her responsiveness and the color of her skin. He assures me that chest compressions are the best thing we can do for her until they get here, and that warming her very slowly and making sure she stays still and horizontal are important as well.

When I hang up, I start off back toward the side door, only to find Cole rushing in with Emmy. He takes her into the living room, kicking the coffee table out of the way so that he can lay her flat on her back on the floor. Without a word, he resumes chest compressions immediately.

As I watch, my eyes are focused on my daughter. The bluish cast to her skin, the darker purplish color of her lips. The closed lids, the lifeless limbs.

I'm not even aware of my legs giving out until I'm on my knees within a few inches of her body. I take her cold hand in mine and bring it to my trembling lips. "Please come back to me, Emmy. I can't live without you, sweetpea. You're my whole world," I tell her tearfully. "Please, God, don't take her! Don't take her from me!"

"Get her clothes off," Cole says quietly. "Then we'll cover her with blankets."

When I glance up at him in question, he's looking at me. In his eyes are the pain and loss and utter devastation that hovers around the corners of my heart. And in these few seconds, I know why. I know why he is here. I know why he won't leave. I know why he can't give up.

His daughter. My daughter. Blood of our blood. Death doesn't change that kind of love. It doesn't really separate parent from child. Not in the heart. Not in the soul.

I set to work on getting Emmy's clothes off her without disrupting Cole's life-saving cycles of pumping her heart and filling her lungs with air. I don't know how long has passed when the knock sounds at the front door, followed by a harsh, no-nonsense voice, announcing, "Emergency Services."

From the moment I open the door, I'm in a nightmare. I watch men in thick jackets and white shirts assess and treat my daughter, exchanging words like "near drowning" and "hypothermia." I watch from behind the bars of my own personal hell as the two men place tiny pads on my child's chest and feed electricity into her heart, watching for a viable rhythm to appear on the small screen. After the second attempt, I hear the reassuring blip. I hear a strangely haunting howl and I feel arms come around me. It isn't until Cole turns my face into his chest that I realize it was me.

The two men work as efficiently as one, preparing my daughter for transport, continuing every measure to save her life, her brain, her organs. To bring her back to me in as much the Emmy state that she ran away in as possible.

I watch, heartbroken and horrified, wanting to help, wishing I could. Yet knowing there's nothing I can do except stay by her side and pray that she wakes up.

The ride to the hospital is a blur. Speeding and sirens, monitors and vital signs, warm IVs and warm blankets. I vaguely remember Cole saying he wouldn't be far behind, but the memory is as fractured as my mind seems. As my heart *feels*.

I torture myself with thoughts of my life without Emmy, with memories of her most precious moments, with questions about her recent fixation on me being happy without her. Could she somehow have seen this in her future? Could she somehow have known that God would take her from me?

The thought sends me into silent sobs that wrack my entire body. From my perch beside Emmy's stretcher, I fold over at the waist, pressing my forehead to hers, fighting off the hopelessness and nausea that pulls threateningly at my insides. She's not dead, I remind myself. And she's not going to be. Her heart is beating now. Her chest is pumping with her rapid, shallow breaths. Those are signs of life. *Life.* She can still make it.

"Emmy, it's Momma," I whisper, smoothing the backs of my fingers down her cold cheek. "You are strong, baby. So strong. You have to fight to stay with me. Listen to my voice. Feel me touching you. Know how much you are loved. More than any little girl in the whole world. We have too much left to do, sweetpea. We have sandcastles to build, stories to read, cartoons to watch. And Christmas will be here soon. I have so many things for you. I want to watch you open all your presents," I tell her, thinking that I will buy her the moon if she'll just come back to me. "Breathe, baby. Breathe and heal, get warm and cozy, and then you come back to me, okay? Okay, Emmy?"

Tears drip from my lashes into her damp hair. I would give her my blood if it would help, my life if she could use it. If she'll just wake up and ask me for it, I'll give her anything her heart desires. Anything. Anything at all for my little girl.

⌘⌘⌘⌘

They let me stay in the corner of the emergency room bay as they work on my daughter. I'm relieved when I hear things like "sinus rhythm" and "clear lungs" and "core temp is rising." They toss back and forth a thousand terms that I don't understand as they hover over my daughter's still body. All I can do is watch. And listen. And pray.

When she is declared stable, the doctor comes to talk to me. I give him my attention in a way that reminds me of watching a television show–thinking with only half of my brain and listening with ears that hear as though I'm standing at the other end of a tunnel.

I struggle to process what he's saying, latching onto bits and pieces here and there.

Dry near drowning.

Hypothermia.

It doesn't appear she was submerged very long.

Her body slowed blood flow to her limbs first.

Arrhythmia.

Perfusion.

Oxygenation.

Compromised.

Reacting as you did probably saved her life.

Breathing on her own now.

The next eight hours are critical.

Pediatric intensive care.

Talk to her.

Hope she regains consciousness soon.

Take you upstairs with her.

I thank him.

I think.

Calls are made. Report is given. The same keywords used.

A nurse dressed in all blue asks me to come with her. She and another nurse wheel Emmy to the elevators. I follow along behind them.

She's taken to the pediatrics wing and we walk along a hall painted in soothing greens and yellows, and bordered with bears dancing on big red balls. I glance in each door that we pass. I see exhausted parents, some crying, some not as they watch their critical children sleep. They vary in age, the children, but the one constant is in the eyes of their parents. Dejection. Desperation. Frantic worry. It's there in every room, hovering like an unwanted guest.

We turn into the room that will be Emmy's. They ask me to have a seat in the chair in the corner as they move my unconscious child into a different bed and transfer her various tubes and cords to another monitoring station.

When the commotion dies down, I'm left with one nurse, probably ten years my senior. She approaches me with a kind smile, squatting down at my side as she speaks.

"May I call you Eden?" she asks. I nod. "Alright then, Eden, I'm Vera. I'll be watching over Emmy tonight. Would you like to come and tell me about her?"

I do. I walk with Vera to Emmy's bedside and I tell her all about my child as she assesses her from head to toe, gently uncovering small sections of her body as she checks things and then covering them back up. She asks me questions, questions that one mother might ask another. Questions that bring tears to my eyes and panic to my heart. This can't be it for my Emmy. It just can't be.

With Emmy covered and settled in her cheerful room, one soft light shining over the corner where I'll be sitting, Vera takes my hand. "She's going to be fine, Eden. You just spend your time talking to her, being comfort and strength to her. I'll take care of the rest. Can I get you anything? Something to eat or drink? Coffee?"

She must know that I won't be sleeping. I nod. "That would be great, thank you."

She squirts some antibacterial foam in her hand as she approaches the door, and then turns to me again. "Is there someone I can call for you? Anyone that you'd like to be here? For you or for Emmy?"

She's asking about her father.

But I'm thinking of Cole.

Cole.

My heart, my battered, tattered, aching heart squeezes at the mention of his name. It slips off my tongue like a plea. "Cole," I tell her. "Cole Danzer will probably be here soon." How long has it been since Emmy and I left the house in the ambulance? How long has it been since he said he'd be right behind us?

Another shot of panic wrecks my chest, sending bone and blood spraying. What if...? I suck in a breath and hold it to still the throbbing of my insides.

Please God, don't let him be hurt. I couldn't take anything more right now. Nothing more. Please.

"I'll send word to the ER waiting room. He'll probably show up there first."

I try to smile. I'm not sure how effective my efforts are. "Thank you."

She nods. "Of course. I'll be right back with your coffee."

As soon as the door is closed, I head for Emmy's bed. I perch one hip on the edge of the mattress. "Emmy, it's me," I announce quietly.

I listen for a response. Anything. A word, a moan, a whimper. I hear nothing but the soft whir of the Bear Hugger machine that pumps warm air into the plastic blanket that rests between her skin and the cloth ones.

"Can you open your eyes and look at me, baby?" I try to keep my voice steady, even though it wants to tremble. As does my chin. But I hold back the shaking and the tremors, the tears and the sobs. I want to wake her up, not scare her.

"Emmmy. Emmmmaline Saaaage," I say in a sing-song voice. "Wake up, sleeping beauty."

She doesn't stir. I reach under the covers and take her slowly-warming hand, stroking each tiny finger from base to tip, massaging them, trying to help coax blood back into them.

I start to hum her favorite song. It's from a cartoon that she loves. She always sings along to it when it comes on, and then again when it goes off. I stop every few bars to speak her name. To tell her I love her. To ask her to open her eyes.

I smell the coffee before I hear Vera bringing it in. But when I turn to thank her, it isn't Vera holding the steaming cup. It's Cole.

He's pale. His hair is mussed like his run his fingers through the longish locks a thousand times. His eyes are flat when they meet mine.

"Is it okay that I'm here?" he asks, his voice a low, soothing balm to my frazzled nerves.

I nod, unable to form the words that would tell him how very grateful I am that he came when he did tonight, that he helped me find my daughter, that he helped save her life.

"I saw the Sheriff at your house, so I stopped and got that squared away."

Ryan. I'd forgotten about him since Emmy went missing.

Emmy.

My precious Emmy.

I nod as one sob escapes. I clamp it off before it can boom out into the room by tucking my head against my arm and smothering the sound. The coffee smell gets stronger as Cole approaches. And then all I smell is him. Cold ocean and warm skin. Salt and soap. Cole.

He wraps me in his scent even as he pulls me into his arms. I bury my face against his neck and I cry. Silently. My whole body shaking with my efforts to stay quiet. I pray and I scream, I beg and I blame. I love and I hate, all without uttering a sound other than my breath hitting Cole's throat.

When my outburst has run its course, I pull away, sniffing as quietly as I can and then turning back to Emmy. I take her hand back into mine and, together, Cole and I guard her, we shelter her, we love her back to life.

In the stillness of the room, with the muted beeps and whirs of monitors and machines as his only backdrop, Cole tells Emmy a story.

"Once upon a time, there was a lonely man building a sandcastle on the beach. He was used to the cool sand and the cool wind, but never had he felt a warmer breeze than he felt on this one particular day. It wasn't coming from the sea or from the southeast as it so often did. This one was coming from somewhere closer. With his hands in the sand, the man stopped and turned around. Standing right behind him was the most beautiful little girl. She looked so much like someone he loved and lost. She had shiny black hair and big green eyes. She looked just like her mother, who was standing beside her. Both of them took the man's breath away. He started to turn away, but he couldn't. He couldn't turn his back on them. Instead, he gave the little girl a daisy. They were the favorite flower of the child he lost. And then, the little girl and her mother walked away. The man knew when they did, that he would never be the same again. He knew he would never forget the two beautiful girls on the beach that day. And he didn't. He thought about them every day. He even dreamed about them sometimes, dreamed about laughing with them, playing with them. Loving them like families should love each other. He started to worry that he'd never see them again, but God had a different plan. The little girl and her beautiful mother moved into a house nearby and the man got to see them every day. Sometimes just through the window, but it was enough. He knew then that he would fall in love with the little girl and her mother. And he did. Just like he dreamed that he would."

Cole doesn't look at me until his words have died, until they've given way to the heaviness of silence and fallen noiselessly to the floor. But when he does, when he drags his eyes from Emmy's pale face to mine, I feel all the love that he professed to have. I feel it like heat from a flame. I see it like color from a painting. Vibrant splashes of red and green, blue and yellow, dotting the bleak landscape. Cutting through the clouds.

His eyes are on mine when he next he speaks. "I love you, Emmy. And I hope you can love me, too."

A lump swells in my throat and tears well in my eyes. There are still so many things to say, so many questions, so many things to work out, but Cole loves me. He loves *us*. It's there, plain as day. And I love him, too. I have to believe that the rest can be sorted through later. Right now is a time for love and unity and strength. For Emmy. She needs us right now.

It's the twitch of her fingers within mine that stops my heart. But it starts running again, at breakneck speed, when Emmy makes a low whimpering sound.

I stand and bend over her, rubbing my hand across her forehead. "Emmy? Can you hear me, sweetpea?"

She doesn't respond, but her brow wrinkles. I turn to Cole. "Get the nurse."

He leaves immediately, jogging from the room.

"Emmy, can you open your eyes?" I watch. I wait. I hold my breath. Nothing. "Emmy, please, baby. It's Momma. Can you open your eyes and look at me?"

Her eyelids twitch. Or do they? I stare at them. Hard. As if willing them to move. Did I imagine that? Or did they actually move?

Cole comes back with Vera, who moves to the bed and starts checking things. When she goes to lift Emmy's left eyelid to shine the light in, Emmy flinches and turns her head away.

The nurse lowers the light and reaches beneath the mountain of covers. "Emmy, my name is Vera. Can you squeeze my fingers?" No response. "Emmy? Can you squeeze my fingers?"

I feel like my life, my entire existence, is balanced on a pinhead. My heart is beating so hard and so fast, I feel winded. Like I've climbed a hill or run a race. And, in a way, it feels as though I have. And that I'm not yet done running.

"Emmy, ca–" Vera's words are cut off and she smiles. "Good girl. Can you wiggle your toes for me?"

I see the slight movement under the blankets, but it's not until a full two minutes later that I feel true relief. That's when my daughter opens her jewel green eyes, searches until she finds my face and whispers a hoarse, "I got to stay, Momma."

THIRTY-ONE

Cole

IT'S BEEN A week to the day since Eden and I brought Emmy home from the hospital. I've seen them every day. I can't stay away and Eden doesn't seem to want me to. Neither does Emmy for that matter. She's opening up more and more every time I see her.

They invited me over for dinner tonight. The table is set and Eden is waiting for the bread to finish baking. Emmy has been on the floor drawing since I got here. Everyone from doctors to nurses to Eden and me were all amazed and grateful that she had no neurological deficits of any kind. *Your rapid response, getting her out of the water and starting resuscitation immediately, are to thank for that. A few minutes longer and she might not be here today.*

I shudder to think what that might have felt like. I know I couldn't stand it again. And Eden...it would've destroyed her world. And *that* would've even further destroyed mine.

All of a sudden, Emmy hops up and walks a picture over to me, holding it out for me to take. "Is this for me?" I ask. She nods.

There are eight hands, each at a different place around a sandcastle. The positioning is a little clumsy, but for a six year old, it's amazingly accurate and detailed. I can easily make out what it is.

I slide off my kitchen chair and squat down in front of her, intent on thanking her. But before I can, she surprises me by throwing her arms around my neck. Hesitantly, I curl my arms around her thin body and hold her to me. She doesn't move or wriggle or seem uncomfortable. She just squeezes me as tightly as her little arms will allow.

When she lets me go, she puts her thumb in her mouth. "Thank you, Emmy. This is beautiful."

She watches me intently, then, after a few seconds, she reluctantly takes her thumb out and surprises me even more. By speaking her first words to me.

"Do you know who they are?" she asks.

I hear Eden gasp behind me. I don't have to turn to know that she has tears in her eyes or to know that she's wearing a breathtaking smile. One, I'm sure, is hidden by hands covering her mouth. I can picture her standing in the kitchen behind me as clearly as I can see the drawing Emmy made for me, held between my hands.

"No, who are they?" I answer.

She points to the two bigger pairs of hands. "These are yours and Mom's," she explains. "These are mine. And these are your little girl's." Shyly, she raises her eyes to mine. She's standing so close and staring so deep, I can count every darker green fleck around the center of her irises. I smile. I don't say anything for several seconds. I don't quite trust myself to speak yet.

"We're all four building a sandcastle," I surmise when my voice feels steadier.

"Like a family."

I nod to her. I can see her clenching her toes in the rug. She's nervous.

"Like a family. I love it, Emmy."

She doesn't say anything else; she just turns and runs off, leaving me a little mystified as to what I did to make her go. She comes running back, just as fast, a few seconds later, though, and something is dangling from her hands.

She stops in front of me to sift through the necklaces, taking the longer, thicker one from the clutch of chains she holds. "This one is yours," she says, holding it out to me. It's a dog-tag type chain, and at the end of it swings a clear hourglass filled with sand. "We made them for us. So you don't have to put sand in your pocket anymore. You can have it with you all the time. Even at the grocery store."

I glance back at Eden. Her eyes are shining. Obviously she shared my pocketful of sand with Emmy. I don't mind. It's nothing I'm ashamed of or try to hide.

I slip the chain over my head as Emmy pulls hers on, too. It's shorter and thinner, as is Eden's, who comes to get hers next. Emmy picks up her hourglass, kisses it and then trots off to the living room to watch her cartoons.

I turn toward Eden when she speaks. I'm still marveling at the sand, something that's so special to me, trapped safely within the little vial. "The night after I brought her home, she told me that she'd gone to your house for help, but that you weren't home so she decided to hide in the shadows along the surf until it was safe. I guess the water was colder than she thought and she…" Eden's voice trails off on a choking sound and I pull her into my arms. I know it will take time for the shock, for that kind of fear to leave her unshaken. When she collects herself, she leans back and looks up into my eyes. "She wanted to go back to the beach yesterday. She said she wasn't afraid of the sand, that it was where we met you and your little girl. Sh-she didn't want you to forget either of them, so she wanted to make these for us."

Tears well in her eyes again and I kiss her forehead. "I could never forget either of them. Charity was a part of me. She always will be, but

Emmy has wormed her way into my heart, too. I want her in my life. Her and you," I tell her carefully.

I glance behind me at Emmy then I swing my gaze back to Eden. "Can I stay for a while tonight? So we can talk? After Emmy goes to bed?"

Eden's smile is small, but happy. "Of course."

I breathe a sigh of relief. In my mind, I make a list of all the things I want to tell her, all the things I want to say. Like that I told Brooke that it was over. Like that I want to start over with her and Emmy. Like that I just ask for one day at a time, so we can learn and grow and do this the right way. So that I don't screw it up. I feel like I've got a second chance at life and I want to make this work. For Emmy. For Eden. For me. For my daughter. She'd want me to be a better person for Emmy. She was amazingly generous like that. Nothing will ever make me stop loving her. Or missing her. Or wishing that things could've been different. But she will always be alive in my heart. In my soul. I'll never let her go or replace her. I can only prove to her, every single day, that she made me a better man. That knowing her and loving her made me the kind of man who could deserve her. If I had her back again.

And all that starts tonight.

Eden starts to go around me to check the bread. I stop her with fingers lightly gripping her upper arm. "Eden?"

She looks up at me, those big hazel-gray eyes melting me all the way through. This is right. *She* is right. For me. For my life. She's beauty for my ashes. And I'm hope for her heartache. We fit. Like we were made for each other.

"I'm going to make you fall more and more in love with me. Every single day. I promise."

She grins at me, a different kind of grin, and I know I'll remember it for the rest of my days. "I don't doubt that one bit."

EPILOGUE

Eden

Five months later

As LONG AS I live, I don't think the beach will
ever look the same. Especially this one. I look down
the long expanse that stretches out to the left, the
way we walk to go to our little cottage, and I
remember the first time Emmy and I stepped onto
that sand. It was the day we moved here. The third
time we'd moved hoping to find "home." It was the
day we met someone who would change our lives
forever.

At the time, I had no idea that I'd meet someone so broken. Or that he'd be the man who could heal us. Or that this sand could threaten life as well as sustain it. I still feel a thin thread of fear when Emmy gets near the surf. She's declared to me on more than one occasion that she's now seven years old. She knows how to be safe. I never take my eyes off her, though. It'll probably be years before I feel safe doing that. If ever. But there's someone else watching over her now, too.

I glance back to where Cole is talking to Cody and Jordan as Emmy and her two little friends get buckets of water to fill up the mote she and Cole dug. He watches her closely even as he chats with our friends. I feel perfectly safe in his care, and I feel like Emmy is perfectly safe, too.

His eyes follow the girls as they run to the surf and carefully collect sea water. Cole and Emmy made an enormous, very elaborate sandcastle for today's festivities—a beach barbecue out in front of Cole's cabin. I know that if I were to go and pat the pocket of Cole's swimming trunks, I'd feel a lump of sand. He still does that. Still brings daisies for his daughter. But he's now included Emmy. They do it together, the three of them, I suppose.

We invited Cody and Jordan, who are now a very happy couple, as well as Cody's two little girls who have become good friends to Emmy over the winter. Ryan is in prison for child molestation, rape, sexual assault and battery. Lucy is free, but she's paying in her own way, not only with the money she gave me, but in the public eye. I feel like that part of my life, of my past, truly can't hurt me or Emmy anymore.

Brooke signed Cole's divorce papers a few days after Emmy came home from the hospital. It'll be final next month. All in all, it seems that life is pretty close to perfect. Finally. It's like we had to pay our dues up front, a down payment on happiness. As hard as it was, I can say now that it was worth it. The only thing I would change is the scares with Emmy–both with Ryan and the beach. She'll always carry those emotional scars with her, but she's healing more and more every day. I'm just going to do everything within my power to make sure that her life is as smooth as I can make it from here on out.

Emmy and her friends come back to pour their water into the nearly-full mote and I hear Cole tell her to stay put for a few minutes. When he stands and tells Jordan to watch them, I know he's coming to me. We are never far from each other. It seems the longer we are together, the closer we need to be. To touch, to reaffirm. He spends every night at my house and "comes back" right after Emmy gets up. Time apart feels almost unbearable, but we make up for it when we are together. Doubly so after Emmy has gone to bed, when we can touch and taste and memorize every tiny detail of each other. I've never met a more perfect man.

I scan his long, lean body as he jogs down the beach toward me. I can see him in pads and a jersey, chasing a football down the field. Wide, wide shoulders, trim, trim waist, long, powerful legs and arms. That ripped stomach that disappears into his shorts and the magic that hides just inside them.

My stomach flutters thinking about that.

His smile is crooked and cocky when he stops in front of me. "I would ask what you're thinking, but I don't want to get myself into trouble."

"I don't know what you mean," I deny as he wraps his arms around me, presses his chest to mine and lifts me off my feet. I'd like nothing more than to wind my legs around him, but I know that'd be asking for an embarrassing situation to arise.

"Yes, you do, you vicious tease," he says, nipping the skin on my throat with his teeth. "What I wouldn't give for twenty minutes alone with you right now."

His hot breath brings chills to my arms and I can feel my nipples tighten accordingly. "How did you not get enough last night?"

He leans back to look at me. "I could never, *ever* get enough. I thought you'd figured that out by now. But I'll be happy to prove it to you. Over. And over. And over."

His voice has dropped low, into that sensual sandpaper of his. But it's his eyes...*God!* I don't think I'll ever get used to them. They're so deep and intense and...sexy. He can make me feel a million things without ever opening his mouth.

"I love the sound of that," I admit breathlessly.

"And I love *you*."

My heart swells. I can't hide the smile that spreads across my face. "I'll never get tired of hearing you say that."

"Well, it just so happens that I love telling you, so we're a good fit."

"I never thought I could love someone this way," I tell him, dragging my finger along his full bottom lip.

"I'm glad you picked me," he says gruffly, kissing my fingertip.

"I don't think I had much choice."

"No, but I'm glad you didn't put up too much of a fight."

"Me, too."

"I've got a question for you," he says, setting me on my feet and taking my hand. We start to walk, but he doesn't say anything else.

"What's your question?" I finally ask.

He acts as though he doesn't even hear me. We keep walking and he keeps holding my hand. About three minutes later, he steps in front of me and takes me by the shoulders.

"Close your eyes."

"What?"

"You heard me."

I do as he asks and he starts to walk again, slowly this time, with his hands still on my shoulders, him going backward I assume. When we stop again, he turns me slightly and then releases my shoulders.

"You can open them."

I open my eyes to find Cole kneeling in front of me. Behind him, etched in the packed sand, are the words MARRY ME. My heart stutters and stumbles and I gasp. I had begun to wonder if Cole would ever marry again. He's always talked about us being together forever, but he's never once mentioned marriage.

He takes a black, velvet box from his pocket, brushing the sand off it. He kept it in the same pocket as the sand for his daughter, almost as though we really are all together in his heart now.

"Will you, Eden? Will you give me all of your tomorrows? Mine are already yours. Everything I am, everything I have, everything I'll ever be is yours. Whether you say yes or not, I'm all yours. All the broken pieces. Please say yes. Please make my life mean something again."

When I fall down onto my knees in front of him, he takes the ring from the box and holds it out to me. There is a big solitaire in the center and, on either side, four smaller diamonds that trail along the band. The platinum wraps around them in such a way that it looks like two hourglasses on their side, framing the center stone.

"I said yes before you even asked. I've been saying yes every day since I met you. I knew then…somehow, I knew that you'd be the one to fix me."

"And *you* fixed *me.*"

"Together, we aren't broken at all."

"Our pieces fit. Perfectly. As perfectly as you fit in my soul. I love you, baby. So, so much," he says sincerely.

As I watch, heart in my throat, Cole takes my hand in his and slips the ring on. It feels warm and a little heavy and so, so right. I lift my finger to study it more closely.

"Where did you get this? Not at Bailey's, I'm sure." The one thing you *can't* get at Bailey's is a diamond ring.

He grins. "No, not at Bailey's. I drew it up and called a jeweler up in Portland. Said he could do it. Even drove it down here himself when he was finished."

"That was nice of him."

"I think he was curious after I asked him for the second one."

"The second one?"

Cole pulls up the velvet cushion from the bottom of the box and removes a tiny ring that looks like a pink version of mine. Perfect for a little girl.

"Let's go get Emmy," he says.

I'm smiling so brightly, I think the sun might seem dimmer by comparison. I feel it shining from my face like a million-watt bulb.

Cole stands and sweeps me up into his arms to carry me back. As he walks, he seals our deal with a kiss. A kiss that melds together all of our different pieces into the most beautiful whole this world has ever seen.

The End

Dear wonderful reader,

I would LOVE and APPRECIATE if you would leave a review, but please omit any spoilers about what each ending holds so that every reader can enjoy the choice and the surprise for themselves. And if you loved it, please tell your friends. Your words, your recommendations are more powerful than you know☺ Thank you so very much in advance!

TURN TO PAGE 296
For an extended excerpt from
STRONG ENOUGH
book one in the *Tall, Dark and Dangerous* trilogy
coming August 4, 2015 from Berkley

Door Number Two

THIRTY

Cole

I WAKE WITH a start. My heart is pounding and my head hurts so badly my vision is blurry for a few seconds. I close my eyes and cradle the throbbing left side of my skull until the worst of it passes.

I recall the dream, so perfectly clear. So perfectly *real*.

Only it's not. It's only a dream. A sweet dream *and* a horrific nightmare. I've had it dozens, no *hundreds* of times before. Maybe more. It always leaves me feeling wrecked. Panicked. Lost. But even so, I never want to wake from it.

Yet I always do.

It takes me a minute to realize who I am. I'm Cole. The guy in the dream. I look like him–somewhat–

and I sound like him. I *feel* like him. Only I'm not sure I'm him. I don't know *what* my name is.

In the dream, I see and hear and think and feel like Eden, as though I know her every thought and emotion. But I'm still Cole. It's like I'm in the director's chair, directing an intricate drama, enacted only on the stage of my mind. I know all, see all, *feel all*. Only it's not real. None of it.

Minutes pass. Maybe more. Maybe an hour. I don't know. Time means different things these days. But some time later, I crack one lid. When knives don't pierce my brain, I lift the other and glance around. I'm on my back, staring at the sky. I recognize the trees above me. It's a familiar canopy, especially one tree in particular with its gnarled branches that look like an enormous hand reaching for me. I've always found comfort in it, as though something might be coming to save me, to drag me out of the blank hell that I find myself in.

I sit up, each grate of the park bench digging into my back as I move. They're familiar to me, too. I wake here often. More often than not, actually. I think the cops stopped patrolling this park at night, so as long as I'm gone by an hour or so after daylight, they don't give me trouble. But I always come back. After the sun goes down, I come back and I watch. I watch the family across the street, in the brownstone that is as foreign to me as my name or my childhood. It's never in my dreams, only in my reality. Or, rather, *someone else's* reality.

My memory extends five hundred and eight days.
I woke on a riverbank with blood streaming into my
eyes. I was freezing and had a broken arm, a
dislocated shoulder and four cracked ribs. I
remember every day since then–the hospitalization,
the psychiatry, the search for a missing man or a
wrecked car. But there was nothing. For months,
there was nothing. And I couldn't take it any more,
so I ran. I took to the streets because I couldn't stand
the constant feeling that I'd lost something so dear to
me that I didn't want to live without it.

Only I have no idea what–or who–that might've
been. It's enough to drive a man crazy, though, so I
left. I abandoned polite society to hide. Here.
Where I can see that brownstone.

Today, the sun is streaming through the single
tree that dots the landscape out in front of it. It
dapples the front door and the walk with moving
drops of black and white, a kaleidoscope in constant
motion. The wind carries the scent of fresh cut grass
from yesterday, along with something else.

It's baby powder and the soft perfume of the
woman from my dreams. The woman across the
street. Or at least how I imagine she might smell.

I dream of them almost every night–the woman
and her daughter. I know now that they can't mean
anything to me, or I to them. Eden and Emmy aren't
even their names. I heard the man who lives there,
the husband most likely, call them Jovie and Serah. I
wish they were mine, but they're not. I wish they
had answers, but they don't. I know that now. But

still I come. Because the dreams of them, the near-memories of them give me comfort in a comfortless world.

As the sun creeps higher in the sky, it begins to shine on the side of my face, a welcome heat to what skin isn't covered with hair and scar tissue. I know I have to leave. Before they *make me* leave and I can never come back. I don't know much, but I know that I have to come here. I have to come back here to watch them. And dream about them. If not, I'll go crazy. I don't know how I know that; I only know that I do.

I watch the man leave, another face familiar to me only through my dreams. He leans back in and kisses the woman, drawing her into his arms. I can see his passion for her. What I don't see is *her* passion for *him*. Or is it only that I *wish* there was no passion for him? I can't be sure, but it hits me in the chest like a metal slug when he leans away and she smiles at him. That smile is meant for me. I can feel it.

And yet it's not. It's very obviously not.

She closes the door as he jogs lightly down the steps. He's all but whistling, he's so happy. Actually, the closer he gets, the more clearly I can see his face. His lips are pursed. He actually *is* whistling. I just can't hear the sound. I don't hear all that well anymore, truth be told.

When he's out of sight, I drag my eyes back to the house, hoping for one more glimpse of the woman before I retreat into the shadows of a nearby bridge.

That's when I hear an explosion.   It shakes the ground under my feet.

Then I see the smoke. And I hear the scream. And the brownstone bursts into flame.

To Be Continued

Note from the author

Have you ever awakened from a dream and been able to trace many of the various elements to something you heard or read or saw in real life? I have. Many times. And so has Cole. Everything in his dream points to something based in reality. He's not as far from Eden as it seems. He just has to find his way back to her.

Join me in Handful of Tears as Cole traces his dream back to his soulmate. Reality can only keep them apart until destiny brings them back together again.

I would LOVE and APPRECIATE if you would leave a review, but please omit any spoilers about what each ending holds so that every reader can enjoy the choice and the surprise for themselves. And if you loved it, please tell your friends. Your words, your recommendations are more powerful than you know☺ Thank you so very much in advance!

READ ON
For an extended excerpt from
STRONG ENOUGH
book one in the *Tall, Dark and Dangerous* trilogy
coming August 4, 2015 from Berkley

A FINAL WORD

If you enjoyed this book, please consider leaving a review and recommending it to a friend. You are more powerful than you know. YOU–the words from your mouth, the thoughts from your heart, shared with others, can move mountains. You make a huge difference in the life of an author. You have in mine. You do every day, which brings me to my gratitude, my overwhelming, heartfelt gratitude.

A few times in life, I've found myself in a position of such love and appreciation that saying THANK YOU seems trite, like it's just not enough. That is the position that I find myself in now when it comes to you, my readers. You are the sole reason that my dream of being a writer has come true and your encouragement keeps me going. It brings me unimaginable pleasure to hear that you love my work, that it has touched you in some way, that it has made life seem a little bit better for having read it. So it is from the depths of my soul, from the very bottom of my heart that I say I simply cannot THANK YOU enough, which I say a lot of in this blog post.

For the full post, visit my blog at http://mleightonbooks.blogspot.com. You can sign up for my newsletter or find me on Facebook, Twitter, Instagram or Goodreads via my website, www.mleightonbooks.com

ABOUT THE AUTHOR

New York Times and **USA Today** Bestselling Author, M. Leighton, is a native of Ohio. She relocated to the warmer climates of the South, where she can be near the water all summer and miss the snow all winter. Possessed of an overactive imagination from early in her childhood, Michelle finally found an acceptable outlet for her fantastical visions: literary fiction. Having written over a dozen novels, these days Michelle enjoys letting her mind wander to more romantic settings with sexy Southern guys, much like the one she married and the ones you'll find in her latest books. When her thoughts aren't roaming in that direction, she'll be riding wild horses, skiing the slopes of Aspen or scuba diving with a hot rock star, all without leaving the cozy comfort of her office.

Other books by M. Leighton

All the Pretty Lies
All the Pretty Poses
All Things Pretty

Down to You
Up to Me
Everything for Us

Pocketful of Sand

Strong Enough (8.4.15)
Tough Enough (11.3.15)
Brave Enough (TBA)

The Wild Ones
Wild Child
Some Like It Wild
There's Wild, Then There's You

YA and PARANORMAL

Fragile

Madly
Madly & the Jackal
Madly & Wolfhardt

Blood Like Poison: For the Love of a Vampire
Blood Like Poison: Destined for a Vampire
Blood Like Poison: To Kill an Angel

The Reaping
The Reckoning

Gravity
Caterpillar
Wiccan
Beginnings: An M. Leighton Anthology

STRONG ENOUGH

*Is she strong enough to trust the most dangerous man
she's ever met? And is he strong enough to let her?*

How would I describe myself? Well, I'm Muse Harper.
I'm a twenty-something painter who loves red wine, quirky
movies and men with a fatal flaw. But that was before I met
Jasper King. *He* became *my* fatal flaw.

Eight months ago, I had a choice to make– abandon
everything I've ever known to protect my family, or stay and
risk someone getting hurt. I chose the former. My plan was
working just fine until I found out my father had gone
missing.

That's when I met Jasper. A bounty hunter with the eyes
of a tiger and the nose of a bloodhound, he was supposed to
help me find my father. What I didn't know was that meeting
him was no accident. Hunting people isn't all that Jasper
does. And helping me was only part of his plan. I just wish
I'd found out sooner, before my heart got involved. But even
then, I don't know if I'd have done things differently.

Now, I have another choice to make– trust the man that
I'm falling in love with and hope that he'll do the right thing,
or run as far away from him as I can get.

ONE

JASPER

Seventeen years ago

"WHAT'S HE GONNA do, Mom?" I try to wriggle away from her, but she holds me too tight. I feel like something bad's gonna happen, but I don't know why. "Maybe I can make him not be mad. Let me go!"

"Shhh, baby. It'll be okay. You have to stay here with me or he'll take you, too."

My heart's beating so hard it hurts, like it did that time when Mikey Jennings punched me in the chest. Not even my mother's arms around me make the pain go away, and her hugs usually make everything better.

My eyes water as I stare out the window. I can't blink. I'm afraid to. I don't want to see what Dad's going to do to my older brother, Jeremy, but I can't look away either.

The longer I watch, the less I can move, like my feet are glued to the floor and my arms are strapped to my sides. It feels like I can't even breathe. I can only stare at the cold, gray water and the two shapes moving closer to it.

I see Jeremy's fingers clawing at my dad's hand where it pulls him by his hair. It's not doing him any good, though. Dad isn't letting go. Jeremy's feet sometimes drag along the ground, his ratty tennis shoes kicking up mud and grass, but my father never slows down. I can tell by the way his other fist is balled up that he's mad. Madder than usual, maybe.

Jeremy got in trouble at school again today. They called Dad at work instead of Mom, so she didn't even know until Dad brought Jeremy home. By then it was too late.

"No kid of mine's gonna act like a monster. There's something wrong with you, boy," Dad was saying when they walked through the door. Jeremy was in front of him. Dad pushed him so hard, my brother fell and slid across the kitchen floor.

There *really is* something wrong with Jeremy. The doctor said so. He said Jeremy needed medicine, but Dad doesn't care. It just makes him mad, makes him lose his temper with Jeremy even more.

I was standing at Mom's side when Dad stopped in front of her. He put his finger in her face until it almost touched her nose. His eyes were that red color all around the edges like they are when he's getting ready to whip Jeremy. "You'd better hope this little shit doesn't turn out the same way." He slapped me in the side of the head when he said it. It made my ear sting like a bee got me, but I didn't even say "ouch." I didn't say *anything*. I knew better than to open my mouth. "One's enough."

Dad went and grabbed Jeremy by the back of his shirt, pulled him up to his feet and threw him out the kitchen door. Jeremy fell again, but that didn't stop Dad. He followed him into the yard.

"Get up, you worthless little asshole," he yelled. There was something not good in Jeremy's eyes when he looked up. Then I saw him spit on Dad's work boots. I knew he shouldn't have done that. I knew it even more when Dad kicked him in the ribs. Now we're watching my older brother get dragged away for punishment.

Rather than stopping at the old stump that he bends Jeremy over to whip him, Dad keeps walking right out into the lake. He doesn't even stop at the edge.

My eyes hurt while I watch, but I can't close them. Something about this time looks different. Feels different. Something about the hot tears streaming down my face tells me that this time *is* different.

Dad's boots splash through the shallow water. He drags my brother behind him like he does a bag of trash when he's loading up the truck to go to the dump. Jeremy falls and gets back up, falls and gets back up. He's fighting for real now. He's kicking and hitting. I see his mouth open wide like he's screaming, but I can't hear it. The only thing I can hear is my heart beat. It's like drums in my ears, it's so loud.

Dad stops when the water is up to his waist. He pulls Jeremy to him. I see his face from the side, my father's. It's so red it looks purple. Veins are standing out all down his neck. My brother's face is almost white, like he's wearing ghost Halloween makeup. His eyes are dry, though. He stopped crying over the stuff Dad does to him a long time ago.

Dad yells something at Jeremy, his mouth stretching so wide it looks like he could eat him. Like a snake, just swallow him whole. Jeremy just stares up at him with his pale face. Dad shakes my brother hard enough to make his head snap back, and then he dunks him under the water.

I suck in a breath. I've never seen Dad do this before, no matter how mad he gets at Jeremy. Something in my chest burns while I watch Dad hold him under, like *I* can't breathe either. Like air is stuck in there, burning. Just like I'm stuck in *here*. Hurting.

I taste salt from my tears. I lick them away, ashamed to be crying. Something starts pecking the top of my head. A wet trail, like snail slime, slides down the side of my face. I wipe it away and look at my hand. It's just water. Warm water.

Tears. But not my tears. They're Mom's.

I count. *One Mississippi, two Mississippi, three Mississippi.* I wonder how long Jeremy can hold his breath. My head feels like it might explode.

Four Mississippi, five Mississippi, six Mississippi.

Air and sound push past my tight throat to make a weird garbled scream. It lands in the quiet room like a crack of thunder. It's the only noise I make. It's the only noise I *can* make.

I watch Jeremy's hands, beating against my dad's wrist. Dad never budges, though, never lets up. His arm is straight and ruthless, holding my only brother under the water.

Mom's arms squeeze me tighter. It's getting even harder to breathe.

Seven Mississippi, eight Mississippi, nine Mississippi.

I count, even though time stopped moving. When I get to *twenty Mississippi*, I start over at one, start over for Jeremy, to give him more breath. To give him another chance. But he doesn't use it. He can't. His time already ran out. Like his breath did. I know it when I see his hands drop away. They fall into the water and float, like there's nobody attached to them. Like my brother just... left.

Dad lets him go. Sort of pushes him out into the deeper water. Jeremy just drifts there, like he's playing dead. Like he used to do when Mom took us swimming on summer afternoons when our father was at work.

I don't watch Dad walk out of the lake. I don't watch him walk across the yard. I don't even look up when he walks through the back door. I just watch Jeremy, waiting for him to move, waiting for him to wake up.

"Get your purse. We're going out to eat. The boys can have a sandwich here."

Boys? Does that mean Jeremy's okay?

I start toward the door, but Mom grabs me. "Jasper, be a good boy and get my purse for me, sweetie. It's beside the front door."

Her eyes are different. They look scared and they make *me* scared, so I just go get her purse and bring it to her like she asked. When I hand it to her, she takes it and pulls me against her. I feel her arms shaking and when she lets me go, she's crying. But she's smiling, too, like she's not *supposed* to cry. None of us are supposed to cry.

"You sit right there in front of the television, okay? Don't you move a muscle." Her voice is warning me about something. I don't know what's going on, but I'm afraid. She's afraid, too.

"Okay."

I turn on cartoons and sit on the couch until I hear Dad's truck start. When I do, I get up and run as fast as I can, through the kitchen, out the back door and across the yard toward the lake.

It's raining now and the grass is slick. I fall twice before I can get to the edge of the water. When I do, I holler at my brother.

"Jeremy!" He doesn't move. He just floats on the surface like my green turtle raft does. "Jeremy!"

I look back at the house and then back to my brother. I know nobody can help me. Nobody will stand up to my dad. Not even my mom. If I don't help Jeremy, he'll die.

My hands are shaking and my knees feel funny when I step into the water. It's so cold it stings my skin, like when I fell off my sled last winter and snow went up my pants leg. I couldn't get it out fast enough. It was so cold it almost burned. But this time, I keep going no matter how much it hurts.

When the water is up to my chin and my teeth are chattering so hard I bite my lip, I think about turning back. Jeremy is so far away, I can barely see him and I can't catch my breath enough to holler for him.

"J-J-Jer–" I try again.

I paddle out farther. My arms and legs weigh so much I can hardly move them through the water. It's like trying to run in cold, thick soup. I fight to keep my chin up, gulping down the water that laps into my mouth.

I swim and swim and swim, watching the back of Jeremy's head until he's close enough for me to touch. It's raining harder now. Big, fat drops are splattering on the back of my brother's neck, and it's running down my forehead and into my eyes.

I grab a handful of his dark hair and raise Jeremy's face out of the water. His eyes are open, but they aren't looking at me. They're looking at something else, something I can't see. I take his arm. It's cold and feels kind of like that fish Dad brought home and made Jeremy skin.

My stomach hurts and my eyes burn. I feel like somebody's squeezing me around the middle, squeezing me so hard I can't even cry.

I take my big brother's hand and I pull him toward me, toward shore. He floats pretty easy, so I swim a little and tug, swim a little and tug.

After a while, it gets harder and harder to move, harder and harder to keep my face above the water. The shore, the grass, the back door of my house…they're all getting farther away, not closer. I'm scareder than I've ever been before. Even scareder than that time Jeremy made me watch *The Evil Dead*.

Jeremy seems heavy now, like he's trying to drag me down every time I pull on him. "Swim, Jer, swim," I mumble through a mouthful of water. "Please."

I go under. When I try to scream for help I know won't come, water goes down my throat. I try to cough, but I can't. There's no air.

I can see light above me and I use my heavy arms and legs to crawl toward it. When I finally get my face out of the water, I grab for my brother's hand. I hold onto it tighter than I've ever held onto anything before, even my favorite *G.I. Joe* soldier.

I paddle as fast and as hard as I can, pulling Jeremy behind me until I can touch the squishy bottom of the lake. I pull and tug and drag me and Jeremy to the shallowest part of the water and I roll him over.

His lips are blue and his face is still so white. But it's his eyes that scare me the most. They don't look like he's awake. But they don't look like he's asleep either. They sorta look like mine feel–scared. Like he saw something that made him want to hide, but he didn't get away fast enough and now he's just…froze.

I shake his shoulders. I scream my brother's name. I cry even though I don't want to.

I give in and pound on his chest. I know that if he gets up, he'll punch me in the back of the leg until I say "uncle," but I don't care. I just want him to get up. But he doesn't. He doesn't get up. He doesn't move at all. He just slides in the mud until he's back in the water.

I try to reach for him, but my feet slip and I almost fall in. That scares me so bad, I scream my head off. I can't go back in. I won't come back out if I go in the water again. I just know it.

Don't make me go back in! Don't make me go!

But what about Jeremy? What about my brother?

I cry as quiet as I can as he floats away from me again. I watch his white ghost face until the only thing I can see is black. And nothing else.

ONE

Muse

I SHAKE OUT the three hundred dollar sweater I just folded for the third time and I start over. Somehow keeping my fingers busy seems to calm my brain. It gives me something to think about other than the man I'm waiting on and how worried I am about taking this step.

When the icy blue cashmere is folded perfectly–for the *fourth* time–I lay it on top of the others in the stack and check the time on my phone again.

"It's almost noon, dammit!" I mutter, as if my friend, Tracey Garris, can hear me all the way across town. She's the one who knows this guy. I should've gotten more information from her, but she was in a rush this morning and she's in a meeting now, so I'm stuck waiting. Information-less. I only know what she muttered so briefly before she hung up, something about a guy coming by and his name being Jasper King.

I let out a growl of aggravation and grab another sweater, flicking it open with enough force to cause one sleeve to snap against the table like a soft crack of thunder. For some reason, I feel a little better for having taken out a bit of my frustration on *something*, even if that something is an innocent piece of very pricey material.

Rather than climbing right back onto a ledge of frustration, I purposely tune out everything except the words of the song playing overhead, *If I Loved You*. It always reminds me of Matt, the guy I left behind. The guy who should've hated seeing me leave. The guy who *would've* hated seeing me leave *if* he'd loved me like I wanted him to. But he didn't. He let me go. Easily. And now, even after eight long months, it still makes my heart ache to think of him.

I don't shy away from the pain. In some twisted way, I bask in it. Like most artists, I welcome all kinds of emotions. Good or bad, they inspire me. They color my life and my work like strokes of tinted oil on pristine white canvas. They make me feel alive. Sometimes broken, but still alive.

After I finish the sweater, I move through the store, lost in thoughts of my ex and how much it hurt to say goodbye. I'm straightening a rack of ties when the chime over the door signals the arrival of a customer. I catch movement in my peripheral vision and absently throw a polite greeting in that direction. "Welcome to Mode: Chic," I say, feeling both resentful and relieved at the interruption.

I get no response, so with a deep sigh I even up the last row of ties and smooth my vest before turning to find my visitor. When my eyes settle on the interloper, all thoughts of Matt and the past and every trouble in the world melt away for the time it takes me to regain my breath.

A man is standing behind me. I didn't hear him approach, didn't smell cologne or soap, didn't sense the stir of the air. He was just coming through the door one second and looming right behind me the next.

He's tall, very tall, and dressed in black from head to toe. Other than his lean, dramatically V-shaped physique, that's all I notice about his body. It's his face that captivates me. From an *artist's* standpoint, he reminds me of a bronze sculpture, something strong and ancient that was carved by the talented hands of Michelangelo or Donatello, Bernini or Rodin. From a *woman's* standpoint, he's simply breathtaking.

His face is full of angles and hollows–the ridge of his brow, the slice of his nose, the edge of his cheekbones, the square of his chin. Even his lips are so clearly defined that I find myself wanting to stare at them, to reach up and touch them. Find out if they're real. If *he's* real. But it's his eyes that I finally get stuck on. Or maybe stuck *in*. They're pale, sparkling gold, like a jar of honey when you hold it up to the sun. And they're just as warm and sticky, trapping me in their delicious depths.

Despite all my worries, worries that have consumed me for several days now, I am only aware of the raw, primal power that radiates from him like heat from a fire. He doesn't have to say a word, doesn't have to move a muscle to exude confidence and capability. And danger. Lots and lots of danger.

I don't know how long I've been staring at him when I become aware of his lips twisting into the barest of smiles. It's minimally polite, but somehow anything more would seem a betrayal of the intensity that oozes from his every pore. The tiny movement is potent, though, and I feel it resonate within every one of my female organs like the echo of a drumbeat in the depths of a hollow cave. *God, he's gorgeous.*

As much as I enjoy the rubbery feel of my legs, the tingly fizz in my stomach, I pull myself out of the moment. Not necessarily because I want to, but more because I have to. I'm at work. Men don't come in here to be ogled. They come in here to be outfitted.

Unless they come here to see me. The thought hits me like a slap. Could this possibly be the bounty hunter Tracey was telling me about?

"Pardon me," I eventually manage, taking a step back as reality and worry and purpose crash back into my mind in a multi-colored tidal wave. "How may I help you today?"

Dark head tilts. Tiger eyes narrow. Silence stretches long.

I wait, part of me hoping this is the man who will help me, part of me praying he's not.

When he finally speaks, it's with a voice that perfectly mirrors what he physically projects—dark intensity, quiet danger. "I need to be measured for a suit."

I let out a slow breath, oddly more disappointed than relieved. "I can do that for you." I take yet another step away, clasping my hands together behind me, determined to find some equilibrium in his presence. I glance at Melanie the other person working the story today. She's the owner's daughter and for the fourth hour straight, I find her holding down the chair behind the cash register, typing into her phone. I should probably tell her that I'll be in the back getting measurements, but I obtusely decide to let her figure that out for herself when she can't find me. It won't take her long to realize I'm gone when someone else comes in and I'm not out here to do her job for her. "This way," I say turning toward the rear of the store.

All business now, I ask questions as I make my way toward the dressing rooms. Even though his rich, velvety voice warms my belly, I find it easier to concentrate when I can't see the man following quietly along behind me. He answers all my queries politely, seemingly oblivious to the way he affects me.

I take him to the larger dressing room, the one with a platform that rests in the center of a crescent of mirrors. It has enough space for a desk and computer to one side, so we use this room to measure for tailored clothing. That and for special fittings like bridal parties and other groups.

I glance to my left as we enter the scope of the mirrors. My gaze falls immediately on the figure behind me. I look quickly away, but not before I notice the lithe way he moves. With the fluidity of the jungle cat his eyes remind me of.

Like a tiger. Surefooted. Silent. Deadly.

Without turning, I sweep my arm toward the dais. "If you'll stand there, I'll get the tape and be right with you." I don't doubt that he's following my instruction, even though he doesn't respond. I still can't hear him, still can't even detect a disturbance in the air, but now I can *feel* him, as though my body has become perfectly attuned to his within the five minutes he's been in the shop. It's beyond ridiculous, but it's the absolute truth. I've never been more aware of a man before. Ever.

I busy myself gathering the cloth tape, a small notepad and a pencil, doing my best to keep my mind on the task at hand until I'm able to control my thoughts to a small degree. Those wayward thoughts scatter and my mouth goes bone dry when I turn and see him standing on the platform, muscular arms hanging by his sides, long, thick thighs spread in a casual stance. It's not his posture that catches me off guard. It's his eyes. Those intense, penetrating eyes of his. He's watching me like a hunter watches prey. I feel them stripping me bare, asking all my secrets, exposing all my weaknesses.

"Ready when you are," he murmurs, startling me from my thoughts.

"Right, right. Okay," I say, dragging my gaze from his and focusing on his body. As disconcerting as it is to appraise him so openly, it's not nearly as disturbing as eye contact, so I go with it.

As I take him in, I realize that he's a magnificent male specimen. I'd wager that his dimensions are perfect for every kind of clothing, from formal to sleepwear. And, dear God, I can only imagine what a striking figure he'd make in a tuxedo. He'd look like a model. For guns maybe. Or bourbon. Something dangerous and thrilling or smooth and intoxicating.

I clear my throat as I approach, careful of my feet as I step up to stand beside him. I sense his eyes on me as I move, making me feel clumsy and slightly off balance.

I lay the pad of paper on the thin podium to my right and I clamp the pencil between my teeth as I stretch the tape out straight. With movements that I'm relieved to find swift and sure, I measure his neck and over-arm shoulder width, his chest and arm length. I jot down the numbers then make my way to his waist, cursing the fine tremor of my hand when my knuckles brush his hard abdomen.

I note his measurements, mathematical proof of the flawless way he's put together. What I don't write down are things that no numbers could convey. I don't need to. They'll be seared in my brain for all eternity, I think.

Wide, wide shoulders, the kind a girl can hang on to when she's scared. Strong, steely arms, the kind that can sweep a woman off her feet. Long, hard legs, the kind that can tirelessly chase down what he wants.

It's when I get to his inseam that things get...tense. Surprisingly, despite all the other worries that hover at the back of my mind, I can't overlook the heaviness that presses against the back of my hand as I measure. My belly contracts with a pang of desire that rockets through me. *Good Lord almighty!*

I snap into a standing position, turning away to write down the last of his measurements before he can see the blush that heats my face. Normally, I'd love all these "feels," but not now. Not today. Not like this. It seems like a betrayal.

Without another word or glance, I take my pad and step off the platform, moving to the computer to enter them into a New Client form. My pulse settles more and more the longer I keep my eyes to myself. "What's your name, sir? I'll set up a profile for your order." Still, I don't glance back at him. I keep my gaze glued to the lighted screen.

"King," he replies, his voice so close that I jump involuntarily. I don't turn when I feel his hulking presence behind me; I just stiffen.

I type in the name. It's as I'm hitting ENTER that it clicks. *King. The last name of the bounty hunter Tracey told me about.*

I whirl to face him, ready to pin him with an accusing stare, but I stop dead when I see that he's not looking at me. He's looking down at what he's holding. Between his fingers is the pencil that was stuck between my teeth. I can see the tiny bite marks as he rubs over each one.

I watch him move his thumb over the indentions, gently, slowly. Back and forth, like an intimate caress. It's hypnotic. Erotic. A fist clenches low in my core causing me to inhale sharply at the sensation. It feels as though he's rubbing *me* with those long fingers. Touching me, arousing me. It's so physical, so tangible, so *real* that I have to reach back to steady myself against the edge of the desk.

"What sharp teeth you have," he says quietly, *Big Bad Wolf*-style. When he glances up at me, his eyes are a dark and serious amber. "Do you bite?"

"No," I whisper. "Do you?"

"Only if you ask nicely."

Made in the USA
Lexington, KY
15 June 2015